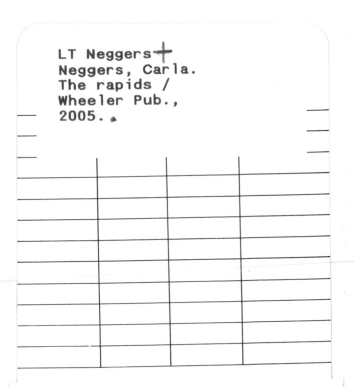

Seneca Falls Library
47 Cayuga Street
Seneca Falls, NY 13148

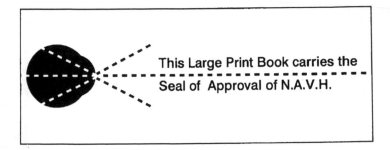

This Large Print Book carries the
Seal of Approval of N.A.V.H.

The *Rapids*

CARLA NEGGERS

WHEELER
PUBLISHING

Published in 2005 by arrangement with
Harlequin Books S.A.

Wheeler Large Print Softcover.

The text of this Large Print edition is unabridged.
Other aspects of the book may vary from the original edition.

Set in 16 pt. Plantin.

Printed in the United States on permanent paper.

Library of Congress Cataloging-in-Publication Data

Neggers, Carla.
    The rapids / by Carla Neggers.
      p. cm.
      ISBN 1-58724-939-1 (lg. print : sc : alk. paper)
      1. Diplomats — Crimes against — Fiction.
    2. Government investigators — Fiction.   3. Security
    consultants — Fiction.   4. New York (State) — Fiction.
    5. Women diplomats — Fiction.   6. Large type books.
    I. Title.
    PS3564.E2628R37 2005
      813'.54—dc22   2005000295

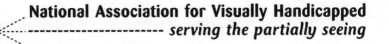

National Association for Visually Handicapped
serving the partially seeing

As the Founder/CEO of NAVH, the only national health agency solely devoted to those who, although not totally blind, have an eye disease which could lead to serious visual impairment, I am pleased to recognize Thorndike Press* as one of the leading publishers in the large print field.

Founded in 1954 in San Francisco to prepare large print textbooks for partially seeing children, NAVH became the pioneer and standard setting agency in the preparation of large type.

Today, those publishers who meet our standards carry the prestigious "Seal of Approval" indicating high quality large print. We are delighted that Thorndike Press is one of the publishers whose titles meet these standards. We are also pleased to recognize the significant contribution Thorndike Press is making in this important and growing field.

Lorraine H. Marchi, L.H.D.
Founder/CEO
NAVH

* Thorndike Press encompasses the following imprints: Thorndike, Wheeler, Walker and Large Print Press.

Acknowledgments

A special thank-you to my Dutch cousins Henk and Christine Nouwen, Jan and Martha van de Leur, Amy Knechten, Sonja van den Akker and Bart, Leo, Marie Louise, Nanny and Rob Neggers for their warm welcome and many family stories on our visits to the Netherlands. Christine was my "Dutch pen pal" when I was growing up in small-town western Massachusetts and she was growing up in Eindhoven. Henk — who for some mysterious reason thinks that the Neggers family is a bit argumentative! — went above and beyond the call of duty in answering my questions for this book, and even put me in touch with a Dutch police inspector, who was equally generous with his time and expertise. I've promised to keep working on my Dutch vocabulary . . . but I'll never get those *g*'s down!

I'm so glad we got to see my cousin Carla, for whom I'm named, before her recent death. I will always remember our lunch in her beautiful garden. She and her husband, Daan, had the most gorgeous roses. . . .

Many thanks to the deputy U.S. marshal who was so gracious and helpful in talking with me, and to my brother Mark and sister-in-law Kathy Neggers for showing me around the scenic and very special Hudson River Valley.

As I write this, hiking season is about to get under way here in northern New England. I'm still determined to hike all forty-eight peaks over 4,000 feet in the White Mountains . . . but it's going to take a while, because I also really like walking on the beach! I'm also diving into my next book, Juliet and Ethan's story — watch for it next summer. For an excerpt, and if you'd like to get in touch with me, please visit my Web site, www.carlaneggers.com.

Thank you, and take care!

Carla Neggers
P.O. Box 826
Quechee VT 05059

One

Maggie Spencer stood paralyzed in front of the glass case in a small Dutch bakery not far from her apartment. *Decisions, decisions.* She'd arrived at the American embassy in The Hague three weeks ago, her first foreign assignment as a diplomatic security officer and already had fallen in love with Dutch bread.

"You'll kill for a Krispy Kreme in another two months."

She laughed as Thomas Kopac, a midlevel diplomat at the embassy, joined her. "Be careful. I'm talking myself out of chocolate sprinkles."

"Ah. *Hagelslag.* It's more like dessert than breakfast."

"So's Krispy Kreme." Maggie smiled at him. "You said that so well. *Hagelslag.* My Dutch vocabulary is improving, but pronunciation? Forget it. Nobody understands what I'm saying."

But she'd had chocolate sprinkles on buttered bread two mornings in a row and decided, instead, on a whole-grain roll with smoked gouda.

9

Tom didn't order anything. "I just saw you in the window and figured I'd make you homesick."

"Do I look like the doughnut-eating type?"

"Uh-uh. I'm not going there."

They headed outside into the late August sun. A midnight rain had washed the humidity and pollution out of the air and perked up the summer roses and hydrangea blooming in dooryard gardens. The embassy was only a few blocks away. Maggie walked comfortably alongside Tom, a balding man in his midfifties who'd never married, a career foreign service officer who'd never rise to the top ranks of his profession. He was the sort who would wear the same suit for days on end. His job was his life. Maggie was trying to have more balance for herself, but it wasn't easy. Still, she'd turned thirty in July and had already learned the hard way that life was too short.

There was, mercifully, nothing romantic in Tom's offer of friendship. "You can eat your *broodje* in front of me," he said. "I would."

"Do I look hungry?"

He smiled. "Starving."

"I'll have to pound the pavement after

10

work to burn off the extra calories."

Dutch breakfasts notwithstanding, she kept in shape. At five-five, she couldn't count on her size to get her out of a jam. Fitness, training, experience and mental toughness were the trick.

And luck.

There was always the luck factor. But since luck wasn't her long suit, she didn't count on it, either.

"Look there," Tom said. "Your hair's the same color as those roses."

She noticed the cluster of orange-red roses in a dooryard. "It's not *that* red."

"Is the red hair from your mother or your father?"

"Father."

He hesitated. "I'm sorry. I didn't mean —"

"It's okay. I don't mind talking about him." She smiled to prove she wasn't just being nice. "My wanderlust is also a Spencer trait."

The day she'd arrived in The Hague was the eighteen-month anniversary of her father's death. Philip Spencer, ordinary American businessman, had walked into the middle of a bank robbery in Prague.

Talk about no luck.

The bank robbers still hadn't been

11

caught. Nobody seemed to be looking too hard for them.

Maggie gave up on resisting, took her roll out of the bag and bit into it, welcoming the smokiness of the cheese and the softness of the bread. Normalcy. She had to establish her routines, focus on her job and continue to move forward with her life. She couldn't dwell on the past. And it wasn't her job to investigate her father's death.

She and Tom walked up Lange Voorhout, a tree-lined street of stately historic buildings that was said to be one of the prettiest in The Hague, or, as it was known formally in Dutch, *'s-Gravenhage*, which meant "the count's hedge." Even the Dutch shortened it to *Den Haag*. Although Amsterdam was the official capital, The Hague was the seat of the Dutch government and the residence of its royal family, as well as home to dozens of foreign embassies and the International Court of Justice.

The functional concrete American embassy was often called the ugliest building on Lange Voorhout, possibly in the entire city. The original embassy — presumably more graceful — had been accidentally destroyed by an Allied bomb during World War Two.

"Enjoy your bread and cheese," Tom said cheerfully when they arrived. "And don't work too hard."

"You're one to talk."

He laughed. "Not me. An eighteen-hour day's my limit."

Maggie made her way to her desk, pouring herself a mug of coffee before she sat down. As a special agent for the U.S. State Department's Diplomatic Security Service, she had a wide range of duties and responsibilities. First and foremost was the safety and security of the embassy's personnel, property and information, whether in or out of the building, and of American citizens in the country. She'd completed six months of training at the Federal Law Enforcement Training Center in Brunswick, Georgia, then worked in U.S. diplomatic security field offices for four years, investigating passport and visa fraud. She'd come to The Hague straight from the Chicago field office, on the heels of a major joint counterterrorism investigation that had culminated in the arrest of a sophisticated trio of Americans producing and selling fraudulent visas.

She ate the last bite of her roll and drank some of her coffee.

Having a father killed by bank robbers in

Prague hadn't hurt her security clearance, nor did it even seem to trouble anyone — at least, not beyond sympathy for her loss.

It troubled her.

But she'd had to put her questions and doubts out of her mind, because there was nothing to be gained by sticking her nose into her father's murder investigation. The American embassy in Prague and the FBI would keep her informed of any progress. She had her own job to do.

She buried herself in it, and by midafternoon, she realized she'd forgotten lunch. She found some peanut butter crackers in her desk and opened up a bottle of water as she scanned her e-mail.

Re: Nick Janssen.

Now, there was a subject heading, she thought, noticing the message was from a free e-mail account she didn't recognize. She opened it up and took in the neatly typed words in a single glance, then read them over more slowly. Twice.

Special Agent Spencer,
You must hurry.
Nick Janssen is in 's-Hertogenbosch near the entrance of the Binnendieze boat

14

tour. If necessary I can keep him there for another hour or so. But please hurry if you want him.

Sincerely,
A friend

Maggie read through the e-mail a fourth time.

A joke. It had to be.

Nick Janssen was an American fugitive with the rare distinction of being on the "most wanted" lists of both the FBI and U.S. Marshals Service. He'd fled the country a year ago to avoid prosecution for tax evasion. That was enough to put him in hot water with the FBI and the marshals, but he wasn't considered violent. Then he tried to extort a presidential pardon, a disaster that had left three marshals wounded and three of his own men dead. That the whole mess had come to a climax in the backyard of the Tennessee boyhood home of the President of the United States didn't help matters.

As if that weren't plenty, Janssen's antics also exposed him as the violent, amoral mastermind of a lucrative criminal network of buyers and sellers of illegal arms, drugs and commodities.

Charlene Brooker, an American army

captain, was the first person to suspect he was more than a simple tax evader. Janssen had ordered her killed last fall while she was in Amsterdam.

He was in Amsterdam himself during the pardon debacle in May and had managed to disappear shortly after it all blew apart.

Everyone wanted his hide.

Since arriving in the Netherlands, Maggie had worked with various American and Dutch investigators on the Janssen case, but she couldn't think of a single "friend" who would know Nicholas Janssen's whereabouts and alert her by an anonymous e-mail.

'S-Hertogenbosch was a small city in the southern Dutch province of Noord-Brabant.

She didn't know what in blazes the Binnendieze was. The name of a canal? A boat tour company?

You must hurry.

It was almost four o'clock.

Maggie abandoned her peanut butter crackers and got up to go find her boss.

Libby Smith welcomed the breeze that seemed to float up from the Binnendieze, the shallow waterway that encircled most

16

of the old city of 's-Hertogenbosch. "What happened to your dogs?"

"What?" Nick Janssen seemed confused, but it was obvious he hadn't liked anything about their meeting from the moment she'd joined him on his bench. It was, he'd said rather pathetically, his favorite spot nowadays. "How did you know about my dogs?"

"Rhodesian ridgebacks, weren't they?"

He'd dyed his distinctive silver hair a stupid-looking black. As notorious as he was, it was unlikely that anyone in the sleepy southern Dutch city would recognize him, even if he hadn't colored his hair.

Tourists — most of them Dutch themselves — stood in line for the boat tour of the Binnendieze.

Libby was bored out of her mind. She'd put on a frumpy denim skirt, a cheap tank top and ergonomic sandals and carried a canvas bag over her shoulder loaded with all the usual tourist paraphernalia. Her .22-caliber Beretta was tucked inside her foldable, packable, squishable traveler's rain jacket.

If necessary, she could get to the Beretta, shoot Nick Janssen and be gone before anyone realized what had happened. If people didn't expect him to be an international fugitive, they didn't expect her to be an accomplished killer.

But she hoped violence wouldn't be necessary. She had very big plans for her new relationship with her fellow American.

"I had to give the dogs away," he said.

She'd almost forgotten she'd asked about them. "That's too bad. Still, it wouldn't be easy to be on the lam with two dogs, never mind ones as large as they were."

"Samkevich shouldn't have sent you here," Janssen said tightly. "We should have met somewhere else."

"That would have had its own risks."

Vlad Samkevich, a Russian who lived in London, was a well-known arms dealer who also had an international warrant out for his arrest. But he wasn't as rich or as desperate as Janssen, and Libby needed someone who was both.

Janssen stared at the tourists talking loudly to one another in Dutch. "Samkevich says you've done work for him. You look like a child. How old are you?"

"Thirty-six."

"You look younger."

It wasn't a compliment. She was small and wiry, and although her very short hair was prematurely gray, it still hadn't added

18

years to her appearance. It was her size and her cute face that made people think she was younger — always *too* young.

"I can do the job, Mr. Janssen," she said. "Just give me your list."

"I'll need you to prove yourself."

She was prepared. "I already have."

He glanced sideways at her. "How?"

"I killed Vladimir Samkevich before I left London two days ago."

No reaction from Janssen. Not shock, not respect, not anger.

Libby responded in kind and kept her mix of satisfaction and fear to herself. What if she'd guessed wrong? But she knew she hadn't. The man next to her had no more feeling for the Russian than she did. "Samkevich wasn't your friend. The authorities don't have solid evidence on you. You were as much a victim in May as anyone else. You didn't shoot the two marshals in Central Park or have the Dunnemores kidnapped in Amsterdam. Your guy had his own agenda."

Janssen made a little noise at her mention of Stuart and Betsy Dunnemore, parents of one of the wounded marshals, friends of John Wesley Poe, the current U.S. president. Libby wasn't sure she should have brought them up. Janssen had fancied himself in love with Betsy, his former college classmate, and tried to manipulate her into interceding on his behalf with Poe.

He'd thought Betsy would dump her elderly diplomat husband and marry him.

But Libby understood what it was to have unrealistic dreams, dreams everyone else thought were insane — not that most people gave a damn about anyone else's hopes and dreams. Nick Janssen didn't. He'd wanted a presidential pardon and let it be known he'd pay for one. He didn't care who got hurt in the process. His blindness to the aspirations of others had backfired on him as well.

When he didn't speak, she went on. "You had a guy use you in May for his own ends. The two men you sent to the States to clean up after him could have been a problem, too, but they're dead. They can't testify against you. They were two of your most trusted bodyguards, but who's to say they wouldn't have turned on you?"

"What does any of that have to do with Samkevich?"

"*He* could testify against you. The authorities were closing in on him. He knew it. He'd have cut a deal in a heartbeat, given them you in exchange for a lighter sentence."

Janssen thought a moment. "You're right, of course."

She hid her relief. "I don't want payment for him."

"His body —"

"He won't be discovered for a few more days."

"You're a very cold woman, Miss Smith."

She tried not to bristle, but she wasn't cold. Not at all. "I'm good at what I do."

"This is a nice town," he said absently. "I could have stayed here for a long time. I was on an island off the coast of Scotland for two months. Did you know that?"

"No," she lied.

He seemed to like that, having one over her. "The food was terrible. Here . . ." He gave a wistful sigh. "I have other safe houses."

"Of course."

"I want to see my mother's grave." His words were soft and yet toneless, as if he'd said them so many times they'd lost their meaning, become an unattainable fantasy. "It's within walking distance of where I grew up in northern Virginia. She died last winter."

Libby squirmed. She'd gone to her father's grave once, just so she could spit on it.

21

"I'm sorry. Do you have your list?"

He looked at her again. "Yes. You really are very cold." But he fished a white index card out of his shirt pocket and passed it to her. "Ten names. A hundred thousand dollars for each."

She tucked the card into her canvas bag. "Excellent."

"You didn't look at any of the names."

"There's time for that. I'll need a deposit of a hundred thousand dollars wired into my account."

He nodded. "I'll take care of it. Should I be arrested —"

"I'll work faster and expect a bonus. Double."

"That's two million dollars."

"You rich tycoons." Libby smiled, hoisting her canvas bag higher onto her shoulder. "Always so good at math."

She slid smoothly to her feet, noticing that Janssen didn't so much as glance at her breasts straining against her tank top. Wrapped up in his own problems, she supposed.

She glanced at her watch. Four-fifteen. What to do with herself the rest of the day?

"I want this all to be over," he said quietly.

"It will be. Patience."

"The bonus?"

She'd started to move away from the bench, but his words — his cool tone — forced her to turn back.

"Any bonus would be paid only upon my release." His eyes, a frosty blue, held her in place. "I wouldn't want you to get any ideas."

"Of course. I understand."

She did, too.

She understood that one or two million — whichever amount Janssen ended up paying her — was a miniscule amount to him. And it wouldn't satisfy her. She was finished being a bit player, a hired gun, an anonymous force in a larger game.

She wanted it all, and Nick Janssen was her vehicle for getting it.

You have no fellow feeling, do you?

The words came out of nowhere. The jolt of memory. Philip Spencer might have been perched on the branch of a nearby linden tree, speaking to her from the dead.

Her heart pounded, and she actually glanced around her, just to make sure he hadn't somehow materialized in her shadow.

He'd tried to save her from herself.

Leaving Janssen on the bench, Libby hurried away. Glancing around, she noticed a balding man in a rumpled suit break off from the boat tour queue and walk down the street.

A prickly sensation crawled up her back. *Something's wrong.*

She walked into a small café and sat at a table inside, with her back to the wall so that she could see out the open front.

The balding man had disappeared.

She had good instincts. She was a superior shooter. But she wasn't trained at surveillance, countersurveillance, any of those tricks of the trade. Mostly, she got along by guts and a willingness to take risks — and the unexpectedness of being a petite woman in her midthirties who killed people for pay.

It was possible she was wrong.

She bit into the small cookie that came with her coffee.

Five minutes later, Nick Janssen got up from the bench and stretched.

He walked to a fence overlooking the narrow waterway.

Ten minutes kicked by. He seemed transfixed. Libby drank her coffee. *Something isn't right.*

Janssen turned and started toward the street. The Dutch police pounced.

An *Arrestatieteam,* their version of a SWAT team. They moved fast, intercepting their target, giving him orders in English, getting handcuffs on him.

Libby joined the onlookers at the outdoor tables.

There was no sign of the balding man. Was he a police officer?

Had he seen her on the bench with Janssen?

Janssen went quietly. He wasn't a fighter. He relied on others to do his fighting for him.

And his killing.

Libby paid for her coffee, wondering if he'd blame her for his arrest.

There was very little she could do if he did.

In the meantime, she had a job to do.

Ten names to memorize. Ten people to kill.

Two

Equal light, level sight.

Falling back on the basics, Rob Dunnemore aimed his .40-caliber Glock and emptied it into the silhouette twenty-five yards away.

Four months ago, he'd been the target. Alive, not a paper silhouette.

Even with ear protection, he could hear the shots echo across the indoor range. He didn't flinch. He was soaked with sweat under his Kevlar vest. He'd popped off a couple of boxes of ammo and felt the burn in his shoulders and back, another reminder that he was out of practice.

He racked back, then made sure he'd counted his shots right and hadn't left a round in the chamber. He didn't want to ruin his practice by putting a bullet in his foot. Shooting was a perishable skill, and he was rusty — he hadn't done this much in one outing since he'd taken a round to his gut in Central Park almost four months ago.

He'd almost bled to death. He'd lost his

26

spleen. Lying in his hospital bed, helpless, he'd nearly lost his family.

Those hadn't been good days.

Shrugging off his goggles and ear protection, he could smell the smoke from the powder and the spent ammunition. His hold on his Glock was tighter than it needed to be. A death grip, like a damn rookie's.

He made sure his gun was clear and safe, then set it on the wood counter in front of him and reeled in his target.

Thirteen in center mass, one a clear miss.

Not bad. Just a hair off a hundred percent.

The rest was a mind game that had nothing to do with technical proficiency.

The door behind him creaked open. "Don't shoot," Juliet Longstreet said in her usual cheeky manner. "It's just me."

But Rob could tell from her expression that something was up with his fellow deputy U.S. Marshal, and he unclipped his target, loosened his vest. "Hey, Longstreet."

She nodded to his target. "How'd you do?"

He showed her.

She whistled. "You'll be back on the street in no time, taking down bad guys."

Her heart wasn't in her words. Something had definitely happened. "Juliet —"

"Nick Janssen's been arrested," she said quickly.

"Where?"

"Some town in Holland. A Dutch SWAT team picked him up on a tip to our embassy there."

"When?"

"A couple hours ago."

Rob pushed back an image of a young Nick Janssen in his mother's college yearbook and studied Longstreet. They'd been an item for a while, splitting up well before the shooting in May. Juliet had her own demons from those difficult days — she'd nearly become one of Janssen's victims herself.

"You okay?" he asked.

"Yeah. It brings it all back, that's all. About time we got the bastard."

"Any word on extradition?"

"Legal eagles are already on it. The Dutch say they have enough to charge him with Char Brooker's murder. If we can't do better than that —" She shrugged, then gave a dry smile. "It's not as if he succeeded in killing any of us over here."

"Not for lack of trying."

Juliet's eyes seemed to flatten. "Yeah,

28

well. The two goons he sent over here to find out what was going on are dead."

And she and a former Special Forces officer — dead army captain Charlene Brooker's husband — had found the bodies. A lunatic out of the Dunnemore past had believed he could use his knowledge of their relationship with President Poe to extract a pardon for Nick Janssen and earn millions for his efforts.

The story, with all its complexities and intricacies, had been fodder for the media for weeks.

"News of the arrest public yet?" Rob asked, keeping his own emotions in check.

Juliet shook her head. "You and I are getting a heads-up before reporters get the bit in their teeth and start calling."

"For what? To ask us how we feel now that Nick Janssen's in custody?"

"Pretty much."

"I'm not talking to any reporters."

"Me, neither."

The shooting range was curiously quiet. Rob still could smell the smoke from his practice. He shoved a full magazine into his Glock, aware of Juliet watching him. "Want to shoot a few rounds?" he asked her.

"I'm a better shot than you."

"Always the ambitious one."

She smiled, not taking offense where she would have six months ago. "Just stating the facts, Dunnemore. Let me get some ear protection and goggles. It's too god-damn hot to wear a vest —"

"Wear a vest, Juliet."

She waved a hand. "Yeah, I guess I'd better, given my luck these days."

"I suppose we should be relieved now that Janssen's in custody."

"I suppose. So why do I feel like another damn shoe's about to drop? I'm not that paranoid."

Rob had no answer.

Whether it was instinct or post-trauma stress at work he just knew he shared her sense of dread.

By the time Maggie dragged herself back up to her small apartment it was after midnight. Without hesitation, Dutch police had followed up on her anonymous tip and arrested Nick Janssen without incident. They had no idea who her "friend" was. Neither did she. She was hungry again and heated up leftover Indonesian fried rice, which she ate standing up, pacing, too wired and uneasy yet to settle down.

Her gaze landed on a picture of her

father on a sailboat in south Florida. Smiling. She remembered how his eyes would crinkle when he smiled. He'd worked as a consultant for small businesses, mostly in eastern Europe and Russia — supposedly. Maggie had had her doubts, more so since his death. Little things didn't add up. She suspected he'd played some kind of role in the multifaceted world of intelligence — one that he couldn't talk about even to his DS-agent daughter. As the sharp edges of her grief had worn down, her questions had become more focused, but answers weren't any easier to come by. She hated the idea that she might have to learn to live with her questions.

But her father had always been a fairly remote figure to her. Even when she was growing up, he was never around. Her mother finally couldn't take his long absences anymore, and they'd divorced when Maggie was in high school. He hadn't changed his ways. He couldn't. She understood that part. She had that same sense of wanderlust.

"Well, Pop," she said, dipping her wooden spoon into her pan of spicy vegetables and rice, "we got the bad guy today."

She didn't know if he'd ever really approved of her career in diplomatic security. He'd seemed okay with her political science degree in college, then her first job at the State Department. She'd hoped her decision to become a DS officer and the prospect of a foreign service career might have intrigued him, but he'd remained outside her life, not disinterested but not a part of it.

The DS special agent in charge of her field office had given her the news of her father's death himself.

Philip Spencer had simply been in the wrong place at the wrong time.

Except Maggie hadn't believed it. Still didn't. Czech authorities, U.S. authorities — she wasn't getting the whole story. She'd pushed and bucked and bitten off heads, and everywhere, from everyone, she got the same line.

Shot by bank robbers who then got away.

Bullshit.

There were no witnesses. Newspapers, even in Prague, barely covered the story. And the reaction she got from investigators — American and Czech — amounted to stonewalling. But she'd finally backed off. What was the point in sticking her neck out for a man she'd seen maybe a half-dozen times in the five years before his death?

Maggie dumped out the rest of her fried rice and ran cold water into the pan, leaving it until morning.

No one — not the Dutch authorities, not anyone at the American embassy — was celebrating Nick Janssen's arrest. As pleased as they were with having him in custody, they all knew his tentacles were far-reaching. There was a lot of work yet to be done.

The media were all over the story. The embassy's public affairs officers as well as the FBI and USMS people back in Washington were fielding questions. Janssen's attorneys had descended, screaming and hollering. News of Maggie's anonymous tip was out.

On her way to bed, she noticed that her solitary plant, an orchid she'd bought in deference to the collective Dutch green thumb, looked dead. It was supposed to be a hardy variety that she'd have a difficult time killing, but she'd killed it in less than three weeks.

She took it to the sink, doused it with water and left it next to her soaking left-overs pan. Maybe it'd revive by morning.

She rolled her eyes. Who was she kidding? The thing was *dead*. To hope other-wise wasn't optimism — it was refusing to face reality.

And if nothing else, Maggie thought, she was a woman determined to face reality.

Libby Smith left her window open in her room at her small hotel around the corner from where Dutch police had picked up Nick Janssen. It was brazen of her. A risk. But there was no reason for authorities to investigate hotel guests. Even if they did, they'd never suspect her of being anything but what she was: an American antiques dealer, a woman looking for off-the-beaten-track bargains.

What if they had him under surveillance and saw you on the bench with him?

If they caught up with her and asked about it, she'd say she'd stopped to rest her feet and they'd chatted for a few minutes about the sights.

She couldn't seem to get cool.

She lay naked atop the cotton duvet and noticed the sheen of her sweat in the light from the street. She could hear the traffic, the sound of music playing somewhere not too far off, the voices of people under her window, out enjoying the warm summer night.

The hundred-thousand deposit had been wired into her account. Janssen must have prearranged the transfer.

Libby had never made such money.

And it was just the beginning.

She'd memorized Janssen's list of targets and burned it, flushing the ashes down her toilet.

Knowing his enemies — and eliminating them — would help her to understand his network and, in time, replace him.

His arrest was inevitable, just a bit earlier than she'd hoped for. Some Dutch Goody Two-shoes must have recognized him and called the police.

The balding man — who was he? Closing her eyes, Libby breathed deeply and tried not to feel as if she were suffocating, told herself the balding man didn't matter. Only her plan did, her next target. The thrill of her work had satisfied her in the beginning. Now she wanted more.

Money.

Power.

She smiled to herself, relaxing, feeling in control at last.

Three

Nate Winter came home to find secret service agents crawling all over his house, a reminder of just how much his life had changed in the past four months.

His fiancée, Sarah Dunnemore, was on the back porch having peach cobbler with President John Wesley Poe, who regarded her as the daughter he'd never had. Being together brought out their Southern accents.

Nate had a feeling he knew why Poe was there.

Nick Janssen.

The rich, murdering bastard was finally in custody.

It was hot even on the shaded porch, but the two Tennesseans didn't seem to mind. While looking for a home of their own in northern Virginia, Nate and Sarah were living in a corner of an 1850s historic house she was researching and getting ready to open to the public. Supposedly it was haunted by both Abraham Lincoln and Robert E. Lee. Poe liked to joke that he wished he could ask both men for advice. But Sarah, a historical archaeologist, was serious about her ghosts.

Before they'd met, Nate had been a senior deputy U.S. Marshal dedicated to catching fugitives and not much else.

He was still a marshal, he was still dedicated to his work — but now he could come home to Sarah, ghosts, peach cobbler and the occasional presidential visit.

"Mr. President," Nate said, "it's good to see you."

Poe, already on his feet, put out his hand, and the two men shook. "It's good to see you, too, Nate. Sarah's ruining my diet with her peach cobbler."

Nate had helped her pick the peaches from one of the trees in the old house's sprawling yard, knowing she expected to make jam one evening. The cobbler meant she was upset, because otherwise she'd still be up to her elbows in the hundred-year-old dump she'd found out back and was in the process of excavating. When she was upset, she dug out family recipes, usually ones involving a lot of butter.

Her gray eyes connected with Nate's for a split second, enough to tell him that Poe's visit hadn't been her idea. She had on cropped jeans and a tank top, barefoot even for peach cobbler with the president.

As welcome as it was, Janssen's arrest had brought back the trauma of her ordeal last spring. Her twin brother badly injured in a sniper-style attack in Central Park, a killer on the loose in Night's Landing, the Dunnemore family's Tennessee home, their refuge. John Wesley Poe happened to have grown up next door.

Sarah was fair-haired and beautiful, and Nate — tall, lean, impatient — hated for those dark days to prey on her again. But he'd learned that Sarah Dunnemore wasn't an ivory tower intellectual who wanted to remain aloof from life. She dove in, sometimes without looking.

"I stopped by to see how Sarah had taken the news of the Janssen arrest," Poe said. "And Rob. I wondered how he was doing."

"I haven't talked to him yet," Sarah said. "I called my parents a little while ago — they're fine."

"I tried to reach Rob on his cell phone earlier," Nate said. "He didn't answer. I left a message."

"How is he recuperating from his injuries?" Poe asked.

Sarah dabbed at the ice cream melting onto her cobbler. "He's doing well, but

38

he's frustrated because his recovery took longer than he expected. At least he's back to his triathlon training."

Swimming, running, biking. From all accounts, Rob was as fit now as he'd been before the shooting. But he'd endured a weeks-long media barrage. Now the whole world knew that he'd graduated from Georgetown and spoke seven languages, that he and his twin sister were like the son and daughter President Poe had never had. Rob often came off in media reports as a silver-spoon, Southern frat boy, but nothing about him was that simple.

"Is he back on the street?" Poe asked.

Nate shook his head. "Not yet."

The president sighed heavily. "I worry about him."

Which, Nate knew, Rob would hate. Sarah knew it, too, but she nodded with understanding. "It's hard not to worry."

"Janssen's arrest will fire up the media again. I hate to see him go through *that.* They'll rehash everything that happened in May." Poe winced. "They'll be calling you, too, Sarah. And your parents."

"The marshals have sent someone to Night's Landing in case it gets crazy. If any reporters show up here, I can handle them." She smiled and licked her spoon.

"I'll have Bobby Lee or Abe talk to them."

Nate could see Poe forcing himself to relax. "I never know when you're serious —"

"*Every* resident of this house since 1875 swears the two of them are haunting the place. I take that seriously." She rose, calmer now herself, and grabbed her bowl. "Are you going to eat your cobbler, Wes? Because if not, I'll take it into the house before the flies get to it. There's no wasting fresh peach cobbler around here."

That elicited a real smile. "Can I take it with me?"

She beamed. A Ph.D. with academic credits up and down both arms, and she loved getting compliments for her cooking. "I'll go wrap it up."

When he heard the screen door shut, Wes breathed out, any hint of a smile gone. "Nate — I hope you'll tell Rob he can call me anytime. I'll make sure he's put through right away."

"He knows that, Mr. President."

The older man nodded. "I'd like to think so. I'd like to think that now that our families' relationship is common knowledge —" He seemed to fight for the right words. "That it won't ruin his life."

Nate had no idea what to say.

A secret service agent stood on the

40

bottom step of the porch.

Time for Poe to leave.

He glanced at the screen door. "You and Sarah are good for each other. After you're married —" He shook his head. "Well, never mind."

Nate thought he understood what Poe was getting at. "We'll want you to be a part of our lives, Mr. President. Both of us."

He sighed. "Thank you."

"Rob —"

"Rob's a different story. He always has been."

After Poe left with his entourage of secret service and staffers — and his peach cobbler — Nate found Sarah in the kitchen, flipping through her grand-mother's recipes. Given the array of ingredients on the table, she was looking for something that involved both cream of mushroom soup and mayonnaise. He slipped his arms around her. "I don't think my arteries can take whatever it is you're about to whip up."

She shoved the cans aside. "I'm missing an ingredient, anyway."

"Dare I ask what?"

"Water chestnuts."

He let his hands move up her midriff toward her breasts. "Do you think Abe and Bobby Lee would object if we made love this early in the evening?"

"If I think about them watching us —"

"I don't know, it could be fun. A four-some —"

She elbowed him in the gut, registering her disapproval, and he laughed, sweeping her up off her feet, getting her away from her cans and her kitchen. He figured he could ease her stress in other ways.

Rob rolled out of bed at six in his first-floor Brooklyn apartment, pulled on shorts and a T-shirt and headed out for his morning paper. He'd ignored all messages from reporters on his voice mail when he got home last night.

A woman in biking shorts was on his doorstep. "Deputy Dunnemore? My name's Patty. I'd like to talk to you about the arrest of Nicholas Janssen yesterday in the Netherlands."

No last name, no credentials. A freelancer. She looked young enough to be a journalism student. She was sweating and panting, indicating she'd pedaled a ways to get to him, which at least meant she didn't live nearby.

Rob picked up his paper and noticed Janssen's arrest had made the front page. No surprise.

Patty frowned when he didn't respond. "Have you and President Poe talked about the arrest?"

Her eyes fell to where his scar was under his shirt. The whole damned world knew the details of his injury. There'd been diagrams of the path of the bullet on TV. Doctors had discussed his prognosis, his recovery, how people could live normal lives without a spleen.

"It's a nice morning for a bike ride," he said. "See you, Patty."

He didn't like shutting the door in her face, but his other options — for example, talking to her — were even less appealing. When he got back up to his apartment, he looked out his living room door and caught her giving him the finger from her bike.

A pro.

No way would he get a bike ride in himself. Or a run. Or even a swim at the Y. There'd be more reporters to deal with. He'd been shot and his family nearly destroyed because of their connection to the president. For months the media had hounded him.

Now Janssen was in Dutch custody.

Due to an anonymous tip to a diplomatic security agent three weeks on the job.

43

Something about it didn't sit right with Rob. He took a shower, got dressed and headed for work, contemplating the unlikelihood of what had gone down across the Atlantic.

He managed to sneak past a throng of reporters outside the federal building where the Southeastern District Office of the U.S. Marshals Service was located. When he got to his desk, a stack of messages, all from reporters, was waiting for him.

Reporters and a day of desk work. He swore to himself and dumped all the messages in the trash.

Mike Rivera stood in his office doorway and jerked a thumb at Rob to join him. Rob doubted it was because the chief deputy wanted to put him back on the street. A heavyset man in his early fifties with bulldog features that his wife seemed to adore, Rivera was well respected but not a soft touch. He wouldn't like having reporters crawling all over his office and harassing one of his deputies.

"Talk to me," he said. "Who've you heard from?"

Rob sat in a spongy plastic chair. "A lot of reporters. I haven't talked to any of them. There's not much to say."

"We can issue a statement. It probably won't do much good while the feeding frenzy's on, but we can try. Do you want to be available for interviews, issue a statement yourself or anything?"

"No."

"Didn't think so."

"I want to do my damn job."

Rivera's eyes flashed. "Yeah, well, you're going to need to lie low for a couple of days until the dust settles on this Janssen arrest."

"I've been laying low since May."

"You've been recovering from a goddamn bullet wound that nearly killed you —"

"It didn't kill me." Rob kept his voice calm. "I'm fit for duty. I don't want anyone coddling me."

"Who the hell's coddling you? You don't want to move too fast, get in over your head —"

"What, with a computer?"

"With another asshole with a gun."

Rob didn't respond. He hadn't had a chance in May. He'd dragged Nate down to Central Park to see the tulips — they'd never live that one down — and gotten shot. No warning, no way to fight back. They'd walked into the park and come out on stretchers.

Rivera sat forward, his chair squeaking loudly. "Why do you look so thin?" he asked, making it sound like an accusation.

"I'm back into my triathlon training. I can pass any test you want to throw at me —"

"Yeah, okay. Don't drop and do push-ups here in my office. You nailed your fitness for duty assessment. I know that. It's your head I worry about."

"I've done everything I've been asked to do, all the desensitizing and reprogramming or whatever it's called. Time for you all to stop walking on eggshells around me."

Rivera grunted. "Today isn't a good day to tell me you're just a regular deputy trying to do his job."

His chair squeaked again when he leaned back, bugging the hell out of Rob. Not a good sign, probably, that a noisy chair irritated him. "I want to get out of here, at least for a few days. Let the dust settle."

"Will you go down to Tennessee?"

"The Hague."

Rivera stood and turned to his grime-encrusted window. "Christ, Dunnemore. You don't make my life easy, do you?"

Rob smiled. "Not my job, Chief. Less chance of anyone getting misquoted or harassed if I'm out of the country."

"So go to Ireland."

"Nick Janssen's not in custody in Ireland. The DS agent who got tipped off about where to find him isn't in Ireland."

"You're serious, aren't you?"

Still in his plastic chair, Rob shrugged. "Sure, why not? I can check with our people in the Netherlands, see where things stand now that the Dutch have Janssen. A Dutch judge is considering our request to interview him. We don't want anything slipping through the cracks."

Rivera shifted from the window and held up a hand. "I get your point. What says a Dunnemore showing up in Holland won't fire up reporters there?"

"Nothing. Janssen's arrest is a public reminder of my family's connections to President Poe. There's not much I can do about that. But the media will be looking for me in New York, not The Hague."

"You want to do this thing?"

"I can be on a flight out of Kennedy tonight."

"Listen, Rob, if this is personal —"

"Of course it's personal." Rob stood, feeling the August heat even in the air-conditioned room. "Janssen put out word that he'd pay for a presidential pardon. He tried to get under my mother's skin. Ulti-

47

mately, he's the one responsible for everything that happened in May —"

"It was a bad time."

"Then there's Charlene Brooker. The
Dutch are charging Janssen with ordering
her murder in Amsterdam last year. We're
all still scrambling to unravel his network."

"None of that is why you're going to
Holland."

Rob shrugged. "Maybe not."

"You want to know who gave that DS
agent the tip."

"Don't you?"

Rivera pulled out his chair and plopped
down with a loud, obnoxious groan of
metal. "Hell." He looked up at Rob.
"Bring me back some Dutch gin."

"Mike —"

"Just a little bottle. I don't drink as
much as I used to."

Rob knew he'd won. There was nothing
to do now except figure out which flight to
take, dig out his passport and pack.

Four

Maggie stared at her boss in disbelief. "Why me?"

George Bremmerton regarded her with a reasonable measure of sympathy from the other side of her desk, but she knew he wasn't about to change his mind. "Because he requested you."

"Why would Rob Dunnemore request me?"

"Because you made the Janssen arrest happen."

"I got an e-mail tip and made a phone call. That was the extent of it." She sat back in her chair. "I can't get out of this?"

"Not unless you find a way to get run over by a bus."

"Great," Maggie said without enthusiasm. "You know Dunnemore's a rich frat-boy type playing marshal until he decides to start living off his trust fund, don't you?"

Bremmerton almost smiled. He was in his late forties and one of the most respected regional security officers ever, a very serious-minded man who was none-theless getting a kick out of her predica-ment. "I met his parents last winter. They're not rich."

"Rich people never think they're rich. And they're friends with President Poe. They don't need to be rich."

"Are you whining, Spencer?"

She groaned. "Yes, I'm whining. How long is Dunnemore staying?"

"Not my problem."

Which meant it was her problem. Maggie had seen pictures of Rob Dunnemore. He was fair and very good-looking, more rugged than she'd expected — or particularly wanted to admit at the moment, since she preferred to think of him in terms of stereotypes.

People said he had gray eyes, but she hadn't really noticed.

"When's he getting here?" she asked.

"Half an hour."

"I like the big warning I get."

Bremmerton shrugged. "I just found out myself."

"You have his flight information?"

He handed her a printout. "Don't treat him like a VIP. He's a federal agent. He's here on business."

"Marshal business? Or President Poe business?"

"Don't go there, Maggie. Dunnemore's main reason for being here is to see you. He's not even being very subtle about it."

Since Bremmerton had more than two decades of foreign assignments behind him and she had three weeks, Maggie trusted his instincts. She was fortunate to be working with him. He'd gone to Nairobi in the aftermath of the American embassy bombing that had killed scores there. From all accounts, he'd been a steady presence amid tragedy and fear. It wasn't a surprise to anyone who knew him or his reputation. No task within the realm of diplomatic security was too big or too small for him to tackle, which, along with his mix of competence and genuine decency, had earned him widespread respect and admiration. He also managed to have a relatively normal family life, with his speech-therapist wife with him in The Hague and two kids in college in the Midwest.

Maggie had worked hard to gain George Bremmerton's confidence in her three weeks at the embassy and didn't take it for granted.

If he wanted her to baby-sit President Poe's marshal pal, that was what she'd do.

"I guess I should get going," she said.

"His twin sister's getting married in a

few weeks to the marshal who got shot with him in Central Park." Bremmerton shrugged at his own non sequitur. "It'll give you something to talk about. She's an archaeologist. Sarah."

"He's going to want to talk about Nick Janssen."

Given the small size of the Netherlands, Schiphol was almost exclusively an international airport — a very busy one — but Maggie had no trouble finding Rob Dunnemore. She recognized him from all the pictures she'd seen of him since the Central Park attack.

He was even more good-looking in person. Tall, very fit. Lightly tanned. He had on a dark suit that had come through the long flight virtually without wrinkles.

His eyes were, indeed, gray.

She introduced herself. "Can I carry something?"

"No, thank you, I've got everything."

She'd expected more of a Southern accent. He had a small carry-on suitcase that she hoped meant he didn't plan a long stay.

But as he observed her, she sensed an air of danger about him that took her aback. She quickly told herself she'd imagined it.

It was just something she'd assumed be-cause she knew he'd nearly been killed in the line of duty four months ago.

"Decent flight?" she asked, leading him out to her car.

"Uneventful."

"That's the way I like it. I always feel as if I've come out of the dryer after a long flight. Did you sleep?"

"I'm fine, Agent Spencer."

But cranky, she thought. "Please, call me Maggie."

He didn't seem too excited about riding in her red Mini. She unlocked the pas-senger door. "SUVs don't work that well in Holland with all the narrow streets and teeny-tiny parking spaces."

"The Mini's no problem. It's yours?"

For the first time, she detected his Southern accent. She nodded. "It's cute, isn't it?"

She thought he might have smiled.

"Jet lag's a killer," she said when she got in behind the wheel. "My father used to swear by drinking a gallon of water on the plane and not eating a bite. I thought he was exaggerating, but he meant it. A whole gallon of water."

"I ate everything that was offered."

Maggie smiled. "That's what I do."

Dunnemore stared out his window most of the drive back to The Hague. She didn't bug him. It was still before dawn his time. His body wanted to be in bed, asleep.

"I'll drop you off at your hotel," she said. "You can get settled, and I'll come fetch you when you want —"

"I can make it to the embassy on my own."

So it was going to be that way. He wanted control. No suggestions from her. She shrugged. "Fine by me."

He sighed. "I'm sorry. I didn't mean to sound surly. Thank you for trekking me around."

"You asked for me. My boss gave the order."

"I asked if I could talk with you. I didn't mean —"

"It doesn't matter." She smiled over at him. "You've got me for the duration of your visit, Deputy."

When they arrived at his hotel, he turned down her offer to make sure his room was ready. He'd see to it. He was definitely independent. Self-sufficient. Not one who played well with others. Maggie hoped it wouldn't become a problem. She didn't want to bump heads with Rob Dunnemore, friend of the president.

Thomas Kopac intercepted her when she got back to the embassy. "Rumor has it you're escorting President Poe's —"

"You shouldn't be listening to rumors."

"Rob Dunnemore. He's here?"

"He's freshening up at his hotel. He's a marshal. We're not supposed to think of him as Poe's surrogate son."

Kopac grinned. "Says who?"

"Says me. Anything I can do for you? Or do I get to do a little work before Dunnemore gets here?"

"Nothing you can do for me, Special Agent Spencer." He leaned in toward her, adding in an amused conspiratorial whisper, "I'll be in my office if you need a place to scream. It's in the bowels of the building. No one'll hear you."

"Very funny."

He laughed. "I thought so."

When she got back to her desk, Maggie checked her e-mail, hoping for another tip, something that would force Bremmerton to find someone else to stick Rob Dunnemore with. The guy put her nerve endings on edge. It wasn't the Poe connection, she decided. It was the gray eyes.

But there was nothing.

Her mobile phone rang, almost as if it knew she was looking for distractions.

A private number.

"Maggie Spencer —"

"St. John's Cathedral is the finest example of Gothic architecture in the Netherlands."

The voice was male, the accent East Coast American, and the words had her sitting up straight. St. John's was in 's-Hertogenbosch, the same city where Dutch police had picked up Nick Janssen yesterday.

"Who is this?"

"I'll be there tomorrow afternoon. It's important that we talk."

"I understand, but I need more information —"

"Just trust your instincts."

"My instincts tell me this is a crank call."

She thought she heard the start of a laugh. "I doubt that. Do people still call you Magster? Your father did when you were small, didn't he?"

Magster.

Her stomach flip-flopped, but she warned herself that using her childhood name could just be a good guess, a way to manipulate her. It didn't mean he knew anything about her father's death. She couldn't let herself think it was anything more.

"Who are you? I need a name."

It was as if she hadn't spoken. "Come alone. If you don't, I'll disappear, and you'll have missed an important opportunity."

"An opportunity for what?"

But he was gone, the connection dead.

A meeting. Was the guy out of his mind?

He must have prepared every word in advance. Of *course* her father called her Magster. What father with a daughter named Maggie didn't?

Some days she couldn't believe it'd been eighteen months since his murder; other days, it was as if her father was more a dream than anything else, lost in a fog of memories and lost possibilities.

Had the caller known him?

Maggie felt a sudden rush of tears that she immediately fought back, impatient with herself.

But Rob Dunnemore materialized behind her, startling her with his good looks. The ends of his fair hair were still damp from his shower. He hadn't wasted any time in getting cleaned up and settled in.

She smiled quickly, hoping there was no sign of even one damn tear in her eyes. "Have a seat, Deputy. We can get started."

"Bad day?"

"What? Oh." She made herself smile. "No, not yet."

He didn't seem to believe her. "That's good."

Maggie wished she'd indulged in chocolate sprinkles that morning, because it was going to be a very long day.

Magster.

She'd figure out what to do about her anonymous caller when she didn't have Deputy Dunnemore's gray eyes on her.

Wide awake despite his overnight flight and long day, Rob sat on a wooden chair at a small table in his room on the top floor of his hotel, a renovated eighteenth-century building. It had low, slanted ceilings and no air-conditioning, but it wasn't a hot night, at least by middle Tennessee standards.

He heard laughter through his open window and looked down four floors at a young couple standing under a linden tree, its branches carefully trained.

Rob turned away from the scene.

His eyes were heavy, scratchy, from fatigue and jet lag.

Maggie Spencer had walked with him back to his hotel, turning down a quick after-work drink.

A woman with things on her mind, Special Agent Spencer.

He'd gone into the dark, quiet bar by himself, but in a few minutes another man joined him, introducing himself as Tom Kopac, an embassy employee. Maggie's friend.

They'd had a beer together. It was clear word had gotten out that the wounded marshal from the Janssen mess in May — the marshal who was friends with the president — was in town and Maggie was stuck with him.

Kopac had decided to check him out.

Their conversation was cordial but superficial. Rob had smiled at the older man. "Maggie's a DS agent. She protects you. You don't protect her."

"She's also a friend."

After Kopac left, Rob had a spicy, meat-filled *kroket* with mustard, then went up to his room.

Why the hell was Kopac suspicious of him when Spencer was the one who had received the damn anonymous tip about Janssen? Not even an hour afterward, he was under arrest. Tips like that didn't happen often, even with minor nonviolent fugitives, never mind with violent fugitives with international warrants out on them.

Was it someone wanting to collect the reward for information leading to Janssen's arrest?

No one had come forward.

Rob put aside his questions and picked up the phone, dialing his future brother-in-law's office in Arlington.

"What do we know about the DS agent who got the Janssen tip? Maggie Spencer." Rob didn't mention her rich red hair, her turquoise eyes, her creamy skin, and chastised himself for his gut-punched reaction to her. "She's gritting her teeth, but she's not complaining about getting saddled with me. At least not to my face."

"Her name's familiar," Nate said.

"Because she's the one who got the Janssen tip —"

"No, it's something else."

"You want to see what you can find out?"

"Sure."

"She's fetching me up in the morning and carting me to the town where Janssen was picked up."

"Her idea?"

"She's finding things to do with me."

The alternative meanings of what he said struck him like a junior high student. *Jet lag.*

"I'm not touching that," Nate said with a chuckle. "I'll check her out, let you know if I find out anything. Has she given you any idea of who she thinks gave her the tip?"

"She's not a talker — she's not easy to read."

"All right. I'll see what I can do. Isn't it midnight there?"

"Just about."

"Go to bed. Take a sleeping pill."

"I don't want to oversleep and miss my field trip."

Then again, Spencer was probably the type to throw a brick through his window to wake him up.

"I'll tell Sarah you called," Nate said.

"And the president?"

Silence.

"He wanted to know how I reacted to Janssen's arrest, didn't he?"

"It's not that simple —"

"It never is with Wes. Yeah. Say hi to Sarah for me."

When he hung up, Rob glanced down at the street and saw that the laughing couple was gone. The street seemed empty, almost too quiet. He lay atop his bed in his shorts. No shirt, no shoes. He'd visited his parents in Holland in April, when Nick Janssen was just wanted for failing to appear in court to face tax evasion charges. He'd made a move on Rob's mother, and Rob hadn't even known it.

61

So much had happened since then.

But his parents were back in Night's Landing, permanently, and his father, in his late seventies, was finally easing up on his schedule. His mother seemed more at peace than she had in many weeks. Neither had wanted Rob to go back to work after the shooting — they hadn't wanted him to become a marshal in the first place.

"Should have called them before you left New York," he said to the ceiling. But he hadn't talked to them at all since Janssen's arrest.

He let his eyes close, pushing back an image of Night's Landing and the old log house his grandfather had built, thinking instead about Maggie Spencer and Tom Kopac and what it was about the diplomatic security agent that bothered him.

Five

Maggie pulled up to Rob's hotel in her Mini at eight. She didn't know what else to do except drag him to 's-Hertogenbosch with her.

He greeted her with a charming smile and two espressos and folded himself into her small car without complaint, handing her one of the espressos. "What is it, about two hours to 's-Hertogenbosch?"

He pronounced the full name of the southern city the same way her Dutch friends did — flawlessly. It translated as "the duke's forest" and was typically shortened to Den Bosch, which Maggie could pronounce easily enough. "Should be," she said, pulling out onto the street.

As he sipped his espresso, Rob dug out a pocket map and checked their route. "Den Bosch was founded in the twelfth century by Hendrik I of Brabant."

"Ah."

"Biggest attraction there is Sint Jan's Kathedraal."

Maggie didn't let herself react to his use of the Dutch name for St. John's Cathedral, where she was supposed to meet her anonymous caller, her ulterior motive for going to Den Bosch on a warm Saturday morning. "You've been reading tourist brochures, I see."

"We might need something to do after we look at the spot where the Dutch police picked up Janssen. Do you know the address of his safe house?"

She nodded. "We could go there, too."

"Maybe it has window boxes."

His sarcasm was barely detectable, which, Maggie decided, only made him more dangerous. She'd underestimated him. Dismissed him as not serious, indulged in stereotypes because she hadn't wanted to deal with him — she'd had better things to do than take care of a deputy marshal who counted among his friends the U.S. president. But Deputy Dunnemore was proving himself to be a much more complicated case than she'd anticipated.

She got onto the motorway, the traffic relatively light on a Saturday morning. "If you don't want to go to Den Bosch, I can drop you off somewhere else."

"I'm into the idea now. Have you seen many sights since you've been here?"

She reached for her espresso and took

too big a sip, nearly burning her mouth, then shook her head, putting the coffee back in the cup holder. "I've only been here three weeks. I haven't had much time. I vary my run just so I can see more of the streets in The Hague." She made herself smile through her tension. She didn't like hiding her real purpose for going to Den Bosch from him. "I could get into castles."

"All work, no play," Rob said, looking up from his map. "Does that describe you, Maggie?"

"I don't know. I'm not that introspective."

"Interesting, since you're the new kid, that you should be the one to get the tip on where to find our guy Janssen."

"Yes, isn't it?"

"Where were you before here?"

"Chicago."

"And you grew up in . . ."

"South Florida, for the most part. We moved around a lot before my parents were divorced."

"They still live there?"

"My mother does." She left it at that.

But Rob persisted. "Your father?"

"He died a year and a half ago."

"I'm sorry." No hesitation, no awkwardness. He had the social graces down pat, when he wanted to use them. "Any theory why Janssen was in Den Bosch?"

She shook her head, reminding herself that Rob's family had nearly all been killed because of Nick Janssen and she should cut him some slack. But he wasn't going to change the subject, obviously. He'd keep grilling her about Janssen and Den Bosch and the tip until she put a stop to it. She didn't know if he was suspicious of her because of the tip or just tenacious — or both.

"Why do you think the marshals sent you here?" she asked casually. "Given your personal connection to Janssen —"

"No one sent me. I asked to come here."

It wasn't the answer she'd expected. "They let you?"

Janssen's arrest stirred up the media. "I had a lot of reporters on my tail. This way I'm out of sight, out of mind."

"Or out of sight and they'll all want to know why and show up here next?"

He shrugged. "I don't think so. Have you had many reporters contact you?"

"Not directly. A few have contacted Public Affairs."

"I guess it's not nearly as interesting to have an international fugitive arrested as a presidential connection exposed."

She tried more of the espresso. Rob had

done fine yesterday at the embassy. He was good at small talk, at ease with people. His connection to President Poe made people eager to meet him and be on their best behavior, but in the end, Maggie thought, it hadn't made that big a difference. The guy was likable. The mistake, she suspected, was to assume that translated into being a soft touch.

He again consulted his map. "Janssen was picked up on a canal?"

"The Binnendieze. I wasn't sure of what it was, either. It's a shallow river, but it looks and feels like a canal. Den Bosch is located in a triangle where the Aa and the Dommel join to form the Dieze River, which eventually runs into the Maas."

"Ah. So I see on the map."

"Water's a big deal in the Netherlands. About a third of the country's below sea level. We tend to think in terms of the North Sea, but river flooding is a concern, too."

"Binnendieze — does that mean 'little Dieze'?"

"Aren't you the one who speaks all the languages?"

He finished his espresso without answering.

"I heard it was seven," Maggie persisted.

"Well, one of them isn't Dutch."

67

She laughed. "*Binnen* means inner, or inside. It's the section of the Dieze that runs within Den Bosch's original city walls — it's sort of a natural moat. They've cleaned it up and run boat tours on it these days."

"Bet it used to be the town sewer."

"That's what I understand. The tour's unusual because it takes you *under* the city, actually under people's houses. For safety reasons, centuries ago, people could only build inside the city walls. When they ran out of room, they started building over the waterway."

"Very clever."

"It sounds like a fascinating tour, doesn't it?"

"Better than the cathedral, if you ask me."

Maggie got off the A2 motorway and drove toward the city center, Rob pointing out a stunning fountain featuring a gold dragon in the middle of a roundabout. Remembering directions she'd gotten from a Dutch police inspector, who hadn't questioned her reasons for asking, she found her way to the boat-tour entrance and parked nearby.

It was a pleasantly warm morning under a clear Dutch-blue sky, a perfect day to play tourist — except that wasn't why she and Rob were there, Maggie reminded herself as they walked along a shaded street.

The narrow, shallow waterway flowed next to them, below street level. Steps lead down to a small dock for the boats, a crowd gathering for the next tour.

"Janssen had two dogs," Rob said, stopping along the open black-iron fence above the waterway. "Rhodesian ridgebacks."

"Big dogs."

"Do we know what happened to them?"

"They weren't with him when he was arrested. I doubt he had them with him when he took off in May."

"How long do we think he was in Den Bosch before you got the tip?"

From his tone, Maggie knew he didn't expect her to have an answer. "Not long, but that's not a guess at this point. Den Bosch strikes me as an unlikely place for the leader of an international criminal network to turn up. It's possible he —"

She stopped. *Who was that?* A man in front of a café just down the street . . . balding, rumpled.

Tom Kopac?

Rob was instantly alert. "What is it?"

"I think I recognize someone. Hold on."

Maggie started toward the café, but Tom had disappeared. She pushed past the outdoor tables, where a few tourists were enjoying coffee, and checked inside, her eyes quickly adjusting after being in the bright sun.

Nothing.

Had she mistaken someone else for Tom?

No. She was positive it'd been him.

He must have continued past the café or cut down another street.

She headed back outside and scanned the scene.

Rob stood behind her. "What's going on?"

"A colleague at the embassy is here. Maybe he's like us, just checking out where Janssen was picked up."

"Did he work the case?"

She shook her head. "No. But he's a good guy. A friend."

"What's his name?"

"Kopac. Tom Kopac. He works in economic relations."

Rob frowned at her. "He came by my hotel last night."

"Tom did? Why?"

"Checking me out. Are you two —"

"No."

She thought she detected a flicker of amusement at her forceful answer. "You DS agents are the expert drivers. Could he have followed us out here?"

"It's not like I'm on a secret mission or driving around the secretary of state. I wasn't paying that close attention, but I

70

doubt —" She realized she sounded very serious and deliberately lightened up. "I'm sure he didn't follow us."

"Did he see you just now?"

"You mean, was he running away from me? I don't know."

At the same time, they noticed a change in the crowd at the entrance to the boat tour. A sudden tension, gasps.

Screams.

Maggie and Rob charged back down the street, heading for a half-dozen people who were standing at the open fence, pointing into the water. A woman was screaming.

"Een man . . ."

A man.

Maggie picked out another word. *Gevallen . . .* Fallen. Fell.

"A man's fallen into the river," Rob said tightly.

There were more screams, excited words in Dutch that all ran together to Maggie's untrained ear.

Rob obviously spoke enough languages that he was able to make out the basics. "They think he's dead."

"Not Tom —"

She didn't know why she said his name.

When they got to the fence and looked down at the river, they could see the body

71

of a man floating facedown in the shallow water, drifting downstream.

The balding head, the stocky build, the rumpled clothes.

"Hell," Rob breathed. "It's him. Kopac."

Maggie turned away and took in a breath, pushing back a rush of emotion, then forced herself to look again at Tom's body.

Blood.

His head . . .

The images she was seeing came together, registered. He'd been shot at the base of his neck, the bullet going upward into his brain.

Tom. My God.

There was almost no hope he was alive.

Rob pounded down the stairs to the waterway, and Maggie jumped after him, a man yelling to them in Dutch. From the tone of his voice, she knew he was worried about them.

She understood his fear. "A shooter. Rob, if there's a shooter —"

But another look at Tom confirmed, at least in Maggie's mind, it hadn't been a sniper attack. There was no one hiding on a rooftop — or in the bushes, as the gunman who'd shot Rob had done in Central Park four months ago.

From what she could see, Tom had been shot up close and personal. She felt a sense of revulsion, anger and grief, even as she forced herself to pull back from her emotions and focus on the problem at hand.

Rob pushed out to the edge of the dock. "Someone will have called the police by now."

As he spoke, Maggie heard sirens. Neither she nor Rob had authority as law enforcement officers in the Netherlands. Given the circumstances, they weren't even armed.

But they had to make sure there was nothing they could do for Tom.

Rob knelt down and grabbed Tom's arm. His body was snagged on a support post, and Maggie helped, taking hold of Tom's belt. His skin was warm, water pouring off his clothes as they managed to get him up onto the platform.

He was dead. He'd probably died instantly.

"I just saw him," Maggie said. "It wasn't, what, even five minutes ago? The killer can't have gotten far. Someone must have seen something, someone —"

Rob glanced up at the frightened and horrified people along the fence. "At least we know one of us didn't kill him."

Maggie nodded. At least they knew that

much, if not a damn thing else. Like why Tom was here. If he'd spotted her, heard her. If he'd taken off because he didn't want to talk to her.

If he'd known his killer.

And if his killer had anything to do with the American fugitive who'd been picked up in Den Bosch two days ago.

"Come on," Rob said. "The Den Bosch police are going to want to talk to us."

A dead American in their small city?

The local police most certainly would want to talk to the two U.S. federal agents who'd pulled him out of the river.

"He was the kind of guy who got homesick for Krispy Kreme doughnuts," Maggie said, realizing her front was soaked with river water.

"A nice guy," Rob said.

"A very nice guy."

It was four o'clock before Rob and his DS escort left the police station, their clothes finally dry, every question asked of them answered. Maggie pushed ahead on the narrow, sunny street. "I need to walk," she said.

Rob didn't object. It was a hot, still afternoon. The city seemed quiet, almost as if it were mourning the violence that had taken place there a few hours ago.

An exhaustive search hadn't produced a single lead on Thomas Kopac's killer so far.

No one saw anything. No one heard anything.

Except for Maggie Spencer.

Rob said nothing as he walked alongside her. She seemed preoccupied. Not, he thought, that she was an easy woman to read.

Various Dutch and American authorities had swarmed the Den Bosch police station, including the FBI and Regional Security Officer George Bremmerton, Maggie's immediate boss. All of them grilled both her and Rob about what they'd seen that morning, what Maggie had talked about with Kopac in recent days, why he'd shown up at Rob's hotel last night.

Although she knew Tom Kopac well enough to consider him her first real friend since she'd arrived in the country, Maggie had been straightforward and professional with her answers. She'd also had her own questions, namely, if there was anything about Tom Kopac that she hadn't been told.

Rob had that same question himself.

Den Bosch police were trying to locate

people who'd been in the vicinity of the boat tour that morning, interviewing the café's wait staff and manager — anyone who might have seen the American who'd turned up in the Binnendieze. Maggie's sighting of Kopac and the subsequent commotion along the river pinpointed the approximate time he'd been killed.

Apparently someone had walked up to him, shot him and disappeared.

Not an easy feat to pull off.

The brutal, calculated murder of an American diplomat had taken Dutch and U.S. authorities by complete surprise. They had Nick Janssen in custody. The killing was supposed to stop.

"Another American in trouble on Dutch soil," Maggie said as she and Rob walked across the street to Den Bosch's market square, crowded with booths and shoppers. She was obviously spent, taken aback by Kopac's death, the loss of a friend. "The second American murdered in less than a year."

"Nick Janssen ordered Charlene Brooker's murder," Rob said unnecessarily.

"No one had a clue that she was on to him. He was still a fairly low-priority tax evader then."

"Has there been any sign of Ethan

Brooker since Janssen's arrest?" Rob asked.

After his wife's death, Ethan, an army Special Forces officer, had made finding her killer his personal mission. It'd taken him to Tennessee, where he'd posed as the Dunnemores' property manager. After helping Sarah Dunnemore, Nate Winter and Juliet Longstreet stop their Central Park shooter — a loose cannon with a crazy scheme of his own — Brooker had simply disappeared.

When things exploded in Night's Landing, Rob was still recovering from his gunshot wound in his New York hospital.

"It's not as if Brooker's kept the embassy informed of his whereabouts," Maggie said.

"Could he have given you the tip on where to find Janssen?"

"I don't know. I suppose it's possible. But nothing suggests he's anything but one of the good guys — he couldn't have killed Tom." Her voice cracked, and she turned away, fixed her gaze on a nearby food booth. *"Damn."*

"Are you going to be all right?" Rob asked.

She nodded. "I'd like to offer up a prayer."

A prayer? "Okay."

She lifted her chin, squinting against the

late afternoon sun. "It'll only take twenty minutes or so. Do you mind?"

"No, of course not."

She smiled faintly. "You can try the fresh herring. It's a Dutch favorite."

"It's raw."

"Yes, but it's good. You salt it, then more or less drop it down your throat as if you were a seal. I like it. The tradition is to chase it with a shot of *genever*. Dutch gin."

"I'll take the gin without the herring."

Her turquoise eyes went distant again. "Twenty minutes."

Rob nodded. "I'll be here."

He saw her relief, as if she'd expected she'd have to fight him for a few minutes on her own. She started through the square, the strong afternoon sun lightening her deep red hair.

Normally he was good at reading people, a combination of training, experience and instinct. But Maggie wasn't easy to read.

Still, as he winced at the lineup of raw herring on ice, all his alarm bells were going off.

Special Agent Spencer had something up her sleeve.

"Prayer, my ass," he said under his breath, deciding he'd try raw herring another day.

Six

St. John's Cathedral was cool and dark, a sharp contrast to the afternoon heat and sunlight on the streets outside. Its massive interior seemed quiet for a summer Saturday. Maggie suspected word of the brutal murder of an American had prompted at least some tourists to change their plans.

Tom . . . I'm so sorry.

Why didn't you answer me when I called you?

She wanted to believe he hadn't heard her, but, as she'd told the Dutch and American investigators, she didn't know for sure one way or the other.

She tried not to think of his easy manner, his smile. With physical effort, she pushed back the personal regrets — the grief — she had for the death of a new friend and focused on the job she had to do.

Could Tom have been the caller who wanted to meet with her? Had he disguised his voice and played on her father's death to lure her to Den Bosch?

Why?

But that made no sense.

She hadn't mentioned the call to anyone. It was a long shot that the lead was legitimate, and there was no reason to believe it had anything to do with Tom's death. The Dutch police would probably be irritated with her for withholding any information, but Maggie had no evidence it had been anything but a crank call.

She hadn't told her boss or the FBI about the strange call, either, or, certainly, Rob Dunnemore.

If it'd been Tom, there'd be no meeting.

If it was a nut, either there'd be no meeting or he'd show up and she'd find out that he was crazy soon enough.

If it was a legitimate informant, she'd get what she could out of him and proceed from there.

She felt the uneven stone flooring under her feet. *And if it's whoever shot Tom in the back of the head?*

Then, Maggie thought, she'd kick herself for not having opened her mouth.

And she'd deal with it.

Bringing Rob along for extra security wouldn't have worked. If her caller was still at the cathedral, he'd realize she wasn't alone — and Dunnemore would have quickly figured out she wasn't there just to pray.

Maggie made her way along the outer aisle of the huge cathedral, aware of shadows and the silence. People were buried here. For eight hundred years, people had worshiped in this place. Its thirteenth-century tower and some of its interior were Romanesque in style, but its more ornate Gothic features from later expansion and rebuilding dominated.

Brochure in hand, Maggie pretended she was a tourist, peeking at the baptistery and the Passion altar, checking out the seven chapels that ringed the cavernous interior, staring up at the medieval figures of saints and the religious reliefs depicting the life of Christ and John the Baptist. There were enormous flying buttresses, and beautiful stained-glass windows let in just a thin filter of light.

She could feel the weight of the centuries, the inevitable flow of history, and thought about how much the world outside the cathedral's thick walls had changed.

She pictured Tom's body in the Binnendieze and wondered how many deaths its waters had seen. Conquerors had come and gone. Liberators, wars, floods, people. Maggie was aware of her own impermanence. Perhaps that was part of the purpose of such a place, part of why it endured.

A few people here and there were kneeling in silent prayer, as if to remind her the cathedral was a house of worship.

Most of the pews in the center nave were empty. Maggie made her way into one near the outermost aisle, with a good view of the major entrance and exit. When she sat down, she felt chilled, suddenly isolated and very tired. *Tom.*

A white-haired man worked his way into the pew and sat next to her.

Five aisles, dozens of pews. He picked hers.

She could smell the stale cigarette smoke that clung to him. Glancing out of the corner of her eye, she saw his yellow-tipped fingernails and the blue veins bulging in the skinny hand on his thigh.

He didn't kneel or pull out rosary beads.

Hell. It's him, Maggie thought

"Where's your marshal friend?" he asked.

His East Coast prep school accent didn't fit with his down-and-out appearance. "I don't have a lot of time," she said, not giving him a direct answer. "I need to know who you are. Your name. Why you sought me out. Why Den Bosch. Start now."

She spoke in a whisper, but her urgent tone — and her skepticism — didn't seem to bother him. "My name is William Raleigh," he said. "I was in the foreign service once."

Oh, God. A nutcase. Some threadbare old guy who thought he was a spy or a diplomat. "For the U.S.?"

"Yes. Then I went out on my own. My specialty is economics." He smiled. "As much as it's anyone's specialty."

Although he sounded lucid, Maggie knew he could just be playing the part, trying to persuade her that he was the real thing. "I was never any good at economics."

"No one is, even the experts. It's just that the experts know it and the rest of us hope it's not true."

There was a hint of humor and irony in his whispered words, but Maggie wasn't willing to bet yet whether he was legit or a mentally ill drifter determined to reel her in to his delusions. "Mr. Raleigh, I need to know what this is all about."

He faced the front of the cathedral, not

looking at her. "I've had an interesting life. I'm an economist. I've traveled all over the world, doing what I could to bring fairness and prosperity to others, first in my work as a foreign service officer, then as an economic consultant. That sounds lofty, but I don't mean it to. I did what I could. I think that's what we all do, don't you?"

"No."

He smiled. "So young to be a cynic."

"It hasn't been a good day."

"No, it hasn't. I'm sorry about your friend."

Then he knew about Tom. Of course, Den Bosch was a small city, and news traveled quickly.

"I've met everyone from small-time warlords to the last five U.S. presidents," the man next to her said. "Not the current one yet. Poe."

Yet. Maggie wondered if Raleigh had brought up Poe's name deliberately, if he knew the marshal with her was Rob Dunnemore. Was Rob's connection to President Poe, ultimately, what this meeting was all about?

She shifted in the pew, studying Raleigh. He wasn't much taller than she was, and he was thin, dressed in a blue madras shirt that must have seen him through at least one of his decades of supposed travels. She noticed that he'd let the hem out of his khaki pants, as if they'd shrunk in the dryer.

Maggie checked for drool and dried fried egg or something on his shirt, and hated herself for doing it.

His belt wasn't pulled too tight or hanging too loose.

His fly was zipped.

He had on sports sandals, a definite surprise. No socks.

He smiled faintly at her. "Do I look dotty?"

"Let's just say you don't look like a retired economist. How old are you?"

"Not as old as I look."

"What kind of economist are you, the kind for or against tax cuts?"

He gave a small laugh. "That's a very American question."

"I'm a very American diplomatic security agent. Come on, Mr. Raleigh. Who are you, really?"

His eyes, a pale grayish blue, focused on her a moment, emanating a warmth and affection — a familiarity — that made Maggie edge away from him.

"My father . . ."

She didn't know if she'd spoken aloud.

"What about your father, Maggie?"

Her chest tightened, and she turned abruptly from him and stared up toward the pulpit. She had to stay focused, on task. She couldn't lose control.

"Did you know him?" she asked.

"I can't say I knew him well. We ran into each other in Prague a few weeks before his death. He told me about his DS agent daughter. He was so proud of you. He called you his Magster." Raleigh's tone was formal and very correct, almost without emotion, incongruent with his tattered appearance. "I believe it's fate that our paths crossed."

"Fate or bullshit."

He didn't respond.

"Thomas Kopac —"

"I had nothing to do with his death. It's a terrible shame. I know he befriended you."

Maggie noticed red veins in Raleigh's eyes, bulging veins in his nose. A drinker. "That wouldn't be hard for you to find out. It's not as if we kept our friendship a secret."

"No doubt." Raleigh went very still next to Maggie, staring down at the bony hand on his thigh. "So many of the people I've met in my day were forgettable. Shallow, venal, selfish, arrogant — I don't want to remember them in my retirement. Others weren't. They were the best. They had honor and integrity. Not all of them went on to live to an old age the way I undoubtedly will, if only because I'm destined to be the one to remember what they were." He didn't raise his voice or ramble. "I'm often haunted by the good people I couldn't save."

Jesus.

"Who are you talking about? Why am I here?"

He inhaled through his nose. "I can feel the presence of the dead here, can't you? Eighteen months. It doesn't seem that long ago —"

"If you're using my father's death to try to manipulate me, it won't work. If you were responsible in some way for what happened to him —"

"He wouldn't have wanted me to put you in danger."

"I have a job to do. I intend to do it to the best of my abilities. That's not up to you."

"It wasn't up to him, either." Raleigh's tone lost its moroseness, became firmer, more serious. "He knew you were like him. You're capable of breaking a few dishes, Maggie."

"I'm a professional —"

"You're a self-starter, an independent thinker. And, yes, a professional. You won't cross the line. But you'll put a toe over it." His tone had lightened, but only momentarily. "You can't tell anyone about me, Maggie. No one. That's very important for your own safety. You have good instincts. Trust them."

"I didn't know Tom Kopac was about to be killed this morning."

"I didn't say you were clairvoyant."

"If you have any information, I can take you to the American embassy and we can talk there." Unless he was already familiar to everyone there — *good old Bill Raleigh, yeah, that head case.*

But he was very convincing. "That won't be necessary."

Maggie knew she'd lost him, that he was wrapping up, but she persisted. "I need more to go on."

His movements unhurried, he carefully, deliberately, stood. She noticed he had a walking stick with him, the retractable kind that hikers use. He turned to her. "There's an inn in Ravenkill, New York. The Old Stone Hollow. I don't know if it's of any significance. Perhaps it's just a pretty country inn."

"An inn? What —"

"It's good to meet you in person, Agent Spencer," Raleigh said, easing out of the pew. "Your marshal friend is here. He's not one to underestimate, is he? I'll be in touch if I have anything else for you."

Maggie whipped around in the pew, but she didn't see Rob.

A trick. Damn.

She jumped up, but Raleigh — or whoever he was — had darted into the outer aisle, moving faster than she'd thought him capable of. He kicked over a kneeler and it landed on her ankle, slowing her down as she went after him. Every fiber of her being told her that he was someone she could trust, but her common sense — her training and experience — warned her not to let herself get sucked into his story all the way.

She wouldn't be the first law enforcement officer to get taken in by a delusional alcoholic.

"Mr. Raleigh," she whispered, "please wait. Rob's not here. You have to give me more. This inn —"

Ignoring her, he picked up his pace. Maggie didn't know what she was supposed to do if she caught up with him. Tackle him and drag him to the Den Bosch police? Shove him in her Mini and drive him to the American embassy? She wasn't armed. She had no arrest authority in the Netherlands.

She heard someone mumbling a prayer in a nearby chapel, then the far-off moan of a door, the echo of footsteps. Her hands were clammy, her fingers stiff as if they'd been in the cold.

"Raleigh!"

She let her voice go above a whisper.

A woman spun around in a pew and glared at her.

He wasn't stopping.

If she tried to tackle him, Maggie figured he'd whack her with his walking stick. He'd make a scene. He'd play the crazy old drunk being attacked by a religious zealot. He'd scream for help, scaring the hell out of the few stragglers in the cathedral, and run.

Trust your instincts.

He disappeared, hiding in one of the thousand nooks and crannies of the massive cathedral, stealing out an exit.

Maybe he'd just gone up in smoke.

Maybe she'd imagined him.

Ravenkill, New York.

Maggie had never heard of it or the Old Stone Hollow Inn.

"Little unsteady on your feet there, Agent Spencer?"

Dunnemore. He didn't bother to speak in a whisper. Maggie recognized his Southern accent even before she swung around and saw him coming through a pew from another aisle.

Obviously he'd been in the cathedral long enough to have seen her trip on the kneeler.

That meant he'd also seen her chase William Raleigh.

"Just a little," she said with an edge of sarcasm. "Have I been longer than twenty minutes?"

"I don't know. I gave you a two-minute head start before I came after you." He stood very close to her, not much charming about his manner right now. "The raw herring wasn't that appealing."

She flexed her ankle, easing out any stiffness. "I should have remembered you track people for a living."

"Probably should have. Who was the old man?"

"William the Conqueror."

He held his suit jacket over his shoulder with one finger, his shirtsleeves rolled up. He hadn't had a particularly good day, either. Maggie felt herself softening as he looked her up and down. "You hurt?" he asked.

She shook her head, wondering if he might be exaggerating his accent just to throw her off balance. "How did you find me?"

"You said you were off to pray. This is the biggest church in the whole damn country. I figured it was a good place to start."

"You shouldn't swear in here."

"You're right. We can go outside, and I'll swear out there." His eyes — they were a dark gray in the dim light of the cathedral — fixed on her. "And you can tell me about the old guy in the madras shirt."

They found a table in the shade at an uncrowded café near the market square. "Get two of whatever you're ordering," Maggie said. "I'm not picky. I don't even know if I can eat."

Rob ordered two bowls of the soup of the day, which seemed to involve chicken, and coffee for himself, a Heineken for Maggie. He'd do the driving back to The Hague.

Their waiter brought the drinks first. Maggie touched a finger to the foam of her beer. She'd had a miserable day, and she looked more shaken than she'd want to admit, worse now that she'd finished with the investigators and the questions — and now that whatever her mission at the cathedral had been was over.

"The old guy looked like he planned to take you out with that walking stick," Rob said.

"For all I know, he thought it was tipped with ricin."

"Is that a joke?"

She sighed. "An attempt at a joke."

Rob lifted his small coffee cup. "I'd say cheers, but it wouldn't sound right today."

"I suppose not." She picked up her beer, hesitating, as if pushing back an intrusive thought, before taking a sip. "It's been a long week. Nothing about it's been normal."

Including having him thrust upon her, Rob thought, drinking some of his coffee. It was very strong, but he figured a jolt of caffeine wouldn't hurt. He was hot from chasing after Maggie, negotiating the narrow, unfamiliar city streets in the late August heat. "Your rendezvous with the old guy at St. John's. That's why we're in Den Bosch today?"

Maggie stared at the disappearing foam on her beer. "I shouldn't drink —"

"Go ahead. I'm sticking to coffee. I'll drive." He smiled, trying to take some of the edge off her mood and maybe his own. "It's okay. I can handle a Mini."

She raised her eyes from her drink. "I know what it must have looked like back there. Just forget about it, okay?"

"Not okay. The old guy's an informant?"

"A wanna-be, I think."

"Any relation to Kopac?"

"I don't know that much about him."

Rob sat back in his chair. "That's an evasive answer."

"Maybe it's a polite way to tell you —" She stopped herself. "Never mind. It's been a lousy day for you, too."

But she obviously wanted to tell him what happened in St. John's was none of his damned business. "Better to evade than to lie outright. Okay. I get that. You don't know anything about me except that I'm a marshal, I was shot four months ago and my family knows the president." He shrugged. "I wouldn't trust me, either."

"It's not a question of trust."

Then what else was it? But he didn't ask. "This guy's contacted you before?"

"First time."

"What'd he do, call, e-mail, send a carrier pigeon? Come on. Throw me a bone. Let me think you're starting to trust me a little."

94

She didn't smile. "He called."

"When?"

"Yesterday."

"So, after I got here."

Their soup arrived in heavy bowls. Cream of chicken and fresh vegetables. It was steaming and substantial, which, despite the heat, Rob welcomed.

Maggie shifted around in her chair. "I wouldn't make too much of this. The timing's bad, I know, but I'm not all that sure he's playing with a full deck." She picked up her beer with such force, some of it splashed out onto her hand. "It's quiet, don't you think? Especially for such a beautiful afternoon. People must be worried after this morning. I guess I don't blame them."

"They'll decide it's an American thing and go on with their lives. In Central Park in the spring, people decided it was a marshals thing. It helped them get past the idea of a sniper on the loose. Someone wasn't picking off people at random."

Maggie took a drink of her beer, then set down the glass and blew out a sigh. "Tom's family must know by now what happened to him. It's an awful experience to go through, having someone come to your house and tell you — well, you know what I mean."

"I called my sister from Central Park so she wouldn't have to find out that way or, worse, see me on television."

"Did you know you were in bad shape?"

"I don't remember what I knew."

She looked away. "You didn't need what happened today."

"Maggie, I didn't come to the Netherlands to run away from anything. I can do my job."

"You're not back on the street," she said.

"That's not my decision to make. Look —"

She faced him again, her creamy skin less pale. "You should be. You didn't hesitate today. The shooter, Tom. You did fine."

He acknowledged her words with a nod. "I still want to know about this Scarlet Pimpernel character of yours."

This time, she smiled. "You marshals. Hound dogs on a scent."

Rob tried the soup, relished the normalcy of it. "Maybe I can help."

"That's nice of you to offer, but there's nothing for you to do."

Clever. It wasn't as if he could order her to come clean. He could badger her for answers, but he'd already seen her help pull a dead man out of a river, deal with the Dutch police and a nervous embassy and chase a white-haired old man. She'd hold her own against anything he threw at her and tell him exactly what she wanted him to know and not one word more.

This wasn't what he'd had in mind when he'd told Mike Rivera he wanted to go to the Netherlands.

"You saw the man with me at St. John's. My wanna-be informant. Did he look mentally stable to you?"

Rob shrugged. "Down on his luck, maybe. Lost his retirement, got a little daft. Could just be on a tight budget."

"I suppose." She picked up her spoon, held it in midair and sighed. "I shouldn't have wasted my time. I just ended up putting you on high alert, got you into tracking mode."

"Kopac's murder did that."

Her eyes shone, but she covered her emotion by dipping her spoon into her soup.

"This guy," Rob said. "Does he have a name? Besides William the Conqueror."

"That was snotty of me. I apologize." She left it at that. "How long were you in the cathedral?"

"Obviously not long enough."

"Did you see anyone else, anyone who could have been with my guy?"

Rob remembered the scene when he'd walked into the cathedral, his eyes adjusting to the dim light, his sensibilities to the atmosphere. It was quiet, removed from the murder investigation outside its doors. When he spotted Maggie in a pew, at first he thought, guiltily, that she had, indeed, come there to pray.

Then he'd noticed the white-haired man sitting too close to her. In the next second, she was chasing after him.

"I should have followed your guy," Rob said. "But I didn't see anyone who might have been with him. Think he tipped you off about Janssen?"

"No. I'm sure he didn't. That message came by a free e-mail account. I doubt —" She topped herself. "I shouldn't make assumptions. He just didn't strike me as someone who would know the whereabouts of an international fugitive."

"But he chose to meet you in Den Bosch, where Janssen was picked up."

"Probably for dramatic effect. He could have read about the arrest in the paper and decided to give me a call. You must know how it is with sources. I'm sympathetic to mental illness — I mean it. But it's not always that easy to sort out the cranks from the legitimate sources." She sighed. "I didn't expect that part of this work, did you?"

Rob didn't answer right away. He'd dealt with his share of delusional would-be informants, from poor, illiterate drug addicts to highly educated society matrons. Getting sucked into one of their wild fantasies and acting on it was the nightmare of every law enforcement officer he knew. "Maggie — "

"I've told you what I can."

He could feel her tension and reached across the table, skimming his fingertips across the top of her hand. Her skin was cooler than it should have been on such a warm day. She didn't pull away, but touching her was an instinctive gesture on his part and took them both by surprise.

She took a breath, looking down at her soup. "It's been a weird day. Surreal, almost."

"I'm not the prosecution or your boss." Rob tried to sound reassuring, not patronizing or irritated by her unwillingness to talk. Still, he could feel his own tension and fatigue clawing at him, and the caffeine had his mind going in a dozen different directions. "You don't have to tell me anything."

She was naturally very fair, with freckles across her cheeks — her appearance could have a tendency to make people not expect her to be an elite diplomatic security agent, not expect her to be as tough and competent as she was. She'd lost a friend today — an embassy employee — and it had to feel like a failure as well as a personal loss.

She raised her eyes, the turquoise, he noticed, softened with flecks of gold. "I know that. But thanks. It's a decent thing to say."

He sat back, letting go of her hand. "Eat your soup. You look like you're about to pass out."

"I never pass out."

But she ate more of her soup, although Rob could see it was an effort for her. She seemed far away again, caught up in something she didn't want to think about but couldn't stop focusing on. He noticed how drawn she looked, how closed off from him. It'd been that way at the police station. Even on a good day, getting anything out of Maggie Spencer wouldn't be easy.

"Want my opinion?" She looked up at Rob, more alert now, less distracted by whatever had her in its grip. "My guy picked Den Bosch and me because we've been in the news, and that's all there is to it."

But she wasn't willing to take the chance that she was wrong. Part of her believed her wanna-be snitch had access and information that could help her, Rob thought, or she wouldn't have stepped foot in St. John's. At the very least, she would have dismissed the guy she'd met there out of hand. Instead, she was thinking about whatever he'd told her, chewing on it, debating whether or not it made sense after all.

Rob finished off his soup. "I guess it would have been tough to frisk him there in the church —"

"Unless he had a gun strapped to his ankle, he wasn't armed."

"Going to tell the Dutch police about him?"

"Only if it's relevant to Tom Kopac's murder. Right now, I can't see that it is."

"I'll bet they'd like to decide that."

She ignored him, abandoning her soup. "We should get back. Sorry for the lousy day. Come on. Half a beer won't affect my driving." She got to her feet, more animated. "I'll pay —"

"No, I'll take care of it." Rob dropped some euro notes on the table, more than enough to cover their tab. "And I'll drive."

"Going to fight me for my car keys?"

An image of the two of them going at it popped into his head, but he stifled it, rising. He was taller than she was — not that she seemed to give a damn. "Sure."

That brought some color to her cheeks. "All right. You get to drive." She smiled brightly, unexpectedly, with a touch of self-deprecation. "*You* know President Poe. *Me* — I know a probable paranoid-schizo-phrenic old man who needs medical treatment, not the ear of a DS officer."

Rob narrowed his eyes on her. "This guy got to you."

"This entire day's gotten to me."

He had an urge to ease some of her emotional turmoil. He wanted her trust and almost asked her for it straight out. But why should she give it to him? They'd known each other for two days. She'd been stuck with him, the wounded marshal whose family was at the heart of the Janssen investigation.

Maybe it was the effects of pulling a dead man out of a Dutch waterway. He hadn't known Thomas Kopac, but, Rob thought as he followed Maggie out to the street, if he got to the point that murder was nothing to him, just another event in a day's work, he'd quit.

She glanced back at him, said nothing.

He took a sharp breath.

And maybe he should pull back from the

effects of those turquoise eyes and that red hair and remember that she'd received the Janssen tip, that she had hidden motives for today's trip to Den Bosch.

Rob had less reason to trust her than she did him.

He had his own contacts.

He'd make a few calls and check out the old guy in the madras shirt himself, see what people knew.

Seven

Ethan Brooker stood next to a subdued William Raleigh on an arched bridge over the Binnendieze, the water dark and quiet with the fading sun. After the discovery of the American's body, boat tours had been canceled for the day.

"Ever do the boat tour?" Ethan asked.

"Once," the older man said, staring down at the canal-like river. "It's fascinating. You see things you never get to see on ordinary canal tours. The waterway runs behind buildings, not in front, and it literally takes you under the city. It's all very clean. You get an up-close view of the architecture of centuries-old buildings. There are many small surprises along the way. An unexpected window box or a pot of flowers, a statue. And it's so quiet." Raleigh glanced sideways at Ethan. "I take it you've never done the tour?"

"No, sir."

Raleigh looked tired. They hadn't expected Tom Kopac to turn up dead. Scooting out of St. John's before Spencer or Dunnemore pounced had taken some doing. Ethan had stood watch in the cathedral, in hiding, and gave Raleigh the high sign when the good marshal showed up. Dunnemore would have recognized Ethan. That meant Raleigh had to get away from the DS agent on his own. If it'd come to it, the old buzzard would have nailed her with his walking stick. It was more an affectation than a necessity, but it would have done the job.

Instead, Maggie Spencer had let him go.

Why? What had Raleigh told her? Their meeting was his idea.

It was to have followed a meeting with Tom Kopac.

"Did you tell Spencer that you and Kopac were supposed to meet this morning, but he was shot to death before —"

"I didn't see how that would help."

"I don't know Dutch law — hell, I don't know U.S. law — but I'm guessing they could haul you in as a material witness."

"I have no information about the murder today."

"What did you tell Spencer?"

"I didn't have much time. She knows my name. That I knew her father."

Ethan turned to his side and leaned a hip against a stone support column of the old bridge. "She thinks he was killed by Czech bank robbers?" he asked. "Or does she know you're a suspect —"

"I'm not a suspect. Not in his murder."

"In fucking up something that led to his murder." Ethan didn't sugarcoat his words, although he and Raleigh had never discussed just how much Ethan had managed to find out in the short months of their acquaintance. "Spencer must not know or she wouldn't have let you go the way she did."

Raleigh didn't react. He was like that. He didn't act on emotion. Which was what made his contact with Maggie Spencer so weird — it was all emotion. That was the only explanation that made sense.

"Right now," Raleigh said, "it doesn't seem prudent or necessary to alert Maggie to all of our actions. I gave her a small mission."

"What small mission?"

"I'd like to keep that to myself for now."

The old man was getting testy. Ethan let it slide. He was thinking he should head for the American embassy and throw himself at their mercy for ever getting hooked up with this guy.

Raleigh pulled himself away from the fence. There was a slight tremble in his hand.

"You're not hitting the bottle, are you?"

Ethan asked, and when Raleigh didn't answer, added, "People say you're a bottle-and-breakdown case."

"People say a lot of things. They don't know me." Raleigh glanced sideways at Ethan and smiled, not nicely. "You don't know me."

It was a fair point. "I want answers about my wife's death. All the answers. That's it. That's all I'm about."

"We're not about to take the law into our own hands," Raleigh said.

"I think we already have."

He regarded Ethan with paternal insight. "Is that what you think?"

"If I had a clue who killed Kopac, I'd be knocking on the door to the American embassy and asking them what the hell to do with what I knew."

"I don't have a clue, either, Major."

Major. Some months ago, Ethan had stopped thinking of himself as a West Point graduate, an army major who'd led covert special operations missions. In the past, he'd done his best to accomplish the mission tasked to him and his men.

His wife's death had changed all that.

Char.

The gut-wrenching anger, grief and guilt weren't there anymore. Just the determination to expose Nicholas Janssen as the person behind her death, and why. All of it, all the answers. Her actual killer — one of the two men Janssen had sent to the U.S. in May — was dead. Nick Janssen himself was behind bars.

It was a start.

Ethan hadn't seen Kopac's murder coming that morning. He'd have stopped it if he had. It had totally blindsided him.

He wasn't sure about William Raleigh.

"Tom Kopac was a good guy?" Ethan asked.

Raleigh didn't hesitate. "Yes."

"Raleigh . . ." Ethan turned away from the river. "You'd better be who and what I think you are."

Which was a spy. For what agency, even what country, Ethan couldn't be sure. But he'd spent a dozen years in the U.S. Special Forces and thought he could recognize an intelligence operative when he saw one. They'd met earlier in the summer when Ethan's personal mission of tracking down Nick Janssen and Raleigh's mission — unknown — had converged.

Unsettling stories about the supposed economist's drinking and mental health problems had reached Ethan, and he hoped he hadn't misplaced his trust. He didn't want to be duped by a delusional man haunted by his own wrongdoings, trying to dig his way back to some measure of self-respect.

"You're sure you shouldn't be in a home?"

Raleigh's eyes twinkled with sudden amusement, the kind of insight that made Ethan continue to work with him. "You are quite a direct man, Major Brooker. If you weren't, I fear I wouldn't have made it out of St. John's today."

"Spencer and the marshal never saw me. If they had —"

"You'd still have found a way out."

"I don't know about that." Ethan was a search-and-destroy specialist, not someone who hid from federal agents — they were all supposed to be on the same side. "I was just playing the hand dealt us back there."

"Yes."

Raleigh grew thoughtful, and Ethan could see he needed rest and a good meal — they both did. "Come on. I'll buy you dinner. Our American friends are on their way back to The Hague. We're not going to run into them."

"Would Rob Dunnemore have recognized you?"

"The feds weren't happy when I took off

on them in May. I think they all had my picture tattooed on various body parts. Dunnemore was still recovering from the Central Park attack, but I lied to his sister. Told her I was a gardener."

"In other words he'd recognize you. You and U.S. federal law enforcement —"

"We're square. They're not after me anymore."

"It's difficult for me to believe anyone would take you for a gardener," Raleigh said.

Ethan grinned. "Why not?"

They started off the bridge, the shadows long in the street with the waning light. "Our job is to keep more innocent people from being killed," Raleigh said abruptly, then glanced at Ethan in that holier-than-thou way he sometimes had, despite the ancient, worn shirt, let-out pants and veins in his nose. "No matter how great our will or noble our cause, neither of us has the power to change the past."

Ethan laid on his west Texas accent, a contrast to the erudite diplomat and economist who'd become his partner of convenience. "Sucks, doesn't it?"

"Yes, Major. It sucks very much."

Rob turned the Mini back over to

Maggie at his hotel, waiting for her at the driver's door before handing over the keys. "Don't want to come in for a drink?"

She shook her head. "Thanks, no."

"You could dump your car at your place and come back."

"It's been a long day."

He smiled at her. "Dinner? A walk? Another bowl of soup?"

That seemed to penetrate her obvious preoccupation. She almost laughed. "You're very deceptive, Deputy Dunnemore. You have this easygoing facade, but underneath? Uh-uh. Not so easygoing at all. I'm going home and taking a shower and having a glass of wine."

"I'm not invited?"

"Like I said, underneath the Southern charm is a very dangerous man. See you tomorrow."

She slid behind the wheel.

Rob shut the door for her and leaned into the open window. "Maggie —"

"I'm fine. I'm sorry about today. I know it's not what you came here for."

Rob stepped back from the small car.

A shower and a glass of wine. Did he believe her?

He could understand her rationale for not bringing up her clandestine meeting at St.

111

John's Cathedral at the Den Bosch police station, before she even knew it would come off. But now that it had? Maggie had made no mention of going to the authorities.

Rob thought he could understand that rationale, too. If she planned to tell anyone, it'd be without him.

When he got to his room, he showered off the river smells, feeling the scar from his bullet wound under his fingers. Tom Kopac hadn't had a chance. His killer must have been standing next to him, unrecognized or a friend? An acquaintance Kopac had never suspected of murderous intent? Had he known, at the last second, what was happening to him?

Rob remembered almost nothing of the shooting in Central Park. The tulips. The miserable weather. So much of his life before and after the shooting was fuzzy, some of it gone forever, due to the trauma he'd endured — the loss of blood, the complications, the long recovery. For some reason, he vividly remembered the shock and determination on Nate Winter's face as he'd dragged Rob, injured only seconds earlier, to cover behind a rock outcropping.

But he couldn't be sure the memory was real, not something he'd pasted together from accounts and descriptions he'd heard and read after the fact.

He toweled off and put on shorts and a T-shirt, walking out into his room. His window was open, and he could hear a toddler squealing. When he glanced down at the street, he saw a towheaded little guy sitting in a child's seat secured to the handlebars of his father's bicycle. Neither wore a helmet. They pushed off, pedaling along on the quiet street on a pleasant summer evening.

Rob felt an urge to rent a bicycle and head off into the Dutch countryside for a few days, go up north to the polders and the lakes stolen from the North Sea. Who'd care? Just so long as no reporters followed him, no one would.

Pushing aside such thoughts, he sat at the small table next to the window and dialed his parents' number in Night's Landing. He pictured them on the porch of their log home, sipping iced tea punch, the air hot, hazy with the oppressive summer humidity. There was often a breeze on the Cumberland River, and the porch was shaded by huge old oaks that beckoned family and friends to leave the comfort of their artificially cooled rooms.

His father answered, a man who'd traveled the world but never considered anywhere but Night's Landing home. "I didn't expect to hear from you," Stuart Dunnemore said. "Sarah told us you were in the Netherlands."

Rob felt a twinge of guilt, knowing he should have got word to his family himself. His father was almost eighty, and he liked to keep track of his only son. "I didn't get much notice that I was going." He hated the note of defensiveness in his voice. "I'm sorry I didn't call. How are you?"

"Just fine, son, just fine."

It was what he always said. "Mother?"

"She's in Nashville with friends, but she should be home for dinner."

His mother was twenty-two years his father's junior, a fact Nick Janssen had tried to twist to his favor — without success.

"The weather's nice here. What's it like there?"

His father, who'd grown up close to the land, loved to talk about the weather. "We're expecting thunderstorms late tonight and tomorrow. It's been hot."

From the tone of their conversation, it was obvious he hadn't heard about the American killed in Den Bosch.

Rob's room suddenly seemed claustrophobic, and he wished for a breeze; but the air was still, the street a few floors down quiet.

"Rob?"

"I'm okay. I wanted to tell you about something before you hear it elsewhere. An American foreign service officer was killed today in Den Bosch. A DS agent and I found him."

"Good God."

"We weren't in any danger." Which, of course, he didn't know for a fact. What if the killer had decided to put a bullet in the back of his head? Maggie's? But he kept his voice calm as he related what had happened. "His name was Tom Kopac. You didn't know him from your time here, did —"

"No. No, I didn't know him. I doubt your mother did, either, but I'll ask her. Are you all right? How —"

"I'm okay. Nothing to worry about."

"Isn't Den Bosch where Nick Janssen was found?"

"That's right. We were there checking out the area."

"You don't think he had anything to do with what happened?"

Rob stared down at the empty street. "I don't know."

After reassuring his father that he was fine, he hung up, feeling guilty. His parents were still dealing with the aftermath of Conroy Fontaine and Nick Janssen's assault on the entire Dunnemore family in the spring.

I shouldn't have come here.

But Rob dismissed the thought before it could take root. His father would have chosen a different profession for his only son. The shooting in the spring and the murder in Den Bosch today would only add to his conviction that Rob didn't belong in the Marshals Service.

He dialed Nate's cell phone. He didn't want his sister picking up their home phone. "Rob. Where the hell are you? I heard about what happened."

"I'm safe and sound in my hotel room, about to head down to the bar for a stiff drink. My sister knows?"

"Yes."

"She's —"

"She wants to get on a plane and fly to Amsterdam tonight. You know she does."

The twin thing, as Nate liked to say.

"Do you want to talk to her?" he asked.

Rob tried to smile. "Why do you think I called your cell phone and not that haunted house you're living in?"

"That's not why. You've never been afraid to talk to Sarah. You aren't now. What's up?"

Rob pushed back from the window. "I need information. Maggie Spencer and Tom Kopac. What do you know about them?"

A half beat's silence. "Why?"

"Kopac befriended Spencer when she got here. No romance, according to both of them. But it's an odd pairing, even for a platonic relationship. I just want to be sure I'm not missing something."

"Talk to me, Rob."

The two of them had worked fugitive apprehensions in New York before the Central Park shooting and Nate's subsequent appointment to USMS headquarters. Rob didn't want to leave anything out. He had no intention of lying. At the same time, until he knew more, he didn't want to interfere in Maggie's business.

Nate, however, would sense that he wasn't getting everything.

"Maggie spotted Kopac minutes before he was killed," Rob said. "She called to him. Either he didn't hear her, or he pretended he didn't."

"Anyone with him?"

"She says she didn't see anyone."

"Any connection between Kopac and Janssen?" Nate asked.

"Not that I know of."

"I'll check on that, too."

Nate wasn't one to get carried away with speculation. Neither was Rob, although he had a thousand different scenarios and conspiracies and possibilities floating through his head, a distraction, perhaps, to stop him from thinking about Tom Kopac dead in the Binnendieze. But Kopac could have been killed today for reasons that had nothing to do with Nick Janssen — or Maggie Spencer.

"What's Sarah up to?" Rob asked finally, changing the subject.

"Planning the wedding of the century and negotiating with her ghosts. Sometimes I think she believes she really is talking to Abe and Bobby Lee."

"Are they talking back?"

Rob could feel Nate's grin. "I haven't asked."

After hanging up, Rob headed down to the hotel's café and sat at an outdoor table, where an accordionist was playing for spare change and accommodating tourists were laughing and clapping, some even dancing. He ordered a beer and watched the show, dispelling images of Kopac's body and Maggie's horror when she realized it was her friend in the Binnendieze, even as she sucked in her reaction and did her job.

As he drank his beer, Rob let a flashback of his first days back in Night's Landing after he was shot roll over him, not fighting it, but not diving into it. He'd been weak and dependant and guilt-ridden, angry at having missed clues that could have spared him and his family so much pain and suffering — that could have exposed Nick Janssen sooner. He remembered staring at his reflection in the mirror and making himself acknowledge that his life would never be the same again. That the shooting had changed him forever and there was no going back to the man he'd been before Central Park.

A fiddler joined the accordionist, then a singer, a plump woman in a ruffled skirt.

There was more laughter, more applause, but Rob had lost any sense that he was a part of the festivities. He left a few euros for the musicians and took his second beer up to his room.

After a simple meal at a nearby restaurant, Libby Smith retired to her room in a small tourist hotel in Brussels, a renovated mansion with antique furnishings and an oddly shaped bathroom. Unfortunately, it had only a shower; she'd have loved to have sunk into a hot tub.

It'd been a close call that morning.

The man she'd killed had known she was in Den Bosch. He'd known *where*.

His name was Tom Kopac. He'd come to Den Bosch to find her.

Why?

He was the balding man in the rumpled suit she'd seen on Thursday before the *Arrestatieteam* had swooped down on Jannsen.

Libby had a compulsion for checking out her surroundings. She'd recognized him early that morning at her hotel in Den Bosch, she'd heard him ask for her — by name — and she'd taken action.

Defensive action.

It was the man's own damn fault he was dead.

He was a diplomat, she'd learned later from news reports. An American. And he was friends, obviously, with Maggie Spencer, who was herself in Den Bosch for reasons unknown.

Philip Spencer's daughter.

After dealing with Kopac, Libby had checked out of her Den Bosch hotel, speaking with the desk clerk, in English, about driving to Belgium. She'd played the lonely solo American traveler wanting a chance to chat with someone. A normal conversation with a woman who had nothing to hide. The clerk, who spoke little English, gave no indication he realized the balding man who'd come in that morning was the American murdered steps away on the Binnendieze. Libby didn't bring up Kopac's name or ask what he'd told the clerk. She'd spotted Kopac when she came down from her room and overheard him ask for her by name. He obviously recognized her — or guessed who she was — and followed her when she ducked onto the street. His mistake. Minutes later, he was dead.

Lying atop her bedsheets, Libby noticed their lace edging and wondered if it was Belgian. Undoubtedly not. Too expensive for repeated washings, especially in a moderately priced hotel. She hadn't wanted to go rock bottom, though. As a woman traveling alone, that would have drawn attention — but she hadn't wanted to stay somewhere exclusive, either. Again, more attention.

If Maggie Spencer had spotted Kopac even a minute earlier, everything might have gone differently that morning.

"What if she becomes a problem?"

Libby spoke out loud, articulating her concern in a calm, focused voice that by itself steadied her.

She sighed. "Then you'll deal with her."

Just as she'd dealt with Miss Maggie's father.

And would have to deal with his friend Bill Raleigh sooner or later.

Her head throbbed. She blamed it on the sunlight during her drive to Brussels.

She'd booked an afternoon flight back to New York tomorrow. Soon, she'd be home, back in her bed in Ravenkill. That had its own set of problems, but they seemed to pale now against what she faced staying in Europe.

It was always the same, the restlessness and obsession after a killing. This time, she had acted out of necessity. She'd had no time to plan. Had she left behind clues, evidence, witnesses?

Should she have killed the desk clerk?

She shut her eyes, trying to rid herself of the repeated images of that morning. The American asking for her. Maggie Spencer calling him. He hadn't heard her. He'd been focused instead on his quarry.

"On me," Libby said quietly.

She wondered if she'd have acted differently if she'd known who he was. She'd motioned to him to join her along the river, and he'd come straight to her — which at least suggested he didn't know she was a hired killer. He must have seen her with Janssen on Thursday and somehow figured out who she was. Perhaps he'd followed her to her hotel, but she didn't think so. She assumed he wanted to talk to her about the now captured fugitive, but why? Kopac wasn't in law enforcement.

Libby had no choice but to put aside her questions. Tom Kopac was dead. He couldn't harm her from the grave.

She racked her brain for anyone who could have seen her with Kopac that morning and replayed every move she'd made in Den Bosch. If she'd screwed up, Nick Janssen would find someone else to do his killing, and *her* name would go onto his target list.

She squirmed in her bed, knowing sleep would elude her.

Maggie Spencer wasn't on Janssen's list, which didn't necessarily mean he wouldn't consider the DS agent a threat if he found out she'd been in Den Bosch that morning — with Rob Dunnemore. *He* was on the list. Libby wished she'd seen him in time to cross off his name. It was a missed opportunity, but she'd had her hands full dealing with Kopac and avoiding Maggie Spencer.

Janssen was in a Dutch jail. Janssen wouldn't like the idea of an American diplomat tailing her, never mind turning up dead. But that, at least, bought her some time to get started on her work for him and, finally, deal with the blowback from Prague and what she'd done eighteen months ago.

Maggie unzipped her suitcase on her bed at midnight, trying to think what she should pack. She'd made a reservation over the Internet for three nights at the Old Stone Hollow Inn in Ravenkill, New York. She hadn't used a false name — she signed up as Maggie Spencer and gave her current address as The Hague, the Netherlands. She might not need to stay all three nights. Once she was convinced Raleigh's tip — or whatever it was — was off the mark, she'd leave. But she wanted to check out the inn and Raleigh's veracity herself. She owed her father that much if Raleigh indeed had tracked her down because she was Philip Spencer's daughter.

What did people wear for a stay at a country inn in the Hudson River Valley? Shorts, pants, shirts. Maybe a skirt. Underwear. Nightclothes. Her running shoes. According to the inn's Web site it had woodland trails where she could go for a run. With any luck, this expedition would turn into a minivacation.

The inn looked like a nice place. A reno-

vated upscale nineteenth-century farmhouse with pale green clapboards and
white shutters. Sunflowers. Vegetable gardens and orchards. A path along Ravenkill
Creek.

If it'd been a fleabag, Maggie thought,
she might not have been so quick to go.

George Bremmerton had found her at
her computer at the embassy, doing a
search for information on William Raleigh.
If he was an economist, he wasn't a very
famous one. She couldn't locate a single
speech, article, book or mention of him.
But that didn't mean he'd lied about his
identity.

She'd told Bremmerton she needed to
take a few days off and let him think it was
because of Tom's death.

"Planning to leave the country?" he'd
asked.

"I'd like to go to New York. Someone else
can keep an eye on Deputy Dunnemore. I
think he'll understand, actually."

"You've only been here a few weeks.
Homesick already?"

"It's not that . . ."

"Then what is it?"

His eyes had bored into her, telling her
he knew her story was, at best, incomplete.

"All right. I've got a guy who thinks he's

a spy or something whispering in my ear." She remembered how Rob had called him her Scarlet Pimpernel, but William Raleigh wasn't nearly as romantic a figure as the fictional character. "He's not the source of the Janssen tip —"

"You're positive?"

"Fairly. I want to follow up some information he gave me."

Bremmerton had stiffened. "What kind of information?"

"Highly questionable." But, she thought, the e-mail that led to Janssen's arrest had sounded nutty, too, and yet it had turned out to be legitimate. "Give me a few days to find out for sure if there's anything to it."

Bremmerton had looked at her for a long time. "Is this personal or professional?"

"Both."

"I don't like that."

"Neither do I."

"Why not blow off this guy?"

"I can't. He could be a drunk or crazy, I don't know, but I feel like I have to check this out. I've typed up everything I've got and put it on your desk." She'd debated explaining further, then decided to leave it at that. "Let it just be me sticking my neck out."

"If you're going to work for me, I need your trust."

She'd kept her eyes on him. "That's a two-way street."

"A name, Maggie."

She'd looked away. "Raleigh. William Raleigh."

Bremmerton hadn't responded at first. Then, quietly, he'd taken in a breath, his decision to go along with her obviously made. "You're on an early flight?"

She'd nodded.

"I have a meeting first thing in the morning." His misgivings showed in his clipped words, his straight back, but his answer revealed he trusted her. "I'll read your report after the meeting gets out."

"Thank you."

He wasn't looking for thanks, though. "You get a whiff — one goddamn whiff — that you're not on a wild-goose chase after all, I want to know about it. First."

That Bremmerton had gone along with her was a demonstration of his faith in her — and in his own judgment, his own instincts, not to mention his power and influence within diplomatic security. He had twenty years of experience and built-up goodwill on her.

Maggie pulled a pair of black pants out

of a dresser drawer and tossed them in her suitcase.

If a head rolled because of her excursion, they both knew it'd be hers.

She grabbed a pair of jeans. Basically, she was packing what she owned. It wasn't as if she had a lot of wardrobe choices, and there was no time to go shopping. She'd need her weapon, too. She placed it beside the suitcase, to remind herself of the protocol she'd need to follow to take it on the flight.

She'd be on her way to Schipol airport in the morning when Rob started looking for her. She hated to sneak out on him. He'd been decent to her that afternoon — suspicious, but decent, buying her a bowl of chicken soup, rubbing her hand.

And those eyes. She couldn't get over them. Gray with blue flecks, darker lashes than she'd have expected given his fair-haired good looks. Her own lashes were almost invisible without mascara.

"God, you *are* tired."

She almost banged her fingers shutting the drawer.

Her friendship with Tom would lend credibility to her cover story of needing a few days off.

"Cover story" at least sounded better than "lie."

It was after one before she finally collapsed into bed, the mix of crushing fatigue and grief and agitation reminding her of her first days of training, when becoming a DS agent was still not quite a dream come true and when everything she might see in her work — everything she might screw up — was still only theoretical.

When her father was alive, and she'd looked forward to meeting him on a level playing field.

Things change, she thought. Things always change.

Eight

Maggie dragged her suitcase out to the street at six, uncertain she wasn't acting precipitously, even less confident in William Raleigh and his "tip," now that she had some rest.

When she got to the curb, she found Rob half sitting on the hood of her Mini, drinking coffee, and she stopped abruptly. "What are you doing here?"

He smiled at her. "I guess we'd better get moving if we're going to make our flight. I thought I might have to pound on your door. Up late?"

"*Our* flight? How —"

"I'm good at what I do. I've never tracked a DS agent before."

She noticed that he had his carry-on bag with him. "You just got to the Netherlands. You're not even over your jet lag."

"Don't mind if I ride with you, do you? Or are you taking a cab?"

Her suitcase was upright next to her. He had her flight information. There was no way she could deny she was heading to the airport. "Cab. It should be here any second."

"Good. We can split the fare."

Her head felt pinched, tight. If she told Rob to get his own cab, she wouldn't be able to grill him about how he'd found out about her flight. And since he'd apparently already wrangled a ticket for himself, she'd only postpone having to deal with him.

He was getting on that plane with her.

"I thought you went back to your hotel and had a couple of drinks."

"I did."

"Someone gave me up. You must have made a few calls."

"Maybe I got a call or two myself."

Bremmerton? Had he sicced Rob on her?

Rob spoke amiably, as if he expected her not to mind his interference. But Maggie had no intention of discussing her plans with him on the street, or at the airport, or on the flight. She peered down the narrow street. There was no sign of her taxi.

"You could be heading to New York on information from a man who needs psychiatric care," Rob said.

"I'm taking a few days off."

"Ah."

He didn't believe her, not even for a split second. That much was obvious. Not that she'd expected him to buy her story. She was just letting him know she wasn't playing by his rules.

Fortunately, the cab arrived. Rob grabbed both suitcases and dumped them in the trunk, then joined her in the back seat. The dark charcoal of his suit drew her attention to his eyes, a misty gray in the morning light.

"Where are you staying in New York?" he asked as the cab pulled out into the street.

Maggie decided to take a more direct approach. "I'm not telling you. You're suspicious enough as it is." Although not without cause, she thought with a minor stab of guilt. "Yesterday was a tough day. It must have rekindled bad memories for you. I'm sorry I dragged you to Den Bosch. I don't blame you for looking for excuses to get out of here."

He shrugged. "I didn't have to look far, did I?"

She gave him a long look. "You're going to bird-dog me until you're satisfied, aren't you? I don't need you snooping into my private life."

"I'm not so sure this trip of yours is personal. According to my sources, you don't have much of a private life. All work, no play."

"Did you stay up all night checking me out?"

"People say you're at the top of your game. You made the Chicago bust happen. You got the tip that took Nick Janssen down. Yesterday was tough, no doubt about it. But an officer even half as dedicated as you are wouldn't take off for a few days the morning after finding a friend dead. It just wouldn't happen."

"It *is* happening."

"You've been on the job here, what, three weeks?"

"About that." He settled back in his seat, the cab on the motorway now, speeding east toward the airport. "No way are you taking a few days off, Maggie. No way."

She didn't take the bait and respond. If Ravenkill was a wild-goose chase, it was going to be *her* wild-goose chase. Until she knew what she was dealing with, she wanted as few people to know about her little adventure as possible.

It wasn't that far to the airport. Even if Rob had managed to get a seat on her flight, odds were it wouldn't be right next to her. She just had to endure the cab ride, then avoid him on the flight across the Atlantic and shake him when they arrived at JFK. She'd reserved a car rental. With a

133

little luck, she'd be on her way to Ravenkill with Rob Dunnemore none the wiser.

Magster.

She told herself she'd have gone to Ravenkill and shut out the marshal next to her over the reasons for her trip even if William Raleigh hadn't mentioned her father, alluded to his death. Whether Raleigh had ever been to Prague — had ever met Philip Spencer, murdered American businessman — mattered, but it wasn't her only reason for heading to New York. She also owed Tom Kopac.

"Your mother's a painter in Boca Raton," Rob said. "Pretty good, too. She and your dad were divorced when you were in high school. He died eighteen months ago in Prague. Some story about bank robbers."

He didn't believe it, either. Did he know something she didn't? But Maggie forced herself not to respond.

"Must have been rough, losing him that way."

She took a breath. "It was. My family doesn't have the greatest luck. I've never assumed I'll be drinking lemonade in the shade and writing my memoirs at eighty."

"You just described my father." His tone was gentle, as if he didn't take his father's

134

long life and good health for granted. "Why New York? Why not visit your mother?"

"It's hot in south Florida in August."

He drank the last of his coffee and crushed the cup in one hand. "I can't see you leaving town after yesterday. I can't see Bremmerton letting you leave. So this trip isn't without his blessing."

"Maybe it was his idea. Stress."

"Right."

Again that open, amiable disbelief. Maggie glanced over at him, wishing he wasn't so damn attractive. "Why are you leaving?" she asked him.

"Because you are."

Dumb question. "How did you find out?"

"I know people."

He was matter-of-fact, not smug. After yesterday, she couldn't blame him for checking her out. She'd hauled him to Den Bosch, on the pretense of seeing where Nick Janssen had been picked up, only to come upon a murder and a bizarre rendezvous with a man who was, at best, an eccentric.

That she'd let Raleigh go without a fight couldn't have helped Dunnemore's early impression of her.

"You're not going to give me your source?" she asked him.

"No, ma'am."

"You think that Southern charm's going to work on me, don't you?"

He smiled. "What Southern charm?"

"It'll only get you so far when you're sticking your nose into someone else's business. Is the source who finked me out someone you know because you're friends with President Poe, or someone you know because you're a marshal?"

"Could be someone who's worried about you and called me."

"I doubt that."

A very short list of names came to mind, any of whom could be charmed by the fair-haired U.S. Marshal.

When they reached the airport, Rob offered to carry her suitcase. Maggie refused, politely, trying not to let his easy manner and good looks get to her — or to go overboard in the opposite direction and be a witch. Either way, he won. She didn't need a well-connected marshal following her, especially when she was on her way to check out a dubious tip from a man anyone else might have dismissed as mentally ill. But William Raleigh had brought up her father, and he'd been in Den Bosch the same morning Tom Kopac had been killed. If she could be sure going to New York was smart, having Rob as a witness might be more appealing.

But she told herself it wasn't just a matter of sparing herself a little embarrassment. If this escapade blew up in her face, she didn't want Rob getting caught in the shock waves.

There it was, she thought. She was being altruistic.

"You can't tell anyone about me, Maggie. No one. That's very important for your own safety."

Histrionics. If she really thought safety was a serious concern, she'd have had more reason to let Rob in on Raleigh's tip, or at least given Bremmerton more details.

When they boarded the plane, it turned out Rob had the seat directly across the aisle from her.

For the next seven hours.

He'd probably planned it that way, Maggie thought. All feelings of altruism left her. If he wanted to interfere in her business and call in favors to find out what she was up to, fine. Let him. If he wanted to track her to Ravenkill, that was fine, too. His neck, his choice.

Trying to ignore him, she thought about

Ravenkill. The Old Stone Hollow Inn's Web site had a picture of the room she'd reserved. It had forget-me-not wallpaper, a private bath and a view of a sunflower garden.

And it had a four-poster, queen-size bed.

Maggie felt a jolt of heat and awareness so powerful and unexpected she glanced across the aisle at Rob to see if he'd noticed. But as good as his sources were, he couldn't read minds. *Thank God.*

He gave her a half smile. "Long flight ahead of us."

A very long flight. She hoped she got a grip before they landed in New York.

Sitting across from Wes Poe at the White House was just about the last place Nate Winter wanted to be on a Sunday morning. But the visit was Sarah's idea, and he'd promised to go along with her. Slowly but surely, he was getting used to her relationship with the president.

Sarah sat forward on her chair across the dining room table from the president. Her honey-colored hair was pulled back simply, and she'd put on a sundress for her trip to Pennsylvania Avenue. She was happiest digging through musty diaries, old family attics and backyard dumps, piecing together the lives of ordinary people. But Nate knew it was a mistake to forget that Sarah, like her twin brother, had the blood of the Dunnemores of old running through her veins. They'd been loggers and riverboat workers, adventurers who'd worked hard and played harder, and too often died young.

"Rob's on his way back to New York," she said. "He didn't even have a chance to recover from jet lag before he turned around and flew back."

"It works that way sometimes," Poe said gently. He was dressed casually in a polo shirt and khakis. Evelyn, his wife, was out for the day. "I don't think Rob ever intended to stay that long."

Sarah hardly seemed to be listening to him. "You heard what happened yesterday? About the murder?"

He nodded. "It was a stroke of bad luck."

But she obviously suspected more than luck had been involved. "The DS agent with Rob knew the victim. He was a diplomat. He worked at the embassy."

Wes's expression gave away nothing. Nate had no idea what the president knew about Tom Kopac and Maggie Spencer — if anything. Sarah had pieced together her

139

information from talking with her father, whom Rob had also called, and from news reports. Nate had kept his conversation with Rob to himself and intended to continue to do so until he knew more himself. Sarah would understand, but she wouldn't like it.

"I don't have any information you don't have, Sarah," Poe said gently. "I'm sorry."

"I'll call Rob when he gets in," she said half under her breath. "I'm not sure why he went to the Netherlands in the first place. I know reporters must have been calling and pounding on his door — I'm a little harder to find, but I've had my share. And I know he's been restless —"

"He'll find his way," Poe said. "You both went through hell in the spring."

"Rob insists he's fine. He thinks he's found his way. You and my father want him to be a diplomat type, but it's not him. I don't care how many languages he speaks. He likes law enforcement."

"I have complete faith in him, Sarah. If Rob wants to stay in the Marshals Service, that's his choice. He can go far there. If not —"

"The shooting's changed him." Sarah looked away, her concern for her brother not something she could hide, but she shifted back to Poe. "I'm not sure anyone's giving me the full story about what happened in Den Bosch."

Nate knew he hadn't. It hadn't occurred to him that her twin radar would go wild just with the information she had. He didn't have much more himself. He planned to make some calls once he got the hell out of the White House.

Poe didn't answer but kept his gaze on Sarah, as if he expected her to continue without hearing from him.

She frowned. "Wes?"

"Go on," he said.

"Is Maggie Spencer trouble?"

"In what way?"

"Any way."

"I don't know her," Poe said.

But Nate suspected the president knew that Maggie Spencer's father had been killed in Prague eighteen months ago under circumstances that just didn't add up. Nate had dug up that much himself. Whether the Prague murder and the Den Bosch murder yesterday were connected was anyone's guess, But toss in a DS agent, Nick Janssen and Rob's abrupt return to New York, and Nate had his questions, to say the least.

"Did you know Tom Kopac, the diplomat who was killed yesterday?" Sarah asked.

"No. I know very little about him. I expect to hear more today." Poe kept his tone steady. "His death is a tragedy. Our people in the Netherlands are doing everything possible to get to the bottom of what happened. Right now, I don't have any more details than you do."

Sarah swallowed visibly. "What about Nick Janssen? I know he's in jail, but he was arrested in Den Bosch. Could he be responsible somehow?"

Nate sat forward. "There's no evidence to suggest Kopac had anything to do with Janssen or his arrest. We don't know why he was in Den Bosch."

"Why was Rob there?" she asked sharply.

"Because Maggie Spencer took him to see where Janssen was picked up," Nate said.

Sarah spun around at Nate. "You've talked to him. When?"

Nate sighed. "Last night. He called on my cell phone."

Poe looked at Nate, then turned to Sarah, but she pushed back her chair. "You marshals," she said, not sounding that annoyed. "You all stick together. Was he okay?"

"It hadn't been a good day, but yes, he was okay."

"On the case?"

Nate nodded, not expanding.

Sarah frowned at him. "You're not going to tell me. Or you can't tell me. Okay, that's fine. It doesn't change what I already know." She glanced from Nate to the president, her expression one of resolve and deep concern. "Something's wrong."

"Sarah," Wes Poe said. "I know it's hard not to worry, to feel as if you're out of the loop."

"I *am* out of the loop. For good reasons or bad."

The president's eyes bored into her. "You were sitting on your porch in Night's Landing when out of the blue you got a call that Rob was shot. It's going to take a while for you not to go on high alert every time —"

"Every time he finds a dead man in a Dutch river?"

Only Sarah Dunnemore, Nate thought, could challenge Wes Poe like that. But Poe took it. "It would irritate the hell out of Rob if he could hear us now. You know it would."

"You're right about that." She blew out a breath. "I should let him do his job, right? Trust him. All that."

Poe smiled. "We all should."

She shot Nate a glance. "What did he want with you last night?"

"Just to check out Maggie Spencer and Tom Kopac."

"I could have figured that out myself. It's common sense. Why not tell me?"

But Nate knew she didn't expect an answer. On a gut level, she would already have it. She wasn't in law enforcement. She was a historical archaeologist working on a new project. And her brother had called Nate, not her.

"Rob knows better than to try to protect you," Wes said.

"He's protecting himself. He doesn't like for any of us to worry about him. He can take anything but that." She sighed again, no longer as frustrated. "Actually, I understand."

Poe quickly changed the subject, asking her about the wedding, then ushered her to the door, hugging her goodbye. He said something innocuous about Night's Landing that brought a small spark of pleasure.

But when Sarah wasn't looking, Poe let his eyes connect with Nate in a way that communicated in no uncertain terms: they needed to discuss Rob's DS agent, Maggie Spencer.

Nine

Ethan Brooker caught up with Raleigh in Amsterdam's historic *Begijnhof*, an enclosed cluster of perfectly kept, very old houses built around a trim, green courtyard. It was open to tourists, although there weren't many on the humid Sunday afternoon, just a few stragglers wandering along the walkway, checking out the bright gardens and the lace-curtained windows.

But Ethan had never been much of a tourist. "Why can't we meet at a café?" he asked. "I walked by the entrance to this place three times before I found it. It's like its own separate world here."

"Do you know what the *Begijnhof* is?"

"Can't say I do."

"It's where the Beguines lived. They were an order of religious women who dedicated themselves to charitable work but didn't take monastic vows."

"Good for them."

"There's a *Begijhof* in Breda as well. The Beguines died out around 1970."

Ethan couldn't drum up a lot of interest

and didn't want to set himself up for one of Raleigh's history lectures. The guy couldn't put enough of a living together to buy himself decent clothes, and he might or might not have all his marbles, but he knew the history of a tucked-away Dutch courtyard.

Still, it was a pretty spot. Quiet, removed from the city's congested streets.

"It's strange, isn't it?" Raleigh ambled along, touristlike. "The work we do. Yours as a Special Forces officer, mine as an economic consultant privy to government workings, diplomatic communications. We're so tapped into what's going on in the world and yet, at the same time, isolated because of our knowledge and experience."

"I was all about accomplishing the mission."

Raleigh smiled faintly. He had on the same clothes as yesterday. "You still are, I believe."

Ethan changed the subject. "Spencer and Dunnemore got on an early flight this morning to New York."

Raleigh stopped in front of a black wooden house. "This is the oldest house in Amsterdam," he said, but his voice faltered — Ethan's news had surprised him. "It dates from around 1475. You'll note it's constructed of wood. Even then Amsterdam was a crowded city, and wood burns. After huge fires did enormous damage, wood construction was forbidden. I believe there are only two wooden houses in all of Amsterdam. The Dutch are a sensible people. They . . ." He abandoned any pretext of interest in the historic site. "New York?"

"Uh-huh."

"Then you must go."

"I've got a ticket for a morning flight. You?"

He shook his head. "I can't right now."

"Hook up with me when and if you get there. I'll need more information. What did you tell Spencer, Raleigh? It's time to talk. Why New York?"

"Ravenkill. That's where she's headed. She must be."

"It's a town?"

"Yes. It's on the Hudson River about an hour, perhaps a bit more, north of the city. I saw it — the name of an inn —" Raleigh couldn't seem to go on and stopped in front of an attractive, spotless brick house, frowning. "The Old Stone Hollow Inn."

Ethan stared at him. "What? An inn?"

"Tom Kopac had printed information about Ravenkill and the inn off the

Internet. I saw it in his apartment when I confronted him about why he'd been asking questions in Prague about Maggie, her father." Raleigh paused again, almost as if he were talking to himself. "I still have friends. They told me he'd been making calls."

"When the hell did you see Kopac?"

Raleigh seemed momentarily confused, flustered. "Was it Friday? Yes, it must have been. It was after Janssen's arrest. I dropped in on Mr. Kopac before he went to work that morning. He wouldn't talk to me. We arranged to meet in Den Bosch the next day. Then I called Maggie."

"Christ, Raleigh. I should haul your ass to the embassy —"

He waved a hand irritably. "It would only waste time. The police must have searched Kopac's apartment by now. They must have the printout. If they don't — if someone cleaned out his apartment . . ." He was talking to himself, but stopped, shooting Ethan a distressed look. "Do you suppose she's gone to Ravenkill on her own? Maggie? I thought she'd do some checking. The Internet, friends, see what she could find out from her desk at the embassy."

Ethan felt the sun hot on the back of his

148

neck. He wasn't fond of Amsterdam. His wife had died here, only blocks away from the quiet, isolated courtyard. "What did you tell Spencer back at the cathedral?"

"Very little. There was no time."

"You used her father's death to manipulate her, didn't you?"

No answer.

"Come on, Raleigh. You let her think this inn holds the secret to what really happened in Prague. You know goddamn well —"

"I never said it did —"

"It's what you intimated. It's what you *wanted* her to think. That's why she got on that plane."

The older man pursed his thin lips as he moved along the walk, past a small church, in thoughtful, troubled silence.

Ethan knew he had to be merciless. "If you think you could have sent her into danger, she needs everything you have. *I* need it if you expect me to help her."

Raleigh shook his head, as if to counter something he was telling himself. "Agent Spencer's prepared to handle difficult and dangerous situations. I have nothing that would help her." He glanced at Ethan. "Or you."

"You're so used to manipulating people you don't even know anymore when you're doing it. You're using her — me — to clear your name. Was Kopac on to Philip Spencer's real killer? Is that what you think?"

"I don't know what to think. For all I know, Mr. Kopac had that printout because he was planning his next vacation. Yes, he gave me an excuse to make contact with Maggie." He gave Ethan a stubborn look. "I have my reasons for wanting to meet her."

"She's in the dark —"

"I don't have all the answers, Major Brooker. I have more questions than anything else."

"That's not the point."

But Raleigh would know it wasn't. "Philip Spencer had an uncanny ability to make things happen. His instincts were flawless. His energy. His timing." Raleigh turned to Ethan, as if it would help convince the younger man of his certainty, his righteousness. But tears rose to his red-veined eyes. "I believe his daughter is the same way."

"Let's hope she's better at staying alive."

Rob walked with Maggie to her car-rental agency at JFK, the airport bustling on a hot Sunday afternoon. "It's an expensive cab ride to Brooklyn," he said. "So why don't you drop me off on your way to wherever it is you're going?"

Maggie got into line. "You're kidding, right?"

"No, ma'am."

"You're trying to talk me into giving you a ride."

It wasn't working very well. A seven-hour flight was enough to make him antsy by itself; seven hours on a plane, anchored across from Maggie, had about done him in. There were times he thought the flight attendants would read his mind and make him change seats.

He should have just told them he kept fantasizing about whisking the passenger across from him off to a quiet beach somewhere and watched how fast they moved his butt to another part of the plane.

Something about Maggie had gotten to him. He wasn't sure he wanted to know what it was, since it would probably only mean trouble. She was a federal agent on a questionable mission. He was determined to find out what that mission was. That didn't leave much room for quiet beaches.

"I'll drive to Brooklyn," he said. "Then you can go on your way from there."

She angled him a not unfriendly look.

"You're not going to give up, are you?"

"Not until I see you lock your doors and drive off —"

"Okay, okay." She rolled her eyes, but she was smiling. "I'll give you a ride back to your place. Then you'll leave me alone, right?"

He didn't answer.

She glared at him. "Right?"

He shrugged. "If you want me to."

Twenty minutes later, she was swearing at the Long Island Expressway traffic in her little rented car. "I'm not used to SUVs and great big trucks," she muttered. "You'd be surprised how unused to them you can get in three weeks."

"I offered to drive. Sure you don't have the jitters? I noticed you ate a *stroopwafel* on the plane."

Mention of the syrup-filled Dutch cookies made her smile. "No jitters. I'd have offered you a bite —"

"Except you were pretending I wasn't there."

"Fat lot of good it did me. A break from Dutch goodies will do my waistline good." But she pulled her top lip under her teeth, holding back a sudden sigh of regret. "Tom teased me at the bakery the other day. Damn. I wish he'd heard me yesterday.

152

I wish I'd at least seen something."

"You did what you could."

"It wasn't enough."

"There was no reason to suspect someone was about to kill him."

She'd let the speedometer creep up and eased off the gas, calming down. "I still have no idea why Tom was killed. Why he was there. Why he was targeted — if he *was* targeted."

Rob had done enough obsessive speculating of his own on the long flight. Maybe Kopac had provided the tip about Janssen, and Janssen had found out and had him killed. Maybe Kopac had stuck his nose where it didn't belong in some naive effort to impress Maggie Spencer and ended up in the path of one of Janssen's cohorts, and it got him killed.

Maybe he'd hooked up with Maggie's guy in the cathedral, and it got him killed.

Maybe he'd been in the wrong place at the wrong time in a quiet Dutch city that had a random killer on the loose.

Given Tom Kopac's solitary life and dedication to his embassy work, none of the scenarios felt right. He wasn't, as far as Rob knew, an intelligence, military or law enforcement officer. He was one of the countless career foreign service workers

153

who kept U.S. embassies running all around the world.

"What will you tell your bosses about why you're back so soon?" Maggie asked.

"I'll see if anyone asks, first."

"Are you a hundred percent since the shooting?"

"Yes."

"But you're not back on the street," she said.

Rob admired her directness but didn't want to get into a discussion of his status. "Not yet. Mike Rivera, my chief deputy, isn't one to rush something like that."

"He's worried about post-traumatic stress disorder?"

"It's just the way he is."

"He must have heard about Tom's murder." Maggie gave Rob a dry, pointed look. "Are you concerned people are going to start thinking of you as a shit magnet or something?"

He didn't answer.

"Sorry. That was unfeeling. I'm not going to interfere with your business. Just like you're not going to interfere with mine. Right?"

"Apples and oranges."

She ignored him. "What if we get to your place and it's crawling with reporters?"

"I'll duck," he said mildly.

But his street was quiet on a hot August Sunday, with no one hanging out on his building's front stoop wanting to talk to him about anything, never mind Nick Janssen's arrest.

"Why don't you give me your cell phone number?" Maggie stared straight ahead, both hands gripping the wheel as if she was saying something she knew she had no business saying. "I can call you if I get into any trouble."

Rob jotted his number down on the back of the car rental agreement and handed it to her. "Anytime."

She smiled tentatively. "Thanks."

"Maggie —"

"A few days off," she said stubbornly, "probably wouldn't hurt you, either."

That was the end of it. She wasn't budging on telling him her real reasons for flying to New York — or where she was headed. Getting his cell phone number was as far as she was going. Since there was nothing else he could do, Rob grabbed his suitcase out of the car and thanked her for the ride.

When he got into his apartment, he could smell the milk he'd left on the counter, and his voice mail was full. Reporters and more reporters.

He called Nate. "Anything on Kopac or Spencer?"

"Nothing specific."

Something was in his tone. "What?"

"Your sister talked to Poe."

Christ. "That's not what I needed."

"Poe didn't say as much, but Spencer's name rang a bell with him. Her father was killed in Prague a year and a half ago. Got caught in a bank robbery." He paused. "Business consultant."

"Does Sarah know?"

"No."

"What kind of business consultant was the father?"

"The kind that travels a lot and talks to a lot of people."

"You think —"

"I'm just guessing."

Nate was just guessing that Maggie Spencer's father had been on the government payroll — a spook.

"Maggie?"

"A-plus DS agent."

Did her father — his death — have anything to do with her abrupt departure from the Netherlands? Rob had no idea. He could feel his frustration mounting. For all he knew, Maggie was worried her encounter in the cathedral would make her an A-minus DS agent.

His head felt squeezed. "She met an older guy in Den Bosch after we finished with the police. White hair, red nose. She won't even give me a name. I think he was the reason we went out there in the first place."

Nate was silent.

"She says she's here to take a few days off. Wouldn't tell me where she's staying. Thinks I'll be a pest, I guess."

"Is she out of control?"

Rob pictured her behind the wheel of her car rental and shook his head, as if reassuring himself. "No."

"Keep me posted," Nate said. "Here, your sister wants to say hello."

She came on the line. "Rob? Damn it, are you okay? What's going on?"

"I'm good, Sarah. You don't have to worry —"

"I do have to worry. You go to Holland and end up in the middle of a murder scene." Her tone softened. "I'm sorry it happened. It must have been awful. But Rob — this isn't going to work if you tell Nate things that you don't tell me."

"He's my superior —"

"You don't report to him."

She had a point. "What did you and Wes talk about this morning?"

"You. Lately, that's all we talk about."

"Well, change the subject," he said testily. "You and Wes talking behind my back is worse than me talking to Nate behind your back."

His sister wasn't bothered by his mood. "That's not the way I look at it."

Rob grinned at her lack of remorse. "Of course not. Look, it wasn't pretty yesterday. Now we're all probably getting our knickers in a twist over nothing. Relax, okay? Enjoy playing in your old dump. Is it bearing fruit?"

"It's amazing. Totally. I couldn't be happier."

"That's great, Sarah," Rob said, meaning it. But when he hung up, his body didn't know what time it was, and his head was spinning with thoughts and possibilities, none of them worth a damn. He finally gave up on making sense of anything and pulled on his running clothes and headed out.

Maybe a five-mile run would help clear his mind.

Maggie put together her Glock while the lace curtains of her forget-me-not room billowed in the afternoon breeze. She couldn't relax. The Old Stone Hollow Inn was idyllic. Gorgeous. Sunflowers, dahlias, herbs, orchards. It was a perfect spot to rejuvenate.

So why had William Raleigh mentioned it to her in a clandestine meeting in a Dutch cathedral?

What did it have to do with her father, Tom Kopac, Nick Janssen? Any of them?

"Nothing," she muttered. "The guy needs a psychiatrist."

The inn was located at the end of a long gravel driveway flanked by an apple orchard and a cornfield that opened up into a beautiful yard of flower and herb gardens and huge shade trees, with stone paths and fences, cedar benches and screened gazebos. It all felt more remote than it was. The village of Ravenkill, with its antiques shops and attractive houses, was less than a mile down a country road.

Maggie could see the Hudson River from her bedroom window. According to her brochure, a smaller creek was just through the woods along the orchard and cornfield. She was in Ichabod Crane country. She could almost picture a headless horseman charging across the countryside and had the unsettling sense that anything could happen here.

But it had been that kind of week, she told herself, strapping on her holster. She slipped her Glock in place and put on a lightweight denim jacket that draped over it, then checked her reflection in the bathroom mirror.

Not good. She looked like her body thought it was the middle of the night.

She dabbed on some blush, not sure it helped, and headed downstairs.

The inn itself was a sprawling, elegant mid-nineteenth-century farmhouse with celadon-green clapboards and white trim. Any additions and renovations to the original structure were seamless. The cherry floors gleamed, and the tall windows sparkled. The downstairs rooms — a kitchen, dining room, living room, library, den and music room — were decorated with a mix of antiques and contemporary pieces, everything light, airy and comfortable-looking.

The owners, Andrew and Star Franconia, lived on the second floor of a picturesque red barn. An informal antiques shop on the first floor included everything from rusted farm tools to delicate tea sets. A separate outbuilding had sports equipment for guest use — cross-country skis, snowshoes, giant inner tubes, kayaks, canoes, mountain bikes. If nothing panned out, Maggie figured she'd have plenty of things to do before she headed back to The Hague.

She had a choice of eating inside or outside on the back porch and decided on the porch. A waiter led her to a small table covered with a white cloth, with an oversized hydrangea growing up over the balusters. She ordered iced tea and sat back in her chair, welcoming the clean, warm summer air.

The Franconias came over to introduce themselves. Andrew was in his early fifties, stocky and handsome, Star perhaps a few years younger, blond and very thin. They both were dressed casually, relaxed and friendly among their guests.

"I understand you're from the Netherlands," Andrew said.

"I work there, yes," Maggie said.

"Did you have a good flight?"

"No problems. Thanks for asking." She'd never been good at small talk. "It's a beautiful evening."

"It's been beautiful all weekend," Star said. "We were lucky. We had a full house. Weekdays tend to be lighter. It should be quiet while you're here."

161

Her husband cleared his throat, suddenly looking awkward. "Um — are you in law enforcement?"

As discreet as she was, he must have noticed that she was armed. Maggie sipped some of her iced tea. "I'm with the U.S. Diplomatic Security Service."

"I've never heard of them," Star said, obviously intrigued.

"A lot of people haven't."

Andrew bristled. His wife seemed to be getting on his nerves. "I don't want any trouble. I don't like guns."

"I certainly don't want any trouble, either," Maggie said, deciding to change the subject. "I was just looking over the menu. What do you recommend, anything in particular?"

"It's all good."

Star's cheeks reddened in embarrassment over her husband's curtness. "The lobster bisque is particularly wonderful tonight. I would think it would go down well after a long flight. Andrew and I often travel together on business — well, we used to. Now one of us tends to stay behind to keep an eye on things here." She smiled, as if making an effort to be cheerful. "A case of 'be careful of what you wish for.' We always wanted our own inn, and now we've got one."

"How long have you been open?"

"Almost two years. It's gone fast."

Andrew straightened, posturing for both women. "Enjoy your visit, Agent Spencer. Don't hesitate to let us know if there's anything you need."

"I appreciate that."

Once they left, Maggie ordered the lobster bisque and a salad made with greens from the inn's own gardens, although she wasn't that hungry. She supposed disguising her identity in Ravenkill would have been simpler, but perhaps not as effective — this way, she could stir the pot, see how people reacted to her presence.

But for all she knew, Ravenkill or the Old Stone Hollow Inn had been in the news recently, and Raleigh — drunk or delusional or both — had mixed it up with something he'd seen about her father or Nick Janssen or God only knew what and come up with some bizarre conspiracy theory.

Maggie finished her soup, surprised to find she was hungry after all. Then, because she was jet-lagged and the *stroopwafel* was a long time ago, she ordered the plum tart special for dessert. It arrived warm, topped with homemade vanilla ice cream.

The smell alone was worth the price. She smiled to herself. So what if she was on a wild-goose chase?

After dinner, she took a walk along a stone path, puffs of white clouds high in the sky, the air still as dusk gathered, crows crying in the distance.

As she passed the barn, she could hear the Franconias arguing upstairs, their exact words muffled but the tone unmistakable. They'd lose business, Maggie thought, if they didn't get a rein on their marital tensions. Nobody wanted their country inn escape marred by the owners fighting.

She made her way upstairs to her room, hooking the chain on the door.

It wasn't even dark out yet. If she went to bed now, she'd be up before dawn.

She checked a small bookcase. *The Three Musketeers. The Complete Works of Jane Austen. Othello.*

Her bathroom amenities included a small bottle of bug repellant and a warning note about West Nile virus and Lyme disease.

Maggie doused herself, put on running clothes and headed back outside. A jog into the village and back would clear her head.

If not, at least she'd stand a better chance of getting to sleep.

Ten

Libby lifted a heavy tray of breakfast dishes and carried it into the kitchen of what had once been her family home and now was the Old Stone Hollow Inn. The affront was fresh again. It was always this way after she got back from a trip. The insult of her situation would be raw and biting, the reality of what her life had become something she had to get used to all over again. Yet she'd watched it coming for years. Even as a little girl, she'd seen this future for herself with a brutal clarity.

Death, poverty, betrayal, humiliation.

No way out but surrender.

Her parents were dead. Her father had squandered her future. She'd had to sell her childhood home in order to save it.

And everyone knew her sad story.

She set the tray on the granite counter. Jet lag brought her emotions that much closer to the surface. She'd be all right in a day or two. And she had work to do. Targets to assess.

Her father was the one who'd taught her

165

to shoot, she thought bitterly, even as she smiled at Star Franconia. "Good morning. It looks as if you have a few guests, anyway, for early in the week."

Star tugged at an apron that was too long for her. "Thanks for bringing in the dishes, Libby. I haven't seen you in a few days. Did you have a good weekend?"

"Yes, thanks. I was checking leads on some wonderful new pieces."

"Were you?" Star picked through a colander of herbs in the sink. "You must be getting quite an inventory by now. Soon you'll open your own shop. You wait."

Star liked to consider herself Libby's mentor. Libby knew she was supposed to be grateful. But there'd have been no inn for the Franconias if she hadn't kept her father from selling it to developers years earlier, or burning it down in a drunken party or letting it become condemned.

"How was your weekend?" Libby asked.

"We were busy, but most guests left yesterday. We had one new one arrive. She's a diplomatic security agent, in fact. Isn't that interesting?"

Libby grabbed a chair and jerked it out from under the round table, sitting down before her knees could go out from under her. She made herself smile. "I don't believe I've ever met a diplomatic security agent. Aren't they supposed to be overseas?"

"She came from The Hague. She's staying for three nights. Isn't that wild? Having a federal agent here makes Andrew nervous, of course, but I think it's great." Star lifted a few dripping sprigs of orange mint from her colander and set them on paper towels. "I'm sure you'll get a chance to meet her."

Maggie Spencer.

Philip Spencer's daughter was in Ravenkill.

Libby fingered a saltshaker in the middle of the table. Her eyelids were heavy, and she felt as if she were stuck in a soupy fog, unable to move or think fast, clearly.

William Raleigh.

The DS agent's presence had to be his doing. Libby pushed away the saltshaker and gazed out the window at the sunshine and shade trees.

Raleigh had been nipping at her heels for months.

She had to deal with him. She'd known that, but could never seem to get him out in the open, to a place where she could kill him or win him over or do *something* to end this dance they'd been doing. She knew

167

who he was. He didn't know who she was. She had the advantage. How hard could it be?

Damn hard.

"I think I'm going to need more mint," Star said. "Libby, would you mind?"

She eased to her feet, careful to hide her agitation — another perverse skill she had. "No, of course not."

The warm temperatures and the soft breeze in the shade helped restore Libby's equilibrium. Avoiding the stone paths, she made her way through the lush, clipped grass, remembered doing somersaults in the yard as a little girl, and came to the herb garden. It was Star's pride and joy, classically arranged and at its peak on the late August morning. The orange mint was in a separate bed to keep it from spreading.

Libby closed her eyes and smelled it. She felt her energy return. Her natural sense of hope and optimism.

Maggie Spencer, William Raleigh.

Her list of targets.

She'd rise to whatever challenges her job presented, just as she always did with every hardship she faced.

Rob headed to the USMS office in the morning because he didn't know what the hell else he was supposed to do. He could have taken the day off. Then he'd be climbing the damn walls for sure.

"When did you get back?" Mike Rivera asked, standing over Rob's desk.

"Yesterday."

"They kick you out, or you left on your own?"

"On my own."

"Finding a dead guy twenty-four hours after you land in the country —" Rivera sighed heavily, shaking his head. "Not good. I read the report. You and that DS agent could have had your heads blown off, too. You're okay?"

Rob nodded.

"The DS agent? Spencer?"

"We took the same flight to New York."

Rivera straightened. "What's she doing here?"

"Says she's taking a break."

"Where?"

"Wouldn't say. Rented a car and took off. She's not the most open type."

"She gets the Janssen tip. She drags you to this Dutch town where Janssen was hiding, and within a few minutes of your arrival, she spots this friend of hers from the embassy. Next thing, he ends up with a bullet in his head."

169

"Maggie didn't kill him. She couldn't have."

But Rivera didn't trust anyone. "You watched her every second?"

"Yes."

"So she decides, in the middle of all this, to fly to New York and take a break? Come on. You don't believe that. That's why you came back, isn't it?"

"I think she's following another lead, but I could be wrong."

Rob thought of Maggie's smile and that red hair, the gold-flecked turquoise eyes, and figured the effects of his whirlwind trip were to blame. His head was mushy. He felt like Maggie was two beats ahead of him. But he'd find her.

Rivera suggested something along those lines himself before stalking back to his office.

When Juliet Longstreet arrived in the office twenty minutes later, she had a similar reaction. Bad luck in the Netherlands. Not good to have Maggie Spencer on the loose given the circumstances. In her usual blunt fashion, Juliet added, "I think she's up to something. So do you."

"Federal agents get to take time off."

Juliet rolled her eyes. "Within a few hours of finding a body? The body of a *friend?*"

It was a fair point. It was a point Rob had made himself. "I'm on her," he said.

"But of course."

He was still contemplating just how he'd go about finding Maggie when he answered a call from a guy who identified himself as Andrew Franconia.

"My wife and I own an inn in Ravenkill, New York," Franconia said, sounding stressed and irritated. "We don't want any trouble."

"What can I do for you, Mr. Franconia?" Rob asked.

"Diplomatic security agents deal in passport and visa fraud, don't they? Are we under investigation?"

Rob sat forward. "Why are you asking me?"

"Don't be cagey, Deputy. You know goddamn well why. I've read the papers. You and a DS agent came upon a murder on Saturday in the Netherlands. I didn't make the connection at first, but I think it's awfully damn coincidental she shows up here —"

"Who?"

"Agent Spencer." Franconia gave a hiss of impatience. "I'm sorry, it's been a difficult morning. I knew something wasn't right yesterday when she arrived, and I did some checking. I read about the diplomat's murder. Kopac. I'm very sorry. It must have been terrible. But I have my own considerations."

"I understand," Rob said. "What's the name of your inn?"

"The Old Stone Hollow Inn. It's about a mile from the village. I'd feel better about having Agent Spencer here if she hadn't just been involved in two high-profile criminal events. She got the tip that led to Nick Janssen's arrest, too, as I'm sure you're aware."

"Mr. Franconia, I can't speak for Agent Spencer, but if you're concerned that you or your wife or your guests are in any danger —"

"It's not that. We just don't want any trouble. We run a quiet inn here, and we're law-abiding —" He broke off. "Christ, that sounds stupid to say. But we are. We're law-abiding citizens."

"What's Agent Spencer doing now?"

Franconia paused. "Taking a walk in the herb garden."

Hell, Rob thought. Maybe she *was* just taking a few days off to clear her head. He smiled into the phone. "That doesn't seem too suspicious, does it, Mr. Franconia?"

"No, I suppose not."

172

He sounded only slightly chastened. Rob decided to give him a little more to chew on. "I flew back with her yesterday. She told me she was taking some time off."

"Did you believe her?"

Not even a little, Rob thought. "No reason not to. Why did you call me?"

"It seemed the thing to do. I wasn't sure if you were still in the Netherlands. Thanks for your time."

After they disconnected, Rob didn't have a chance to stand up before the phone rang again. He picked up and identified himself.

"Andrew Franconia beat me to you, didn't he?" Maggie said, not sounding remorseful at all.

"You're scaring the hell out of him."

"Upsetting his applecart, maybe. He's not scared."

"What are you doing?"

"Right now? Looking at the sunflowers from my bedroom window. I just got in from a walk in the herb gardens. It's a beautiful day, Deputy. But I almost wish it was snowing. Then you'd be more likely to stay put in New York."

"Don't count on it."

Just a half beat's hesitation. "How long do I have before you get here?"

"Ninety minutes at the most, unless traffic's bad."

"Good," she said. "I won't tell you where I'll be. You can find me. It'll be more fun for you that way."

He almost smiled. "I'll try the sunflowers first."

A click told him she'd hung up.

Rob stood in Rivera's office doorway. "She's in Ravenkill. It's on the Hudson."

"Ravenkill?" Rivera squeaked back in his chair. "My wife dragged me up there once to go antiquing. I thought I'd hang myself, but it's a cute village. Your DS agent into antiques?"

"No idea."

"Go up there," Rivera said. "Find out."

Maggie was sitting in a screened gazebo, amid summer roses and ivy, when Rob found her. He had on sunglasses that only made him look sexier, reminding her — as if she needed reminding — not to get ahead of herself around him.

"You haven't been here a full day," he said, "and you're already scaring the locals."

"They're more irritated than scared." She'd put on capri pants, a tank top and her denim jacket and wondered if he was thinking she looked sexy — or if he, too, was irritated with her. "At least they won't be calling the media. I figure the Franconias don't want reporters sniffing around here any more than I do."

"The old guy in St. John's sent you here?"

She angled a look up at him. "You cut to the chase, don't you? Have a seat. Enjoy the moment. You can smell the roses and listen to the birds twittering."

"I like birds," he said, but didn't sit down.

"The Franconias have bluebird houses set out on the edges of the fields and orchards. It's a different kind of life, isn't it?"

He shrugged. "I used to live this kind of life, except not this fancy."

"On the Cumberland River, you mean."

"That's right."

Next to President Poe's boyhood home. "There are snakes down there."

"Mostly you don't see them." He seemed to be laying on the Tennessee accent. "The snake you see first is always better than the snake you surprise."

Maggie smiled. "That could be my motto. Well, I didn't grow up in a country inn or on a Southern estate. We moved around a lot. Don't you want to sit?"

"I've been in the car for more than an

hour, and I sat all day yesterday." The knotty cedar floor creaked as he moved toward her. "Nice spot."

"The inn's lovely. I only had a peek at Ravenkill. I'm not much on shopping, even if I lived here and didn't have to haul my purchases back to the Netherlands."

"First time here?"

"First time in the Hudson River Valley at all."

He was silent.

"I talked to George Bremmerton this morning," Maggie said. "Tom left the embassy early on Thursday. Right after lunch."

"The day Janssen was arrested."

"Tom was such a loner. No one knew where he went. He didn't say anything to anyone. He didn't leave a note." She paused, physically forcing herself not to picture him in the Binnendieze. "He came to work like normal on Friday. Then he shows up in Den Bosch on Saturday."

"But he had nothing to do with the Janssen case?"

She shook her head. "Not even remotely."

"Investigators will be all over him taking off early."

"He wasn't the type to take off, ever. He loved his work. He —"

"I know. I'm sorry."

"It can be a damn cruel world," she said tightly, leaving it at that.

"Bremmerton knows where you are?"

"Yes."

"But it wasn't his idea for you to come here," Rob said.

She burst to her feet. "Come on, let's have lunch. The food here is very good — lots of stuff from the garden. Makes me want to be careful where I step, in case it lands up in my salad."

"Maggie —"

"I don't know anything, Rob. Nothing worth knowing, anyway."

He followed her out of the gazebo and onto a stone path warmed by the midday sun. A tidy vegetable garden with carefully staked and marked plants sprawled to one side, with grapevines and gladiola in a half-dozen colors on the other. Maggie wondered what it'd be like to spend three days here on a romantic getaway, then pushed the thought far away. Men and romance were not in her cards, at least for the immediate future. She needed to get her feet under her in her first foreign assignment. Then, maybe, she could consider a relationship.

"No dogs?" Rob asked in that slow, Southern way he had. "You'd think a country inn would have dogs. My granddaddy had hounds. I never knew him. Died before I was born. Some kind of logging accident. We Dunnemores live long if we don't get killed."

"My father was only fifty-seven when he died."

The path widened, and Rob eased in next to her. "What was he doing in Prague?"

"He was a business consultant. He traveled a lot. It finally drove him and my mother apart."

"You joined diplomatic security because of him?"

"Because I have the same sense of wanderlust, yes." She smiled suddenly, trying to lift her mood. "As you can see —"

"Being here has nothing to do with wanderlust." He glanced at her, gave her one of his half smiles. "Or with just lust, from what I can see."

She could feel heat on the back of her neck. "What, you don't think I have a guy hiding in my room?"

"No, ma'am."

Since even the way he said *ma'am* got to her, Maggie decided she had low blood sugar on top of jet lag and mounted the steps to the back porch. She could hear the clicking of ice in glasses and smelled mint and charcoal, as if someone had been grilling. Three tables were filled. Breakfast was for guests only, but lunch and dinner were open to the public.

A slender woman cheerfully seated them at a small round table. "I may have gotten you in trouble, Agent Spencer," she whispered; despite her short gray hair, she couldn't have been more than in her midthirties. "Star and Andrew are in such la-la land, they might never have known about the shooting if I hadn't said anything. I saw it on the news."

"That's not your fault," Maggie said.

"I feel bad. They're under a lot of stress." She handed Rob and Maggie each a printout of the day's menu. "I understand the victim was a friend of yours."

"We'd only known each other three weeks, but, yes, Tom was a friend."

"What a shame. My name's Libby, by the way — Libby Smith."

"It's nice to meet you," Maggie said.

"You're smart to get away for a few days after such a tragedy. How'd you end up in Ravenkill? Do you have family here?"

Maggie shook out her napkin and placed it on her lap, noticing Rob eyeing her over the top of his menu, wanting answers himself. "No, no family here. It's just something I picked on a whim. I'm glad I did. It's beautiful."

"Well," Libby said, obviously not satisfied, "enjoy your stay. What can I get you two to drink?"

"Iced tea would be fine," Maggie said.

Rob smiled up from his menu. "Make that two, Miss Smith."

"Just Libby is fine. My family owned this place for generations." She grinned irreverently. "Star and Andrew saved it from a wrecking crane. I help out when I can. I live on the first floor in a little ell my dad used as his trash room. He had problems. Two iced teas it is."

When Libby withdrew to fetch their iced tea, Maggie leaned over the table. "I think there's a subtext around here, don't you?"

"I'd say that's a fair guess, Agent Spencer."

She smiled. "At least you still have a sense of humor."

Libby returned with two glasses of tea with sprigs of orange mint, and Maggie, starving now, felt like ordering everything on the menu. She settled on the carrot-orange soup, the walnut-pear salad with goat cheese and the grilled salmon.

"The goat cheese is local," Libby said. "Star toasts it."

"Sounds wonderful."

Rob chose the chicken salad with grapes and pulled off his sunglasses after Libby left with their orders. "Nate Winter has my description of your old guy. Nate's my future brother-in-law, and a marshal. We're going to find out who your guy is."

"You're relentless, aren't you? I suppose it's a good quality in someone who catches fugitives for a living."

Maggie tilted back her iced tea and wished she could just keep drinking all afternoon and avoid those eyes. But she set the glass down, observing a middle-aged couple sharing a salad at another table.

Rob said nothing. He was, she suspected, trying to use silence to his advantage.

"He says his name is William Raleigh. He's a retired economist." She ran a finger down the frosty side of her glass. "He gave me the name of the inn. It was my decision to actually come here."

"Any contact with him before Saturday?"

"No."

"He had to have said something significant to make you go to the trouble of flying to New York at the last minute, giving me the slip —"

"He referred to my father and his death." She heard the sharpness in her tone but couldn't do anything about it now. "You saw him. He's down and out. He smelled like stale cigarettes and looked like he just finished a drinking binge."

"You think it could be a bad lead."

She tried to smile. "I've been to worse places on wild-goose chases. I have a four-poster bed in my room and forget-me-not wallpaper."

"Do you?"

"Damn it, Dunnemore —"

"You're the one who brought up beds and forget-me-nots."

"Do you even know what a forget-me-not is?"

"Flower." He grinned at her. "Bluish purple."

Andrew Franconia trotted up the porch steps and beelined for their table, saving Maggie from further talk of her bedroom. But he was annoyed. "I didn't mean for the marshals to come up here," he said through clenched teeth. He was sweating, in shorts and an orange polo shirt that was neatly tucked in. "You're Deputy Dunnemore, aren't you? I recognize you from the news —"

Rob got to his feet and shook hands politely, taking some of the steam out of Franconia's irritation. "Maggie and I are enjoying your inn," he said. "We just ordered lunch. Would you care to join us?"

"No, no, that's all right. Thank you. I was just —" He glanced around at the occupied tables, then lowered his voice. "It struck me that whoever murdered that diplomat on Saturday is still at large. If Agent Spencer is someone who protects diplomats —"

"I'm not here because of Tom Kopac's murder," Maggie said.

Andrew glanced at her. "But you made your reservation just hours afterward."

"It'd been a bad day." She kept her tone even. "Have you ever been to Den Bosch? Its full name is 's-Hertogenbosch. There's a lovely gothic cathedral there, and they do boat tours on the waterway —"

"No, I've never been there, but I've been to Holland, of course, many times. Star and I travel frequently in our work — well, we used to." His voice softened slightly, became less rat-tat. "It's harder for us both to get away now that we have the inn."

"You go on solo trips?" Maggie asked.

He narrowed his gaze on her. "Is this an interrogation?"

"A friendly conversation, Mr. Franconia."

"I'm sorry," he said in a half whisper. "I

183

don't mean to be rude. Please, enjoy your lunch."

He couldn't get away fast enough.

"He embarrassed himself," Rob said. "You make him nervous."

"You don't help matters," Maggie said. "He knows marshals arrest people, but he's not sure what diplomatic security agents do. And he knows you're pals with the president. That'd make anyone nervous."

"Doesn't seem to affect you."

"Sure it does. I'm just better at containing my emotions."

Libby Smith returned with the carrot-orange soup, a dollop of sour cream melting in its center.

"I'm not that hungry anymore," Maggie said. "Maybe I should cancel the salmon."

"As you wish," Libby said, smiling. "Don't you just hate jet lag? I never know whether I'm supposed to eat, sleep or just be cranky."

Maggie laughed. "Some people would say I always know when to be cranky."

Libby laughed, too, but when she left, Rob picked the mint sprig out of his iced tea and set it on his place mat. "I want to know everything you know about your Sir Walter Raleigh character. Start to finish.

When he contacted you, how, what he said, why St. John's, what happened there. All of it."

Maggie dipped her spoon into her soup. "Why should I tell you?"

"Because we're in this thing together."

"That's what I was trying to avoid —"

"Not that hard. If you'd wanted to disappear once you got to New York, you'd have figured out a way to do it." He nodded to her. "Go ahead. Eat your soup and talk to me."

Whether he meant to or not, he managed to sound rational and calm and reasonable — not dictatorial, not panicked, not annoyed. It was a skill, Maggie thought. If their positions were reversed, she'd never have pulled it off.

"It's William," she said. "Not Walter."

"He doesn't think he defeated the Spanish Armada?"

"As far as I know, no."

And she told Rob everything.

Start to finish. All of it.

Eleven

After lunch, they ran across Libby Smith folding cloth napkins at the dining room table, and she offered to show them around the place. "I'll give you the secret grand tour."

She had an eager but somewhat self-deprecating manner that Rob attributed to the awkwardness of being reduced, basically, to the live-in help in a house that had been in her family for generations. She pretended not to mind, that she loved what the Franconias had done to the place and appreciated having it off her hands. But it had to stick in her craw.

Before Rob could bow out of any tour, Maggie accepted for both of them. A minute later, they were standing on the front steps and Libby had them listening for sounds of the nearby creek.

"Its official name is the Raven Kill," she said. "*Kill* is an old-fashioned Dutch word for river or creek, but nobody knows that anymore. So, we generally say Ravenkill Creek. Technically it's redundant, but otherwise, who'd know what we were talking about? Do you speak Dutch, Agent Spencer, since you're assigned to the American embassy in The Hague?"

"I've picked up the grammar, and I know a few words."

"And you, Deputy," Libby said. "They say you speak eight or nine languages."

"Not quite that many," Rob said.

"It's such a gift. I can get along in French, but that's about it. Anyway, it used to be farmland right down to the creek. The woods are relatively recent. They've grown up in the past seventy years or so. The orchards and gardens are all my family's doing, revitalized, of course, by Andrew and Star."

"When did your family arrive in Ravenkill?" Maggie asked.

"Just before this house was built in 1846. There wasn't a lot of money until my great-grandfather's day in the early 1900s. My grandfather added on to the house and turned it into more of a country estate — a gentleman's farm — than a homestead." She trotted down the steps onto the front lawn. "Then my father squandered the family fortune. You know the old adage. First generation makes it, second generation spends it, third generation loses it.

That about sums it up as far as the Smiths go."

Rob followed Maggie down the steps. "What was your great-grandfather's fortune in?" he asked.

"Investments. I don't know." Libby waved a hand, her tone cheerful and dismissive. "It doesn't matter now."

Rob noticed the grass was virtually without weeds. Everything about the Old Stone Hollow Inn was picture-perfect. "Your parents —"

"Dead. First my mother, then my father. They were both gone before I was out of college."

"When did you sell the property to the Franconias?" Maggie asked.

"Four years ago. It was that or the wrecking crane. I never thought I'd stay here, but Andrew and Star wanted someone on the premises during renovations and I didn't mind. It was fascinating, actually." She shrugged. "I just haven't left yet. I'm collecting antiques to open my own shop. Quality stuff. My father was a drunk, but he knew a bit about antiques and taught me. It's taking some time to pull the right pieces together. I do a little dealing, but it's not enough so that I can afford to strike out on my own."

"Are those your pieces in the barn?" Maggie asked.

Libby shook her head. "No, they're Andrew and Star's. They made their money in the antiques business. They think of themselves as sort of my mentors. Come on. I'll show you my pieces. They're on the tour."

She led them around to the side of the house, pointing out old rose bushes and lilacs, a sugar maple where her grandmother had once had a swing and a marble fairy statue that her grandfather had picked out because it so looked like her grandmother. She was still talking when she led them down a slope to a full-size cellar door.

"You *have* to see the wine cellar," she said, hefting the heavy door open. "My grandfather had it built almost a hundred years ago."

A switch just inside the door turned on a naked yellow lightbulb in the middle of a narrow hall. An old dehumidifier rumbled against one wall. Maggie sneezed. "Dust sensitivity," she said, sneezing again.

"You can't keep the dust out of here," Libby said. "The original cellar is all stone. Can you imagine? They built it one big old rock at a time. There was a dirt floor, but it got paved over with concrete. This part's

189

newer, but, still, there's just not much that can be done about the dust."

Rob nodded to an arched wooden door. "Is that the wine cellar?"

Libby smiled. "Good guess. Doesn't it remind you of a Vincent Price movie? Alas, no bats and vampires down here."

She pulled open the door, which was heavy for her. The room was small and windowless, naturally cool, its concrete walls lined with mostly empty wooden wine racks. Only a few dust-encrusted bottles remained. Libby pulled on a string, and another naked yellow lightbulb came on.

"It gives a lot of people the creeps to be down here, but not me," she said. "During the winter and bad weather, I'd hide in here with a book. Of course, my father cleaned out any last remaining bottles of wine. Andrew talks about actually using it again, but he's very picky about temperature and humidity controls."

"What's through that door?" Maggie asked, pointing to a more ordinary door in the corner of the small room.

"Storage. It's interesting to see a house from the inside, don't you think? But maybe I'm just a frustrated architect. My antiques room is just up the hall."

They returned to the hall, passing a battered wooden canoe and broken paddles. "Are these some of your antiques?" Maggie asked.

"Junk. Andrew thinks he can restore the canoe. I don't."

"Was it in your family?"

"Everything down here was in my family."

Rob didn't think the canoe had much hope. "Are the Franconias originally from Ravenkill?" he asked.

"Poughkeepsie," Libby said, tackling a combination lock on another door. In a few seconds, she had it unlocked and the door pushed open. "Voilà."

The room was stacked nearly floor to ceiling with old furniture and crates of glass pieces. Another dehumidifier rumbled and rattled in a corner. Rob noticed desks, tables, chairs, dressers, sofas, cupboards and bookcases, but he couldn't place any value or determine the origin of any of them.

Libby sighed proudly. "I know it all looks like dusty old junk to most people, but I can see how it'll all fit into a shop in the village. I even know which one I want."

"Do you specialize in a particular country or era?" Maggie asked, peering at the eclectic jumble of pieces.

"I just buy what I like. I spend a lot of time and money traveling to find things, keep track of all the documentation. There's a lot to it."

More, Rob was certain, than he wanted to know.

But the cellar tour ended, and they made their way up the back stairs to a small laundry and supply room, then continued their tour through the main rooms of the first floor. Libby pointed to the door to the ell where she had her minisuite. "It's very cute," she said.

"Anyone else live here full-time?" Rob asked.

Libby shook her head. "Just the Franconias and me."

"Do they have any children?"

"Two grown daughters. I'm sure they'll end up inheriting the place." She spoke without apparent bitterness. "Andrew and Star are such planners. I'm more spontaneous — which is probably why I don't have a husband, kids or much money."

She pointed out several items the Franconias had ended up buying from her, never mind their own expertise in antiques. An early twentieth-century sofa, a Victorian piano stool, an 1840s quilt. "I'd dreamed for so long of what this place could look like," Libby said. "It was easy to come up with the perfect pieces."

They headed upstairs, where she took them through unoccupied guest rooms and sitting rooms, pausing at a hall window with a breathtaking view of the Hudson River. They were near the narrows, Libby explained, where the famous river forced its way between the Appalachians and was at its deepest and most treacherous.

She turned away from the window. "I never thought I'd have to give up this view."

They returned to the main floor and wandered out to the back porch. Libby put her hands on her hips and breathed in the summer air as if to counter all the dust and the nostalgic memories stirred up on her tour.

Rob dredged up something to say. "It's humid. Maybe we'll get rain." God, he thought, he sounded like his father, talking about the weather. "Think it'll storm?"

"A forty-percent chance of thunderstorms, according to the latest weather report," Libby said. "I should pick the beans before one hits. Thanks for indulging me."

"Our pleasure," Maggie said.

"That's very gracious of you to say."

Libby gave an irreverent smile. "I've never shown the place to a couple of feds. Enjoy the rest of the afternoon."

She set off happily down the driveway.

"Either it doesn't kill her that she lost the place to a brittle couple she doesn't like that much," Rob said, "or she's good at hiding it."

"Maybe she knows that without the Franconias the gardens and orchards would be a golf course by now."

He shrugged. "The golf course might have kept the fairy statue."

Rob said he wanted to check in with Mike Rivera, and they ended up in Maggie's room. He didn't comment on the four-poster bed or the forget-me-not wallpaper. Maggie ducked into her bathroom while he made his call and checked her face for dust and smudges after crawling around the inn's cellar.

Libby Smith. Andrew and Star Franconia.

A country inn.

Antiques.

It wasn't a lot to go on.

"It's not *anything* to go on," Maggie said to herself, then rejoined Rob in the bedroom.

He'd finished with his conversation and

stood at her window. "Juliet Longstreet thinks Ethan Brooker must have had something to do with the Janssen tip."

"Brooker? We don't have any indication he was even in the Netherlands last week, never mind on Janssen's heels. I doubt he'd have bothered with a tip."

"He wouldn't have killed Janssen —"

"I didn't mean that. I meant he'd have grabbed Janssen himself and hauled him to the police station. He wouldn't have risked an anonymous e-mail tip. I could have not gotten it in time, I could have ignored it, the Dutch SWAT team could have missed Janssen. Brooker doesn't sound the sort to take that kind of chance."

"Maybe he had a contingency plan if the tip didn't work out."

"Possible. Does Deputy Longstreet trust him?"

"She doesn't trust anyone."

Maggie hesitated, remembering what she'd read about Rob and Longstreet. "You two —"

She didn't have to go further. Rob shook his head. "Long and well over."

"I don't even know why I asked."

"Because you're curious," he said. "You want to know."

She licked her lips, her mouth suddenly

dry. "Why would I want to know?"

"Because you want to dismiss me as some stereotype —"

"The well-connected Southern frat boy who speaks five languages —"

"Seven."

"And who's friends with the president and is a guest at diplomatic receptions, not just the protection —"

"I can be the protection, too. But, yes. That sums up the stereotype you want to lay on me to keep from getting too close —"

"Rob, you *are* a well-connected Southern frat boy who speaks seven languages."

He smiled. "I never joined a fraternity. And it doesn't matter. You like me, anyway."

"I suppose one shouldn't mistake charm for a lack of confidence —"

"No, one shouldn't."

He spoke with an ease and natural humor that somehow only underlined the edge to him, the air of danger that had nothing to do with posturing and everything to do with self-assurance and purpose.

He'd had a hell of a year, Maggie reminded herself. He'd been shot. His family had nearly been destroyed. He'd had a long recovery that, in some ways, was probably still ongoing.

A little flirtation and attraction that she could keep under control she could handle. But they were fast passing that point.

"Your father's a diplomat," she said.

"The first in the family. My ancestors were riverboat workers and brawlers. Most of them probably looked like Southern frat boys, too."

"Okay. So I won't pigeonhole you."

"It'd be smarter not to. Less likely you'll get in over your head."

"How would I —"

"By thinking I'm something I'm not. Like not interested in redheaded DS agents who have clandestine meetings in Dutch cathedrals and a penchant for trouble —"

"I don't always have that penchant. Only this week."

He touched her hair. "You're not that easy to draw out, are you, Maggie?"

The way he said her name. She shut her eyes a moment to collect herself. "Christ, Rob. I'm supposed to be checking out this inn."

"You did check it out. You had a tour of the cellar and you saw the fairy statue and the view of the Hudson."

His voice was so quiet, and he was standing close enough to her that she could feel his hips, the brush of his chest against her. He let his hand linger on her arm. Even as she warned herself against the impulse, Maggie leaned into him, and he dropped his hand to her waist, gently turning her into him. She thought he whispered her name. She could feel the warm air, moist and heavy with the increasing humidity.

"Rob . . . it's okay, it's . . ." She smiled, raising her mouth to his, answering the unspoken question. "Yes."

Their kiss started out tentative, but that didn't last. Maggie opened her mouth, eager to taste him, let him explore her. He lowered an arm to her hips and pulled her against him. She felt the tight, strong muscles in his shoulders and back, the tautness of his hips as her hands skimmed over him, everything about him suddenly firing her senses.

He lifted her onto him, and she could feel that he was as aroused as she was, as if their close proximity to each other since he'd arrived in Holland — together with the violence and chases and diversions — had built up, erupting now with more intensity than either of them could have anticipated.

He skimmed his thumbs over her breasts, eliciting a soft moan from her that had nothing to do with fatigue or jet lag. It would be so easy just to fall into bed with him. Her pretty four-poster was right there, a few feet way, in the path of the afternoon breeze.

But they broke apart as suddenly as they'd come together. A timer might have gone off, or an alarm reminding them of who they were and what they were about.

Rob backed up a step, exhaling as he ran a hand through his hair. "I didn't expect that to happen."

Maggie took in a ragged breath. "Ha."

He grinned at her. "Okay, I didn't expect it to happen the way it did. I've been thinking it might sooner or later, but —" He smiled at her, not even breathing hard. "I don't want to get you fired."

"Trust me, Bremmerton can find more reasons to fire me than sneaking a kiss with a good-looking marshal."

His expression turned serious. "Maggie —"

She didn't let him draw her out. Just stick to the facts. "You must need to get back to New York. Did you tell Chief Rivera everything?"

Rob pulled open the door to the hall.

"He doesn't know you're a redhead with the most beautiful turquoise eyes —"

"That charm again."

He laughed. "It's a killer, isn't it?"

They walked downstairs, past the view that Libby Smith had said she loved so much. When they reached the back porch, Maggie felt the carrot-orange soup burning up her throat. "You're going to look into William Raleigh, aren't you?"

"Discreetly, but yes."

"Let me know —"

"Of course." There was no sarcasm in his tone. "Bremmerton?"

Maggie thought a moment. "I think he knows more than he's saying, but I can't be more specific than that."

Rob sighed. "Fair enough. You've got my cell phone number. You know the number at the office. Call. I can be back up here in less than an hour if I break the speed limits."

She walked with him to his car.

He winked at her. "I'd kiss you goodbye —"

"We've given the locals enough to talk about, don't you think?"

After he left, Maggie felt the afternoon humidity in the air. There was no breeze. She heard bees in the dahlias and a crow far off in the distance, but no birds, it seemed, nearby.

Libby waved from the vegetable garden, but kept to her task which seemed to be picking loose leaf lettuce. Maggie continued on to the back porch, where Star Franconia was cleaning tables and taking in short, quick gulps, as if she were trying to keep herself from crying. Maggie didn't disturb her and ducked inside.

There was no sign of Andrew in the garden, on the porch or inside.

Maggie had no idea what to do with herself. There was no evidence the Franconias or their staff or any of their guests were engaged in criminal wrongdoing.

Why had William Raleigh sent her here?

Who the hell was he?

When she and George Bremmerton had talked that morning, he'd all but vouched for Raleigh. That counted for something, even if he was being vague.

She headed back up to her room, telling herself that it was necessary, okay and actually quite smart of her to be in Ravenkill on her own.

Twelve

It was early evening when Ethan arrived at JFK.

He didn't know what'd happened to Raleigh. Probably wandering around Amsterdam, checking out the sights and talking to himself. Maybe hitting the bottle. Trying to talk himself out of a psych ward. Ethan was a decent judge of character, but the year since his wife's death had left him less certain about everything he'd once taken for granted.

He paid a fortune for a cab to take him to the Upper West Side building where Juliet Longstreet was borrowing an apartment from a friend who was off to Hollywood for six months.

Deputy Longstreet wouldn't be happy to see him. But he didn't have money for a New York hotel, and he'd be happy to see her.

He didn't know why.

He talked his way past the doorman. It wasn't that hard, which made him think she needed a new doorman. When he got up to her floor, her door was shut and locked up tight, and it occurred to him she could be on vacation.

But surely not Deputy Longstreet. It'd been just four months since two of Janssen's goons had dragged her off the street into their car with every intention of killing her. She'd escaped, jumping into oncoming traffic and getting a hell of a road rash on her upper thigh. Ethan'd seen the rash when it was still raw and bloody, because she'd also turned up in a limestone cave in Night's Landing, where he'd been posing as the Dunnemores' property manager.

She'd still be trying to prove to herself and all the other marshals that she had handled herself well back in May. She had — she'd done great. But she wasn't going to take his word for it.

Ethan plopped down on the floor in front of Julia's door. He hadn't been at his best when they'd met, either. He'd been playing a good ol' boy from west Texas working as a property manager while he tried to make his mark in Nashville as a songwriter. He *had* written a few songs, all bad.

Juliet had come to Night's Landing already beat-to-shit by Janssen's goons.

Then she and Ethan had found them dead at President Poe's childhood home.

Ethan was convinced Juliet had saved his life by giving him a chance to jump into the Cumberland River and escape certain death.

Then he got to save her life when he found her tied up, gagged and left in a cave on a vertical bluff above the Cumberland. Not that she saw it that way.

He'd done what he could to help and took off a little later the same day.

He hadn't seen Deputy Longstreet since.

He leaned back against the door and wondered if she'd cuff him when she saw him. Arrest him for something. Breaking and entering. Harassing a federal agent. Annoying her.

The elevator dinged and she got off, blue eyes on him, blond hair sticking out every which way. She looked like August in New York had gotten to her. Her arms were loaded with, as far as Ethan could judge, a bag of perlite, a flyswatter, a jug of organic skim milk and a bag of Hershey's chocolate nuggets.

She dropped it all and went for her gun.

"Jesus Christ, Longstreet," Ethan said, not moving, "you have great reflexes. Unbelievable. Where were you when I needed you in Afghanistan?"

She didn't draw her weapon, just finally stared at him, her stuff all over the floor. "Brooker. Goddamn it. What are you doing here?"

"Waiting for you. You're not a moment too soon. Nature calls."

"I should arrest you —"

"You should not arrest me. I'm not wanted for any crimes." He nodded to her milk jug. "Look, it didn't break. Is that because it's organic?"

"It's because it's a good bottle." She had a red spot on the V of exposed skin above her shirt. Sunburn or emotion. "You skipped out on the scene of a double homicide."

"Ancient history. I've talked to the FBI and the marshals. We're square."

She pointed a finger at him. "I'm going to see to it nobody wants to talk to you. Understood?"

"If I can use your bathroom, I'll tell the FBI and the marshals everything I told them all over again."

"When did you talk to them?"

"Two days after I skipped out on the caves and the snakes and the fried apricot pies in Night's Landing. Didn't they tell you?"

She sighed. "Sort of. I wasn't sure I believed them."

"Figured they were coddling you? You

205

know, about that bathroom . . . I wasn't kidding."

He thought she might have smiled. "All right, all right. Help me pick up this stuff. And if you're carrying, you'd better have the right paperwork. New York gun laws are very strict."

He knew all about New York gun laws. He wasn't armed, but that wasn't something he planned to tell her, federal agent or no federal agent. He picked up her perlite and the milk; she grabbed the chocolate and the flyswatter.

"You've got something like sixty-five locks on that door," he said. "I'm pleading with you."

"You're not the pleading type."

Although she was armed, he expected he could get her keys off her. He had at least four inches on her, not to mention combat experience. But Juliet Longstreet was tough and he didn't want to fight her.

She unlocked her door, and he followed her into her apartment. She had on jeans and a tank top under a dark pink shirt that draped over her gun.

"How's the road rash?" Ethan asked her.

"Healed."

"Leave scars?"

"A few."

It'd been nasty, he remembered. "You look better than the last time I saw you."

"That's because I'm not beaten and bloodied."

He glanced around her living room, plants and fish tanks on every available surface. The place was small and probably way overpriced, even for New York.

She gestured toward a door up a short hall.

"That's the bathroom."

"Going to get out your cuffs while I'm in there?"

"I might."

She wasn't softening.

He ducked into the bathroom. His reflection in the mirror above the pedestal sink wasn't reassuring. If he were Longstreet, he'd cuff him and haul him to the FBI just on looks alone.

She was leaning against the wall in the short hall, arms crossed on her chest, when he finished. He liked the direct way she looked at him. Not intimidated. "Where'd you come from?" she asked.

"West Point, by way of west Texas."

"Since then."

"Classified."

She rolled her eyes. "Since Tennessee in May. Where were you, say, last night?"

He ignored her question and studied her, wondering why he'd come here and not some flophouse of a hotel. He saw that the paleness and sunken eyes, the pained expression that had been there in May were gone. Her cheeks were pink, her skin lightly tanned. "The marshals wanted to know what you and I did in that cave."

"For God's sake, I was tied up —"

He grinned. "Like I said."

She cleared her throat, dropping her arms to her sides. "They wanted to know why I let you go."

"You didn't. You had to prioritize. It was more important to help Sarah Dunnemore and Nate Winter get your bad guy. I wasn't a threat."

"I'm calling the FBI and Chief Rivera —"

"Can we eat first? I haven't eaten all day."

"Brooker —" She kicked the wall with her heel. "What do you want?"

"Dinner. A night." He left her to chew on that while he walked back to her small kitchen, calling back to her over his shoulder. "How much you pay for this place?"

"Not nearly what I should."

"No air-conditioning, no view —"

She followed him and stood next to a

counter. "No garbage disposal, either. But there's an elevator and a doorman."

"Doorman's useless. He let me in." Ethan pulled open her refrigerator and frowned at its limited contents. One Amstel Light, eggs, a head of lettuce. "There's nothing in here."

"Another thing about New York, you can get whatever you want delivered."

He shut the fridge door. "That works." He smiled at her. "You look like you want to frisk me, Deputy, and not for all the right reasons."

"It's Juliet," she said tightly. "I'm not dealing with you in any official capacity. You're a guest in my home."

"Now you're getting the idea."

"Don't you have a home of your own, somewhere?"

"No."

"The family ranch in west Texas —"

"My brother runs it. I could pitch a tent there if I wanted to."

"I checked out your ranch, Brooker. You could build a mall there."

He walked past her, back into the living room, and stood in front of one of her four fish tanks, bending down so that he was at eye level with a goldfish. "I had a goldfish once. Bought it at a fair. The bowl wasn't

209

big enough, I guess, and it jumped out. The dog got it."

Juliet ran a hand through her short blond curls, a gesture Ethan found very sexy. But it'd been a long couple of days — a long year. She blew out a sigh. "It'd be easier if you gave me a reason to cuff you, read you your rights and get you the hell out of my apartment."

"Wouldn't it, though."

"You heard about Nick Janssen's arrest in the Netherlands?"

"I did."

"That wasn't you who provided the tip on where to find him?"

He didn't want to encourage her to think he planned to tell her a damn thing. The more questions he answered, the more she'd ask. The camel's nose under the tent. He moved to another fish tank, then fingered one of her spider plants. "Pretty much into fish and plants, aren't you?"

"One fish led to another, one plant led to another. You know how it is."

"They look like a lot of work."

"An American diplomat was murdered Saturday morning in Den Bosch, the Dutch town where Janssen was picked up. Thomas Kopac. He worked at our embassy in The Hague."

Ethan didn't respond, instead walking over to her cluttered table, where he started flipping through a stack of take-out menus. "You weren't kidding about the options. Any place you can get a burger?"

"Lots."

"Would that suit you? A burger, fries, salad?"

"You're avoiding my questions because you don't want to lie to a federal agent."

"I'm hungry and tired, Juliet. That's it."

She gave up. "A burger and salad. No fries. And you get the futon." She paused a beat, her gaze not as direct now. "I'm still checking with people."

But not right away, he realized. Not tonight.

An act of trust.

Ethan picked up the phone and handed it to her to call in their order. Her trust had to be a one-way street. At least for now. And tomorrow he had business to attend to that didn't involve any marshals, even one willing to feed him and put him up for the night.

Maggie waited until nightfall to call her mother, using her cell phone as she sat cross-legged on her bed. A passing shower had left the air moist and a bit cooler, the wind sucking her curtains against the wet screen.

If the light was just right, her mother wouldn't pick up the phone. At night, Maggie thought, her odds of reaching Cora Spencer, painter, were better.

She answered on the second ring.

"Hey, there," Maggie said. "It's me."

"Maggie! I'm so glad you called. I just got in from a walk. It's hotter than blue blazes here. How are you?"

"Doing fine. You haven't heard?"

A half beat's pause. "Heard what?"

Her mother didn't watch the news. If the world were ending, if a hurricane were bearing down on her, she would rely on a friend or neighbor to let her know. "Nothing. Never mind. You're doing okay?"

"Great. I'm working hard, teaching at the community college. Isn't it the middle of the night where you are?"

"I'm in New York," Maggie said.

"Oh. On business, I assume? Well, I know you've got an important job to do."

And she didn't want to know any of the details. She never asked questions. It wasn't that she didn't care — she was tired of caring, worn out from it. She wanted a quiet life with routines. She liked painting pretty pictures of gardens and beaches and flamingos and visiting with friends, talking about nothing more serious than whether there was a riptide or it was safe to swim in the warm water outside her apartment.

If she was a little self-absorbed these days, she was allowed. Or so Maggie told herself. Her mother had been married to a man with wanderlust and secrets, and her only child was the same. She'd figured out a way to have a life of her own and to let them — now just Maggie — have theirs.

"I was wondering," Maggie said, "did Dad ever mention Ravenkill, New York?"

"Not that I recall, no."

"The Old Stone Hollow Inn. Does that sound familiar?"

"No." She didn't ask why Maggie wanted to know.

Maggie unfolded her legs and stretched out on the bed, leaning back against fluffy pillows with lace-trimmed cases. "Do you ever recall meeting a man named William Raleigh?"

"I'm sure I haven't met him, no."

"He's in his midsixties, maybe late sixties. White hair. Red-faced, probably from drinking —"

"Maggie, I don't know him. I'm sorry I can't help you. If he's a friend of your father's, I've put that part of my life behind me."

213

"I understand. Thanks."

Maggie knew there was nothing more to talk about. Her mother wouldn't ask questions. She didn't know about Tom Kopac and Nick Janssen. She'd listen if Maggie wanted to tell her, but the most basic information would suit her. Her daughter was fine. She was in New York or The Hague or wherever.

Her problems were her own, for her to solve.

Even before her father had wandered off from his marriage, Maggie had known that her mother wouldn't be there for her. She didn't mean not to be. She just wasn't.

But Cora Spencer didn't expect Maggie to be there for her in return, either. At her father's funeral, Maggie remembered, she and her mother had been more like two old friends who'd cared for him rather than mother and daughter.

After they hung up, Maggie wondered what her mother would have done if she'd asked to spend a few days with her after pulling a new friend out of a Dutch river minutes after he'd been murdered.

It would have been fine. They'd have gone for walks and talked about her latest paintings.

★ ★ ★

Libby winced at the creaking sound the door made when she opened it.

It's past midnight. No one can hear you.

She ducked into the tiny, dark room and shut the door behind her before fumbling for the light string. She felt something on her neck and suppressed a shudder.

Cobwebs. The cellar was full of spiders.

Bats had got down here before, dropping between the walls. She'd screamed and screamed while one had flapped over her head when she was ten, but no one had heard her. Finally, exhausted, she'd pulled her shirt up over her head, believing that would keep the bat from getting tangled in her hair, and had crawled outside.

She caught the string, pulled on it and welcomed the dull light.

Her workroom.

It was barely eight square feet, its outer wall part of the original stone foundation, but it contained everything she needed. Worktables. Her laptop. Boxes of ammunition. Her first pistol, a Smith & Wesson her father had given her for her fourteenth birthday. He'd instructed her in gun safety. At least in that respect, she thought, what she'd become wasn't his fault.

She had supplies. Her experiments. She

was increasingly confident with what everyone knew now as IEDs. Improvised explosive devices. In other words, homemade bombs.

But she preferred her .22 Beretta, perfect for her tried-and-true tactic of surprising her prey and putting a bullet in the back of his skull before he knew she was someone to fear. It was simple, direct and effective.

Bombs were trickier. And messier.

She felt reassured checking her workroom, touching things, and her thoughts, in a frenzy all day, settled down.

Whatever their reasons for being in Ravenkill, Maggie Spencer and Rob Dunnemore knew nothing about her activities. If they did, Libby thought as she brushed more cobwebs off her arm, she'd be under arrest or at least have been taken in for questioning by now.

If William Raleigh had sent Philip Spencer's daughter here, why? What did Raleigh know? Where was he? What was he up to?

Libby opened the file she had on him on her laptop and recoiled at his face, those awful, knowing eyes. Her stomach muscles clamped down on her.

"You won't be the ruin of me."

Not another man, she thought. Not another drunk.

She'd kill him first, even if there was no money in it.

She closed the file and brought up the one on Philip Spencer. She touched his beautiful mouth and remembered the feel of his lips on hers, before he'd known what she was — before, she thought, she'd really even been what she was. He'd thought of her as an antiques dealer from upstate New York. He'd thought of her as a much younger woman he'd meant to resist.

He *had* resisted her. They'd had dinner a few times in Prague, but never slept together.

Their relationship felt like unfinished business, a bitter regret that Libby wished now she could go back and correct.

He was dead because of William Raleigh.

As she closed the file, she noticed how like her father Maggie Spencer looked.

Feeling better, Libby switched off the light and felt her way along the wall, creaking open the door, then tiptoed through the dark wine cellar and back upstairs to her room.

Thirteen

Maggie had apple-cinnamon muffins and fresh blueberries with water-buffalo yogurt on the back porch and found out from Star Franconia that there was only one other guest at the inn, who'd be leaving later in the day.

"You have the place to yourself," she said, heading down to the flower gardens with a pair of clippers in hand. "We have a full house starting on Thursday — it's a two-night minimum on weekends, which helps."

"But the inn's holding its own?" Maggie asked.

"Oh, I think so. We have to watch cash flow, of course, but who doesn't? And we put a lot into renovations. Too much, according to Andrew, but it was better just to go ahead and do everything at once. You can't do renovations in stages when you're trying to run an inn. No one wants to wake up to the sound of power saws and hammers."

"I suppose not."

"What do you think you'll do today?"

Two more nights, Maggie thought. George Bremmerton would expect her to make progress or get back to The Hague, and she had the same expectation. But what was progress? Deciding Raleigh had pulled Ravenkill and the Old Stone Hollow Inn out of thin air?

"I thought I'd take a walk," she said.

"Have you been down to the creek? It's my favorite place to stroll. They say the sound of water somehow produces the same chemical changes in our brains as Prozac. It's a natural antidepressant." She caught herself, her very pale skin blushing easily. "Not that you're depressed, I mean."

"It's okay. I could use some positive energy."

Maggie returned to her room and changed into shorts and trail shoes, noting how quiet the sprawling old house was. She debated calling Rob but decided it was better she didn't. There was no point in him getting any wrong ideas about her or their relationship. A kiss was one thing. Of the moment. Over and done with. But she was a DS agent posted overseas, and he was a U.S. Marshal posted in New York. End of story, as far as she was concerned.

Except, on another level, he felt like just

the kind of man she'd always wanted — charming and sexy and not to be underestimated.

And carrying the baggage of being seriously wounded on the job.

A "mustn't touch," she thought, then warned herself that she was jumping the gun, to say the least. She and Rob had been through a trauma together. A tragedy. Tom's death must have stirred up everything Rob had gone through in the spring. A quick kiss when the opportunity had presented itself had been inevitable.

Maggie didn't want to make more of it than was there.

She scooted back downstairs out the front door, the air warm and a bit less humid than yesterday. But that wouldn't last. Thunderstorms were forecast again for later in the day and overnight.

Good, she thought. She'd sit through a storm or two, then head back to the Netherlands and admit to Bremmerton that she'd grasped at a mentally ill man's fantasies because he'd invoked her father's memory.

She'd have to admit her mistake to the marshals, too.

That didn't excite her.

She followed the stone path around to

the back of the house past the fountains and the gardens, until it became a wide lane that led through an apple orchard, narrowing when it hit the woods. Soft ferns brushed against her bare legs. She breathed in the earthy smells and heard the rush of water below her, down a steep hill, through the birches, beeches and pines.

When she reached the creek, Maggie slowed her pace, the frenzy of the past week falling away. The coppery water was shallow, flowing over a gravel bottom strewn with rocks and boulders. The raging rapids that came with the early spring runoff had quieted, only a few treacherous stretches of white water now left in late summer.

She stood on a boulder jutting out over the river and listened to the gurgle of water tumbling over rocks, the rustle of leaves in the morning breeze. New York and its millions of people were just an hour or so to the south, but they might have been on another continent, another planet.

But then she stiffened, spotting something in the rocks and shade toward the middle of the river.

A flash of light.

Sun on metal.

Maggie jumped down from her boulder to the riverbank for a better view.

A leg. A running shoe.

Not again.

A body — a man — was caught on the rocks.

She ran into water up to her ankles. It was surprisingly cold, the current pushing at her, but she quickly climbed onto a large, flat rock, slippery from just the film of water that ran over it.

The man was on his back, his face out of the water. His torso had caught on a series of small, jagged rocks, but his lower half was bobbing in deeper water.

There was no obvious sign of injury.

Maggie splashed into the water up to her knees and nearly lost her balance in the current. She made her way to the jagged rocks, squatting down next to the man. He was unconscious, she thought, but not dead. Surely not dead.

She checked his airway.

He was breathing.

He had spots of blood on his neck and arms, and a tear in the shoulder of his black T-shirt.

Had he fallen? Slipped?

His skin was cool to the touch. She needed to get him out of the water, if possible, then find help.

He gave a small cough.

"It's all right," Maggie said, trying to sound reassuring. "I'm going to get help —"

"What're you doing here?"

His question was abrupt, antagonistic. His dark eyes focused on her, but she had no idea if he recognized her.

"Are you all right?" she asked.

She might not have spoken. He latched on to her wrist with one hand and, using it to anchor himself, stood up. Water streamed off his clothes and down his bare arms.

Maggie, rising next to him, noticed the raw, nasty lump on the back of his head and remembered that head injuries could make people belligerent, throw them off for a few minutes or even much longer.

"I must have slipped." His voice was ragged, and he didn't sound or look entirely coherent. He seemed to struggle to focus on her. "What are you doing here?"

"I'm staying at the inn. I was taking a walk."

The dark hair, the dark eyes. The black graphic tattoo.

The Texas drawl.

Ethan Brooker.

In that split second, Maggie recognized him and knew she was too late.

He stepped onto her toes and, with both hands, butted her in the chest. Even before she realized he'd moved, she was sprawling backward into the deep pool of water just past the jagged rocks.

Plunging to the bottom, she gulped in river water. Her arms raked across the gravel bottom. She got control of her sprawling, butt-first dive and burst up and out of the water, coughing and choking for air.

The water was up to her waist, the current slamming her against another rock. She grabbed it, then hoisted herself onto it.

"Brooker! You're hurt! You need a doctor!"

She heard nothing but the crows, the water and the wind.

Ethan Brooker was gone.

Hell.

She charged through the river to the bank, then ran, soaking wet, up the path.

He'd made it to the edge of the apple orchard before collapsing against an oak, still on his feet but breathing unevenly. And swearing.

She heard a crunching sound behind her and spun around.

William Raleigh stood under a pine tree. He had on a red madras shirt, another pair of threadbare khaki pants and his sport sandals, but he didn't smell as much of cigarettes in the open air.

Maggie stiffened. "What in hell —"

"What am I doing here?" He seemed at ease with having a half-conscious former Special Forces officer slumped against a tree and a federal agent dripping wet. "Let me just say, Agent Spencer, that you are as thorough as I'd hoped you'd be. I expected you to make a few calls and check the Internet. Instead, you get on a plane first thing Sunday morning, and now here we are in Ravenkill."

"Brooker —"

"His injuries aren't my doing. I'm not sure they're anyone's doing. He probably slipped."

"That doesn't matter right now. He needs to get to a doctor. If he's not hurt, he's faking it well."

"I'm not faking a goddamn thing," Brooker said, using the tree trunk for support as he got to his feet. He looked at Raleigh. "My backpack's under another tree. Let's go."

Maggie shook her head. "Wait just a minute —"

Raleigh touched her hand. "Ethan's too miserable to talk right now. I'll take care of him and be in touch." He smiled, a twinkle

225

in his pale eyes. "Go get dried off."

The breeze on her wet clothes and skin gave her a chill.

She looked at the two men, and she suspected they both knew fourteen ways to disarm her and tie her to a tree if she didn't cooperate, gun or no gun, training or no training. They'd simply done more dirty work than she had.

But if she'd meant to take either of them in, she'd have handled everything differently.

She nodded, knowing she was taking a risk. Breaking dishes, as Raleigh would have said. "Be in touch," she warned, then let the two men go.

"I just knocked your DS agent in the creek."

Rob braked halfway up the driveway to the Old Stone Hollow Inn. The voice on the other end of his cell phone was male with a Texas accent. "Who is this?"

"Redhead. Real pretty eyes. Armed."

Rob tensed. "Brooker?"

"It wasn't her fault. I thought she was on the attack. I hit my head on a rock or something — I don't remember."

"Where are you now?"

No answer.

Rob checked his cell phone readout. Private number. But Ethan Brooker had shown up at Longstreet's apartment last night. She'd just finished explaining the situation to Rivera before Rob headed north.

"Hell." It was Brooker again, sounding as if he were in pain. "My head's a mess. She hauled ass after me. Thought she might shoot me. She's on her way back to the inn. I don't think she's hurt, but you might want to go find her."

The connection ended. Rob jumped out of his car and ran across the driveway into the orchard, the tall grass almost up to his knees. There were Indian paintbrushes and black-eyed Susans in bloom, and the branches of the old trees were drooping with ripening apples. The ground was uneven, spotted with knobby apples that had already fallen, and he was suddenly aware of just how strange his life had gotten since he'd heard Maggie Spencer had received the tip that led to Nick Janssen's arrest.

What the hell was Ethan Brooker doing in Ravenkill?

But when Rob got to the woods, he found Maggie alone.

She was soaked, with bits of rotted leaves and mud splatters on her legs and puffy, pink scratches on her arms. And when she saw him, she swore under her breath.

"Where's Brooker?" Rob asked.

"On his way to the E.R., if he's smart. He's got a good goose egg on the back of his head." She brushed back a soaked lock of hair, a darker red when it was wet. "I found him unconscious in the creek."

"How did he get there?"

"Says he might have slipped." She didn't sound convinced. "When he came to, he was out of his head. He didn't know if I'd attacked him."

Rob observed her a moment, deciding she wasn't telling him everything. "So he dumped you in the river?"

"Correct. It's my own damn fault."

"Maggie —"

"He's a good guy, isn't he?"

"Yes."

"Then I'm glad I didn't shoot him." She coughed, spitting river scum into the grass. "God. What's in the Ravenkill? Anything toxic? I think I drank a gallon of it. It tastes like trout. Or maybe trout tastes like the Ravenkill."

Rob tried to smile. "I think Ravenkill trout was on yesterday's menu. Maggie —"

"Did Brooker call you?"

"Yes."

"He had your number?"

"I'm guessing he used Juliet Longstreet's cell phone and it's on her caller list."

"How —"

"He was at her place last night." Maggie coughed again, not spitting this time. "They're an item?"

"She says not. She came home yesterday afternoon and found him sitting on her doorstep. She let him spend the night. He took off in the morning."

"With her cell phone?"

Rob shrugged. "He left a note."

"And Longstreet just let him —" But Maggie stopped herself, sighing. "But I did the same thing. I let him go."

"He must be persuasive."

"He didn't persuade me of anything." She wiped a drop of water off her nose. "I need to get on dry clothes."

Rob took a sharp breath. "You need to talk to me."

She nodded. "That, too."

"You're leaving something out. Brooker —"

"My guy from the cathedral was here," she said casually, flicking a glop of mud off her knee. "Raleigh."

Rob tensed, but she started toward the inn, then stopped suddenly and kicked off her wet running shoes.

"They're squishy," she said.

"Maggie —"

"George Bremmerton went to the hospital after Charlene Brooker was killed last fall and helped identify her. He thinks he should have done more to get answers to her murder. Pushed harder." She scooped up her shoes. "Ethan Brooker shouldn't have had to go off half-cocked to find his wife's murderer himself."

"Bremmerton didn't let you come here out of a sense of guilt."

"No, he didn't." She squinted back at Rob, the ends of her hair curling as water dripped onto her shoulder; her soaked cotton shirt clung to her. "Charlene Brooker was on to Nick Janssen before any of the rest of us. I can cut her husband some slack if I want to."

"About Raleigh. He and Brooker are hooked up?"

"Somehow. I don't have the details. Raleigh didn't hit Brooker on the head. Brooker says he doesn't remember what happened."

"Do you believe him?"

She squeezed water out of the end of one curl. "Right now, I don't know that I believe anyone. I'm damn lucky I didn't hit my head on a rock."

"Brooker would have grabbed you before you did. Even half out of his head."

"He's that good, is he?"

"Yes."

They came to the driveway, but Maggie stayed in the grass. "I'll meet you on the back porch. I'm in enough trouble with you marshals without dripping all over one of your cars."

Not that she was worried, Rob noticed. He watched her walk along the edge of the driveway, swinging her running shoes by their laces.

She was wobbly.

But, he thought, probably she wouldn't want him pointing that out right now.

Fourteen

Libby arranged fresh-cut asters in pottery vases at a long wooden counter in the inn's kitchen and tried to keep her hands from shaking with that familiar mix of fear, exertion and exhilaration.

If he wasn't such a damn bull of a man, Ethan Brooker would be dead.

Although he was on Janssen's target list, it was just as well the army officer was still alive. She'd be able to collect her hundred thousand dollars for his death, but there'd be a body to explain. That he'd survived his fall into the creek meant that she'd still have to deal with bereaved, out-of-control Major Brooker — and the DS agent and her marshal friend would want to know what Brooker was doing in Ravenkill.

Libby stabbed a particularly tall red aster into the middle of a vase, pushing back her irritation with Star, who was sniffling and muttering to herself at the sink. "Star, please. What's wrong?"

"Maggie Spencer." Star gulped in a breath, her skinny shoulders hunched against her distress. "Did you see her? She came in just a little while ago. Something happened —"

"It looked to me as if she slipped and fell in the river."

"Why was she armed?"

"Because she's a federal law enforcement agent."

"But diplomatic security —"

"I know, I know." Yanking out the too-tall aster, Libby snipped another inch off its stem and tried to smile through her own tension. "It'd be easier if she were a florist. Which I clearly am not. Do these flowers look okay to you?"

Star sniffled again — it was maddening to Libby — and nodded. "They're lovely. It's hard to go wrong with asters. Aren't they so cheerful?"

Cheerful. Libby hadn't thought of them that way. She'd picked them upon her return from the creek, as a reason for her to have been outside, out of view. It wasn't as if she'd thought through any kind of alibi or even had anticipated needing one. As with Tom Kopac on Saturday, she'd had to think on her feet and take action.

Ethan Brooker was a problem. He'd been since his wife's death last fall.

A pity, Libby thought, that Nick Janssen

hadn't hired her for that job. *And* the one in May. She'd have done far better than the men Janssen had sent. The fools had ended up dead themselves.

How had Brooker ended up in Ravenkill?

Why?

He could be trailing Maggie Spencer, or he could have come here for the same reasons she had.

Whatever those reasons were.

This time when Libby jabbed the red aster into the vase, its stem bent. She tossed it aside, feeling her tension clawing at her. Star's whining didn't help.

Libby had prepared herself as best she could for the inevitable questions she'd be asked if Brooker turned up dead. But how would she explain herself if the police checked into her whereabouts for the past week and discovered she'd been in the Netherlands? In particular, in 's-Hertogenbosch?

Again, she thought, just as well Brooker wasn't lying dead in Ravenkill Creek.

Star sniffled again, loudly, and heaved a dramatic sigh. *"Oh, God."*

"Star, it's okay. Honestly. Nothing's happened on inn property."

Libby tried not to indulge in unnecessary emotion. She was confident, at least, that Brooker hadn't seen her. She'd spotted Maggie Spencer in the apple orchard and had followed her, then taken a different, faster route down to the river. She'd planned to get to a spot that intersected with the path the DS agent was on and wait for her, try to gauge what she was up to.

Instead, Libby had come upon Ethan Brooker, recognizing him instantly from the photos of him she had stored on her laptop.

The rush of water, even in late summer when the river was at its shallowest, must have prevented him from hearing her on the path above him. If he'd caught her, she'd have claimed she was picking wildflowers or off to dip her feet in the Ravenkill on a warm August morning. He'd have no idea who she was.

She didn't know whether she'd panicked or had simply attempted to seize the moment. She'd wanted Brooker dead. She knew that much.

She didn't have her Beretta and silencer with her, but she wouldn't have used it — if Ethan Brooker was going to die in Ravenkill, it had to look like an accident. She had to take her chances and at least disable him, impede him from doing whatever he was in Ravenkill to do.

She'd dismissed jumping him. He'd pick her off him like a bug.

Given her limited options, she'd tossed a pebble into the river in front of him, distracting him for a split second, and pelted him on the back of the head with a baseball-size rock.

He'd had the grace to fall, hitting another rock and landing in the shallow river. As beat up as he was, he'd managed to stagger to his feet, stumble around for a few seconds, then fall on his back in the water, halfway to the other bank.

Libby quickly recovered the rock she'd used to hit him, but before she could finish off Brooker, Maggie Spencer arrived.

Libby managed to slip away without being seen. She'd stayed within the woods and avoided open ground, then walked boldly through the cornfield back up to the asters.

Brooker must have also spotted the DS agent on her walk and planned to intercept her, find out what she was doing in Ravenkill, share notes. Something.

Should have left well enough alone, Libby thought.

"I'll put these out on the tables," she

said, collecting up her half-dozen vases of brightly colored asters.

"Maggie Spencer's upstairs changing," Star said, her voice slightly stronger. "The marshal who was with her yesterday is out on the porch waiting for her."

"Does that make you nervous?"

"It all makes me nervous. Where's Andrew? Have you seen him?"

Libby shook her head. "Not this morning."

"I hope he —" Star pulled her upper and lower lips between her teeth, fighting back tears. Finally, she let out a breath and waved a hand. "Never mind."

God. Libby almost dropped the vases. Star thought that *Andrew* had done something?

Warning herself not to read too much into Star's dramatics, Libby exited to the porch, where, indeed, Deputy Dunnemore was sitting at an empty table. He really was even more good-looking than he was in all the pictures of him in the paper and on TV last spring.

Libby set five of the small vases on one table, then started distributing them one by one to other tables.

"You picked those flowers just now?" Dunnemore asked.

"Mmm. Pretty, aren't they?" She set another vase in the middle of a table, pretending to admire the splashes of pink, orange and red against the pale green and white decor. "I understand Agent Spencer had a mishap in the river. Do you know what happened?"

"More or less."

He left it at that. Did he know about Brooker? Had Spencer told him? Of course — why wouldn't she? But why hadn't she called the police, or at least an ambulance? The only explanation Libby could think of was that Brooker wasn't seriously injured and had told her not to.

Where the hell was the army major now?

"The riverbank can be deceptive," Libby said. "I grew up here and I've made a few wrong steps myself."

Maggie Spencer came downstairs and breezed out onto the porch. She smelled faintly of the lilac soap Star had in all the rooms. Her hair was still damp from her shower, and she'd changed into long pants and a denim jacket.

Libby placed the final vase.

Too bad Spencer hadn't hit *her* head when Brooker pounced on her. Maybe he blamed her for how he'd ended up in the river?

My life's not that simple, Libby thought.

Dunnemore turned to her, his Southern charm, she thought, less in evidence than his marshal demeanor. "Nice talking with you, Ms. Smith."

"Same here, Deputy."

The two federal agents left, and Libby returned to the kitchen, realizing she wasn't shaking or nervous.

If anything, she was exhilarated.

With William Raleigh humming to himself two steps behind him, Ethan staggered out of the woods onto a gravel turnaround that marked the end of the road that led from the village to the inn. The creek, shallower and wider than farther downstream where Maggie Spencer had found him, sounded almost like the wind.

His entire body ached. His head felt like it might blow into a million pieces.

Fine with him, he decided. Maybe it'd end his misery.

"You can't remember anything?" Raleigh asked for at least the third time. "Are you sure?"

"No, I can't. Yes, I'm sure. I can't remember anything after I got to the river." He turned to the older man, pushing back a wave of pain and nausea, trying not to let

Raleigh see just how injured he was. "Relax, okay? You look worse on a good day than I do on a bad one."

Raleigh didn't smile. "Do you need a doctor?"

"I just need some time for my head to clear."

He'd made off with Juliet's cell phone that morning before she woke up. It'd seemed like a good idea at the time. He'd headed to Grand Central Station and boarded a train north to Ravenkill. When he got off in the village, he followed the directions he'd memorized from the inn's Web site and walked the mile to the Old Stone Hollow Inn.

Something had distracted him before he got to the inn, but he couldn't remember what. Had he spotted Agent Spencer taking a jaunt through the woods? It was all a blur.

He'd dumped his backpack out of sight under a tree. For some reason, he could remember that. Next thing he knew, he was looking into Maggie Spencer's eyes and thinking she was trying to kill him.

He'd been out of his head, belligerent, paranoid. His reaction to her had been instinctive and defensive, but he'd known he hadn't wanted to hurt her. Some reptilian part of his brain must have recognized she wasn't a threat, because he remembered checking the water behind her to make sure it was deep enough to take her fall, that she wouldn't hit her head on rocks.

But he'd taken a risk, attacking a federal agent.

He hadn't gotten far before she'd caught up with him. That annoyed him. But if his fall wasn't an accident, he figured Spencer's arrival may have spooked his attacker and saved his life.

That didn't sit well with him, either.

"You have a car?" he asked.

Raleigh shrugged. "Not really."

"What do you mean, 'not really'? That was a yes or no question."

"It means no."

"So we have to walk? Are you up to it? Do you want me to use your cell phone to call a taxi?"

Ethan's head was spinning. "Then what? Even if I could get a taxi to take me, they'd kick me off the train. I stink now, and I'll stink worse when my clothes dry. Hell. I've got dead mosquitoes in my hair. Blood on my shirt." He didn't think he sounded all that coherent but kept going. "And you — you're not much better. You look like you should be sleeping under a bridge."

"Then it's just as well I arranged a ride for you."

"What?" Ethan felt fogged in, as if his vision were being pinched. "What ride?"

"Deputy Longstreet. She was on her way up here, anyway." A flicker of a smile. "On your case, I'd say."

"Fuck. I'm going to barf."

"Sit down. Try to relax." Raleigh half shoved him to the pavement and sighed. "You're a wreck. She can take you to the E.R."

"I'll be fine." It was his mantra, Ethan decided. *I'll be fine.* He closed his eyes, hoping the nausea passed. "It wasn't you who dumped me in the river?"

"We're on the same side, Major."

"Right." Ethan didn't know if he sounded sarcastic and dubious or just half-dead. His stomach rolled over again, but he shut his eyes and went still, managing to keep the contents where they belonged. "Raleigh —"

But when he opened his eyes, the old man had disappeared, and a battered pickup with Vermont plates rattled to a stop in the turnaround.

Juliet Longstreet climbed out, armed and not real happy. "Oh, man. Look at you, Brooker. Your friend, whoever he was, should have called an ambulance."

"I'll be fine."

The mantra again. He got on all fours, then onto his knees, then got one foot flat on the gravel ground. The river water and the New York bagel he'd picked up in Grand Central Station bubbled in his stomach, and his head throbbed. He heaved himself up, staggering toward the blond marshal with the blue eyes and the scowl.

She slipped a shoulder against him and took his weight, easing an arm around his middle. "What are you doing?" she asked, the softness of her voice catching him by surprise. "When are you going to give it up and get your life back?"

"Char . . ." He could see his wife's face, hear her voice, even as he leaned into Juliet and let her take more of his weight. She wasn't a small woman. He wouldn't crush her.

"I know. Come on. Let me help you."

"I don't need help."

"No, you hate needing help. There's a difference."

She tugged open the passenger door of her truck and maneuvered him up onto the seat. "Don't throw up in my truck. Understood?"

As weak as he was, he grinned at her. "How come I keep seeing you after I've ended up in a river?"

"Karma. Watch your foot, I'm shutting the door."

She locked him in, as if he might fall out or jump out on the interstate, and came around to the driver's seat. Her movements were stiff, and he could see she was, on the one hand, irritated with her situation and on the other hand, resigned to doing something she knew she shouldn't do.

She stuck the key in the ignition. "I want my phone back."

"Why'd you let me borrow it?"

"You didn't borrow it. You stole it. That's what I told Mike Rivera."

Ethan felt his eyes starting to close against his will. "You're full of shit, Longstreet. You were awake."

She made a face. "Look at you. Damn, Brooker. Are you done bleeding? I shouldn't get you to the E.R. and get that head looked at? Head injuries can be tricky."

"I just need clean clothes and a cigarette."

"There's no smoking in my truck."

"I only smoke when I'm in pain."

She shifted the truck into Reverse, checking her rearview mirror. "Why Ravenkill? Did you know Maggie Spencer was here? You must have."

Even as out of sorts as he was, he knew not to get into his reasons for being in Ravenkill with a U.S. Marshal. "My head hurts."

"How did it happen? The bump on the head."

"I told you. I fell into the river."

She braked hard, putting the truck into first gear as she glanced over at him. "Like Thomas Kopac?"

"Well, he had a .22 round in the back of his skull. I just hit a rock —"

"Or got banged on the head with one. Which is it?"

"I think I fell."

"You think? You don't know. Goddamn it, Brooker —"

"I've slept with your plants and fish." The contents of his stomach were oozing up his throat, and the pounding in his head hadn't even begun to let up. "We should be Ethan and Juliet to each other by now."

She had a white-knuckled grip on the steering wheel. "You rattled my brain showing up last night."

He smiled. "First piece of good news I've had today."

"You don't remember anything about what happened? Don't tell me you slipped. You *don't* slip. I saw you jump forty feet into the Cumberland River that day in Tennessee. You had a guy with a gun at your head, two dead guys at your feet —"

"At the point I jumped, the gun was at *your* head."

"God." She raked a hand through her short curls. "I don't trust you, Brooker."

"Ethan. And, yeah, you do."

She softened again, and he could see the tension going out of her shoulders, her blue eyes shining with a depth of compassion that he suspected she preferred to keep at bay. He saw it because he was that way himself. It was easier. Less chance of getting your heart ripped out of your chest.

She gulped in a breath and averted her gaze, as if looking at him would just make her fall apart. "Tell me what you want me to do."

He couldn't involve her in his mess. Raleigh, Kopac, Janssen. Ravenkill. Whatever they all amounted to, he wasn't sucking Juliet into it. He'd crossed lines, but he could — he didn't answer to anyone. She did.

"Relax, Juliet," he said. "I've hurt my head worse than this fixing my car. I'll be fine. I just need some time."

"You *are* hurt, then?"

"I don't remember what happened. Until I do —"

"You're not trusting anyone. You're not talking to anyone."

He let his silence be his response.

"Ethan . . ." She sighed. *"Damn."*

His stomach settled down. He wasn't going to vomit, but he couldn't keep his eyes open, felt his body sinking and his fatigue overtake him.

"You don't scare me," she said.

He tried to focus on her through his pain and exhaustion. "I don't want to scare you."

It was all he could manage, but he saw her look of shock and confusion before he closed his eyes again, unable to stop himself from drifting off.

"Sleep well, Major Brooker," she whispered. "You've come too far to get killed on us now."

He didn't have the strength even to open his eyes.

Char . . .

His wife was gone, her memory like a stab of heat and guilt.

He thought he heard Juliet sigh. Or maybe it was his dead wife's ghost, leaving him alone to sleep and dream.

Nate Winter would rather be on Cold Ridge where he grew up in the White Mountains, immersed in a thick fog and fierce wind, than more or less alone in a room with the President of the United States.

John Wesley Poe, however, never showed any sign he noticed Nate's discomfort or shared it. His focus was on his reasons for calling Nate to the White House.

They were in a sitting area, Poe on a wing chair, Nate on a love seat.

Nate was surprised at how quiet it was.

Poe shook his head. "Rob's got himself mixed up with Philip Spencer's daughter and William Raleigh. I can't believe it. It's like I saw this coming, knew it would get here, but couldn't admit it."

Nate shifted positions, trying to get comfortable on the love seat. "Mr. President?"

"They were a pair. Raleigh and Spencer. Before my time."

"Intelligence operatives?" Nate asked, guessing.

But Poe didn't give a direct answer. "Friends. Good friends. Spencer was killed eighteen months ago in Prague." He sighed. "It was before my time in office, not that it matters."

Poe's emotional involvement — his dread — was palpable, beyond what Nate could understand. "Philip Spencer was killed when he walked into the middle of a bank robbery —"

"That's the story."

"There was no bank robbery?"

"Oh, there was a bank robbery." Poe sank back into his chair, looking tired, a rarity for a man with his renowned stamina. "I don't know how much it had to do with what happened to Spencer. Raleigh wants his killer. Some people think he's responsible for Spencer's death — that he screwed up, plain and simple. He'd retired, supposedly. Went back to drinking. Again, supposedly. There are rumors he talked out of turn, bragged to the wrong person."

"So Raleigh's not only looking for a killer," Nate said. "He wants vindication."

"From what I understand, the man's a riddle. I'm not sure anyone really knows what he's up to. He could simply want to look after a friend's daughter, no matter how competent and skilled she is."

"Do you know where he is now?"

Poe shook his head. "I have no idea."

"Mr. President," Nate said, leaning forward, folding his hands over his knees as if somehow it would help him understand this man who meant so much to the Dunnemores, who was so much a part of their lives. "What's worrying you?"

He averted his eyes. "I've been waiting for this moment. It's like watching a drought in the west, knowing the fire season's coming and that there's nothing you can do. The conditions are there. They're perfect. All it takes is a dropped match, a lightning strike, a spark of a dragging muffler."

Poe sometimes had a metaphorical way of talking that he seemed to think drove home his point. He could spin a story — Sarah said it was a Night's Landing tradition, a skill born and developed on their quiet stretch of the Cumberland River. But Nate was from the Granite State, raised by a Vietnam vet uncle. He tended to be more direct. "Mr. President?"

"Rob's not going to stay in the Marshals Service."

There was nothing Nate could add. He knew what Poe said was true. He'd known it the minute he'd met Rob earlier in the year, when Rob had been assigned to the southeastern New York district. It wasn't that he didn't belong in the USMS. He just wasn't staying.

"He's suited to intelligence work. William Raleigh will reel him in, just as he reeled in Philip Spencer. And it scares me." Poe sighed heavily, no longer dancing around the truth about Raleigh and Spencer. "It scares the hell out of me."

"Because Rob's a Dunnemore," Nate said.

"Leola and Violet wanted me to stay in Night's Landing," Poe went on, referring to the two unmarried sisters who'd raised him. "They worried about me all the time, from the day I left home."

Orphaned at seven, Nate had faced different kinds of fears. "I think it comes with the turf."

"I know Rob can take care of himself. It's just —" He broke off. "Damn. He thinks his father and I don't believe in him, but that's not it. It's a visceral thing, Nate. This fear. I've never had a son of my own."

"Is anyone in touch with Raleigh? You could get him to back off —"

"No, I couldn't. Whether I could get in touch with him or not, I could never interfere that way."

"You wouldn't, you mean."

"That's right. I wouldn't."

"I respect that, Mr. —"

"Wes," he said, managing a ragged smile.

"Just once can you call me Wes?"

"Maybe when you're out of office, Mr. President."

Poe rose, and Nate followed his lead, the Washington humidity noticeable even in the air-conditioned White House. "What's Sarah up to today?" the president asked.

Nate relaxed at mention of his future wife. "Digging in her dump."

"She'll know —"

"She already does. She denies there's a twin connection between her and Rob, but it's there. She knows he's in trouble. This Raleigh character — he's not drinking now?"

"There are rumors he had a mental breakdown. But I'm told William Raleigh is one of the most clear-eyed people we have."

"He's back on the payroll?"

Poe didn't answer.

"Then you don't believe he got Philip Spencer killed," Nate said.

"No. I don't."

Poe sounded more presidential just then, less like a tortured friend.

When Nate got back to Arlington, he found Sarah on the back porch in a T-shirt and overalls, her dump-digging clothes. His sister Antonia, an E.R. doctor married to the junior senator from Massachusetts, was there with their new baby, Jill, a bald bundle of drool, gums and bright eyes.

Nate tried to get his head around how much their lives had changed in the past year. Antonia's, their sister Carine's, his own. They'd faced fear and stress and their own deepest desires, their toughest challenges, and come out on the other side — strong, united, ready to tackle a new future.

The Night's Landing Dunnemores weren't anything like the Cold Ridge Winters, except for that one thing — they didn't seem to do anything the easy way.

Sarah had her honey-colored hair pulled back, and she frowned at him. "Rob," she said. "Something's up."

Nate turned to his sister. "Don't you medical types tell me there's no such thing as twin radar."

Antonia laughed, her baby laid across her lap, chubby bare legs kicking. "I stopped trying to tell you anything long before I became a 'medical type.'" She scooped up Jill, who smiled, looking more Callahan than Winter. "Say bye-bye to Uncle Nate. We'll see him another day. Right now, he's got to talk to Aunt Sarah."

Jill was barely two months old and didn't understand a word her mother told her, but she smiled and cooed all the way down the porch steps.

Sarah blew the baby kisses. "I could get into babies," she said without looking at Nate.

Six months ago — before Sarah — he would have choked at such talk. Now he just felt a little tight in the throat. But it wasn't a remark, he decided, that needed a comment from him. "I just came from the White House."

The baby out of sight, his fiancée shifted back to him. "You saw Wes?"

He nodded.

"You talked about Rob," she said confidently.

"It's a complicated situation."

"Meaning you're not going to give me the details." She smiled at him, giving him a knowing look. "You don't think I'd interfere in marshal business, do you?"

"You? Never."

"I haven't seen Rob since Janssen was arrested," Sarah said quietly, serious now. "Since the murder in Holland —"

"You know I'd never stop you from seeing your brother."

But she was suddenly tense, her smile gone. "I won't ask what Wes said."

Which just killed her, Nate knew.

She took a breath, let it out. "But Rob

. . . If he's in over his head —"

"Rob can handle himself," he reminded her gently.

She squeezed her eyes shut a moment and nodded. "I know, I know. But if he's in the dark — if Wes knows something —"

"He won't be in the dark after I talk to him."

She relaxed visibly. "That's what I wanted to hear." She started for the porch door. "I finished up early and made fried apricot pies while Antonia and Jill and I visited."

Fried apricot pies were a Dunnemore family favorite, and a sure sign that Sarah was feeling the stress of whatever was going on with her brother.

"You cooked in this heat?"

That made her laugh. "It's not that hot."

When she pulled open the screen door, Nate noticed the small diamond on her finger, and it was as if he was seeing it for the first time. He'd given it to her on Cold Ridge.

In a few weeks, he and Sarah Dunnemore would be married.

Rob couldn't still be sneaking around with spies and DS agents then. He had to be at his sister's wedding.

Nate knew he had to do what he could to make that happen.

The rest was up to Rob.

Fifteen

Maggie drank unsweetened iced tea on a bench in the village of Ravenkill, the afternoon heat and humidity having built up to an uncomfortable level. She'd left Rob at the inn. The walk had helped her work out the kinks from her encounter with Brooker and settle her mind.

The kinks were easier to deal with than the mind.

Keeping his word, Raleigh had called her at the inn and asked her to come to the village.

Alone.

She'd showered and changed by then, getting her physical reaction to Rob more or less under control. They'd had lunch on the porch, and she'd told him exactly what had happened with Brooker and then with Raleigh.

But when Raleigh called, she hadn't told Rob she was off to the village to meet with the former economist, or whatever he was.

She'd said she needed some time alone.

Her bench was directly across from an upscale flower shop with an attractive sidewalk display of pots, cut flowers and bird-houses. On either side of it were antique shops, which dominated the small, pretty village.

She watched Raleigh come out of the too-cute restaurant where she'd bought her iced tea and cross the street, sitting down next to her with a huge iced coffee. "I didn't think the large would be *this* large," he said. "I've been away too long. I have to get used to American sizing."

"Mr. Raleigh —"

"You can call me William. Most people do. For some reason, I've never been a Bill or a Willie. Just William." He removed the plastic cap from his iced coffee and took a sip. "This is enough for a family of four."

"Where's Major Brooker?"

"Resting."

"Resting where?"

"That's for him to say."

Maggie rolled her eyes. "You two don't have to be so damn cagey —"

"Perhaps not," he said, taking another sip of his drink, "but we're used to it."

"How did you meet?"

"We were both on Nick Janssen's trail."

"I understand why Brooker would be looking for Janssen, but why would you?" She felt the humidity, which brought out the smells of the passing cars, the grass, some of the flowers in the display across the street. "Did he have something to do with my father's death?"

Raleigh lowered his drink and winced. "My calves are acting up. I could have used my walking stick today, tramping out in the woods. I left the bloody thing in Amsterdam. It's more a nuisance than anything else."

Maggie stared at him a moment. Beads of sweat had collected on his forehead and nose and seemed to make the sprinkle of brown spots across his cheeks stand out more.

"Are you CIA?" she asked him quietly.

"I'm just a tired old man, Maggie," he said.

"You're not that old. What, sixty?"

"Sixty-two." He smiled sideways at her. "Sixty. I like that. You know I look older. You're just too polite to say so."

She smiled in spite of herself. "No, you look as if you've had a hard life. There's a difference."

"Most of my hardships were self-inflicted." He sipped more of his iced coffee, but didn't seem to enjoy it. "I'd better restrain myself. Rest rooms in this quaint little village are difficult to come by."

"Why are you here?"

He focused on something across the street, avoiding her eye. "There's been another killing."

"Jesus. Who? Where —"

"London. Your colleagues in federal law enforcement will know soon, if they don't already. A Russian arms dealer named Vlad Samkevich turned up dead there late today. He'd been dead for some time. At least a few days."

Maggie recognized the name. Investigators believed Samkevich was one of Janssen's main suppliers of illegal small arms. Janssen never touched any of the illicit goods he moved around the world. He made deals happen. Already a rich man, he got richer from them.

"How?" Maggie asked.

"A .22 round to the back of the head."

Just like Tom Kopac.

"A neighbor found him." Raleigh made a face at his iced coffee. "How can anyone drink this much of anything? Well. I should talk. If it were whiskey —" He sighed with a sense of acceptance mixed with regret. "There's enough caffeine here to end anyone's jet lag, that's for sure."

Maggie's mind wasn't on iced coffee. George Bremmerton had told her that

Janssen was refusing to cooperate with Dutch authorities. American investigators, in the process of getting permission from a Dutch judge, had yet to question him. His attorneys had vowed to fight his extradition to the U.S. Nick Janssen's criminal friends and associates had to be wondering if he would give them up in exchange for another kind of deal, one with prosecutors instead of extortionists, murderers, drug and arms traffickers.

Maybe they were all jockeying for the top position now that their deal-maker was in custody.

"Do we have a turf war on our hands?" Maggie asked. "Is that what you think? It doesn't explain Tom's death —"

"Perhaps it does."

"Are you suggesting he was working with Janssen? I don't believe it. Mr. Raleigh — William — if you know anything, now is the time to tell me."

He gave her a dry look. "I suppose I should remember that we're in the U.S. now. You have the powers of arrest here. And I see that you're armed. I'm not, in case you were wondering."

"I should take you in and let the FBI and the marshals grill you just for being here and knowing Major Brooker — never mind the rest of it, the kooky phone call, Den Bosch."

"Your instincts tell you to trust me."

"My instincts tell me you're manipulating me." She had an urge to fling the rest of her iced tea in the street and walk away from this man. Tom Kopac. Now this Samkevich. What the hell was going on? And her father. Where did he fit in? "People say you're mentally ill, you know."

"Ah, yes. Of course they do." It didn't seem to bother him. "There are days I wish I were. I wish I could take a pill and discover that all the bad voices and images in my head were imaginary. There are days I wish I were delusional."

"Did you kill Tom Kopac and Vlad Samkevich?"

He set his drink on the bench next to him. "Maggie."

His tone. The lucid blue eyes on her.

"Hell," she said. "You believe we have an assassin at work. You *know*."

"A paid assassin, not someone who believes in any cause but money." He leaned back against the uncomfortable wooden bench, stretching out his bony legs, flexing his feet. "It's someone I've been tracking for eighteen months."

Eighteen months.

Maggie didn't breathe.

"I picked up where your father left off. But I'm the one who put him on the trail."

"How —" She paused, composing herself. "How do you know? Who the hell are you? Who was *he?*"

But Raleigh didn't answer her. "Nick Janssen must have hired our assassin. He must have had a contingency plan in the event of his capture. He wouldn't leave anything to chance. His arrest could only make him more dangerous. It's all or nothing for him now. He has no choice, in his view, but to be bold and ruthless."

"He'll eliminate any rivals who threaten his position, any friends who could turn against him."

"Anyone he blames for his current predicament could also be a target."

But Maggie reminded herself not to get sucked into Raleigh's sense of drama and to stick to what she knew — and to remember what she didn't know. Like whether or not the man sitting next to her was even in sound mental health. He could still be spinning wild fantasies and conspiracies.

"Why are you here?" she asked him pointedly.

"Tom Kopac and I were to meet in Den

Bosch the morning he was killed."

"His idea or yours?"

"Mine. I heard through my contacts in Prague that he'd been asking questions about your father."

"My father? But why?"

"That's what I wanted to find out. I caught up with him at his apartment early Friday morning after Janssen's arrest. He was on his way to the embassy. We agreed to meet in Den Bosch the next day."

"Why Den Bosch?"

"Another unanswered question."

"Then it was Tom's idea," Maggie said.

Raleigh nodded. "I phoned you. I wanted to meet Mr. Kopac first —"

"Where?"

"The cathedral." But he anticipated her next question. "I don't know why he went to the river. Perhaps he was curious about where Janssen was arrested. His safe house was nearby. I'd planned to tell you everything I knew. Then he was killed, and there was your deputy marshal."

"Why Ravenkill?"

"I saw a printout on the inn at his apartment. It was in plain sight. I thought . . . well, I wanted to see your reaction when I mentioned it, for starters. I didn't know if it had anything to do with your father or

263

his death, if it was significant at all. Perhaps a place you and your father went on vacation when he was alive. Something of that nature."

"I'd never heard of it," Maggie said.

Raleigh cast her a steady glance. "Your father never mentioned Mr. Kopac, I take it? I didn't want to use his name. I wanted to see your reaction to Ravenkill and the Old Stone Hollow Inn first."

"No, you didn't. You knew for sure I'd never let you out of that cathedral if you mentioned Tom. And no, as far as I know he and my father didn't know each other." The air was still and very warm, and she hoped for a rumble of thunder, a bolt of lightning — anything to jump-start her brain. "Did you leave the printout in Tom's apartment?"

"Yes. I left everything just as it was."

"Then presumably the police have it now."

"Unless he tossed it," Raleigh said.

"George Bremmerton didn't mention it when I spoke to him this morning. Maybe the Dutch police are still sorting out what they found and don't believe it has any significance —"

"It may not, Maggie. Major Brooker thinks he probably slipped and fell in the river and wasn't attacked."

"Is that what you believe?"

He shrugged. "What I believe hasn't mattered for a long time now. I'm not being morose or self-pitying. It's the truth. You're here in Ravenkill because of me. I'm here because of you. Major Brooker's here because of both of us."

"Janssen's in custody," Maggie said. "You'd think Brooker would call it quits and go do whatever comes next for him."

"I don't think he knows what that is."

"That's a hard way to live."

"I think it's how your new marshal friend is living, too." Raleigh returned the cap to his iced coffee and made a face. "Look, I've drunk it down just an inch and I'm swimming. What a waste."

"Take it with you. Where are you staying?"

"Me? Oh, here and there." He nodded at the shops across the street. "Tom Kopac was a serious antiques collector. He could have been planning a shopping trip to Ravenkill."

Maggie shook her head. "I doubt it. I didn't know him that well, but I understand he didn't take vacations, never mind shopping jaunts to the States. There are plenty of antique shops right in the Netherlands."

"Was your father interested in antiques?"

"No."

"Phil was a good man. Intelligent, interested in everything — he gobbled up information like no one I've ever known." Raleigh seemed to be talking to himself more than to Maggie. But he smiled suddenly at her. "Perhaps our Mr. Kopac had more than a friendly interest in you."

"I can't —" She faltered, picturing him in the Binnendieze. "Please don't. There was nothing romantic in our friendship."

"I'm sorry." Raleigh patted her knee, his hand cool from the massive iced-coffee cup. "I'm very sorry for all of this."

"Tom was just a good guy. Who the hell would walk up to him and put a bullet in his head?"

"He had secrets, Maggie. He didn't tell you he was asking questions about your father, did he?"

She didn't answer. There was no point. Raleigh already knew that she and Tom had talked about nothing more substantial, more important, than doughnuts.

"I know it's difficult," Raleigh said. "I remember early on, someone told me it doesn't get easier. It was a frightening thought to me at the time. I wanted it to get easier. I didn't want to have to suffer so

266

much when someone I knew, someone I liked and admired — a friend — died. But now?" He sighed heavily, sweat dripping down the end of his red nose. "It's a comfort to know it doesn't get easier. That every loss still matters."

Maggie dumped out the last of her tea and melting ice in the grass. Her father was dead. Tom was dead. A Russian arms dealer was dead. She and William Raleigh and Ethan Brooker and Rob Dunnemore were all in Ravenkill. They all could be spinning their wheels in the picturesque little Hudson River Valley town.

"I was hoping if I ended up with egg all over my face over this excursion, it'd be with fewer witnesses," she said, her shirt sticking to her back in the crushing humidity. "This assassin could still be in London, picking out another victim."

Raleigh seemed rooted to the bench, his legs outstretched. "You know your father wasn't killed by bank robbers?"

"I'm fairly certain he wasn't just a business consultant, either. Do you know how he was killed? I was never told —"

"It was a .22 round to the heart."

"Your assassin?"

"I'm sure of it."

"Now you're sounding like a nut again."

She squinted at him against the afternoon glare, realizing she was stiff from her dunking in the Ravenkill. "But you're not a nut or a drunk or a breakdown case, are you?"

He didn't answer.

Maggie watched a middle-aged woman pick up a pot of bright yellow mums, examine them with a skeptical frown, then shrug and take them inside the shop. *I should be buying mums.*

But she glanced again at the man next to her. "How can I believe a word you say?"

His pale eyes twinkled. "Magster. You must have been an adorable six-year-old. Freckles, turquoise eyes, red hair and skinned knees. Am I right?"

"It's not that hard. I still have freckles, turquoise eyes and red hair."

"And skinned knees. Brooker did that?"

"My own damn fault."

"Phil wanted to be a better father to you," Raleigh said softly, seriously. "I suspect when it's all said and done it's what most of us wish. That we'd done better by those we love."

"Listen, okay? I loved my father, and I miss him. I'll always miss him. But I'm not going to let emotion drive my decisions —"

He scoffed. "That's what we always tell

ourselves, isn't it? It's ridiculous. Emotion drives most decisions. We just don't like to admit it."

The woman came out of the shop with her mums, smiling now, no regrets, no second thoughts about her choice. Even if her mums had bugs, Maggie thought, what was at stake? Throw them out, get new ones. A loss of a few dollars.

"So you believe the same person — your assassin — killed my father, Tom and Samkevich. Any proof, any leads we can use?"

"None."

"Brooker?"

"Solid, but he has nothing. We'd tracked Nick Janssen to his safe house in Den Bosch. Before we could confirm it, he was arrested."

"I should take you in —"

"If you do, the stress could cause a relapse of my alcoholism and mental illness." He smiled, almost looking handsome. "You don't want to be the laughingstock of the Diplomatic Security Service."

She scowled at him. "That's so lame."

He got stiffly to his feet, leaving his iced coffee on the bench. "Transparently half-hearted, isn't it? I've told you what I know, Maggie. Every tangible lead I've had on this assassin has evaporated. If I had more, I'd give it to you. I want to find whoever killed Tom Kopac and your father. Vlad Samkevich wasn't a good man, but his murder . . ." Raleigh shook his head. "That wasn't justice."

"I can stop you," Maggie said.

"Of course you can, Agent Spencer. I'm just an old drunk."

He crossed the street, smelled a bouquet of flowers and blew her a kiss.

And she let him go.

Just as he knew she would.

Rob arrived in the village in time to see Maggie's white-haired guy — William Raleigh — turn the corner and disappear up a side street.

She was picking up a huge drink cup off her bench.

"You're not going to chase him?" he asked her.

Shaking her head, she squinted at him. "Are you?"

"No."

"Why not?"

Through Nate, Wes Poe had just vouched for William Raleigh. But Rob shrugged. "Trust in your judgment?"

"Ha."

"You look hot." He smiled at her. "Very hot, in fact."

"As in I could use more iced tea?"

"As in however you want to take it."

"Did you walk?"

He nodded. "Felt good. I needed the time alone."

She winced at his sarcasm. "I'm sorry I lied, but it's just as well you don't get mixed up with this guy."

"Protecting me, are you?"

"Trying. So far, so good. You didn't get killed on Saturday in Den Bosch, and you didn't get killed today in Ravenkill Creek. Okay — who gave you the word that Raleigh's okay?"

"Sure about someone did, are you?"

"Otherwise you'd have gone after him. You got here in plenty of time. You saw him. Did your source also tell you about Vlad Samkevich?"

There was no use pretending he didn't know. "Yes. It was Nate, by the way. He called."

"The future brother-in-law. The marshal of marshals." She smiled. "I'd like to meet him someday. And your twin sister."

"You're changing the subject."

"I need a minute to clear my head."

"Let's walk."

271

She glanced in the direction Raleigh had just gone, wondering what he was up to — if she should change her mind and follow him after all. "I thought I heard a rumble of thunder a minute ago."

"The Franconias said storms are moving in from the west. They're a pair, those two. Stressed to the point of cracking. Libby Smith suspects they're overextended."

"Not enough to kill people for money, I hope."

Rob heard an edge in her tone. "Maggie?"

"Nothing. I'm not serious."

She started up the street, and Rob hesitated, noting the stiffness of her movements. It wasn't just the dunking in the creek. Raleigh had said something that rattled her. But she kept walking, not looking back, and Rob finally got moving and caught up with her.

"Your sister and Nate Winter are getting married in a couple weeks, right? Is President Poe coming to the wedding?"

"That's the plan."

They continued along the country road in the shade of huge old oaks and maples, squirrels chattering at them from overhanging branches. Rob had no illusions that Maggie's mind was on the scenery or the afternoon heat or even President Poe and his sister's wedding.

She kept her eyes pinned to the pavement in front of her. "It's President Poe's doing, isn't it? That Nate Winter got in touch with you about Raleigh."

"I really can't say. I don't know it for a fact." Which was true, as far as it went. He didn't need facts — he knew the information Nate had relayed had come from Wes. "You just let Raleigh go yourself. What did he tell you?"

"That we have an assassin at work who probably killed Tom and Samkevich. And my father."

She spoke briskly, as if she didn't want to dwell on the emotional impact of her words. She picked up her pace, but Rob had no trouble staying with her. He was taller, he was a runner, and he wasn't letting her get too far ahead of him.

"The part about my father could be bullshit —"

"I don't think so."

She stopped abruptly. "Poe? Did he —"

"I haven't talked to President Poe."

"Goddamn it, quit dancing around in circles! What did Winter tell you? We are talking about my *father*." But she put up both hands and shook her head, more at herself than Rob. "Never mind. Forget I said that."

"No one's taking you off this thing, Maggie. You're the one Raleigh will talk to." Rob felt an urge to take her hand, but she had her shoulders squared, her arms tight at her side. Untouchable. "I don't have any specifics about your father."

"He wasn't just a businessman," she said.

"Raleigh isn't just a retired economist, either."

"I knew," she said, almost to herself. "About my father. I've known for a long time. In my gut. He never said anything — he wouldn't. I think my mother was in the dark. But even as a kid, when he was away for long stretches, I'd make up spy stories about him."

"Kids' instincts can be amazing."

She kicked a pebble, sent it flying into a field on the side of the road. "Bank robbers in Prague. Jesus."

"Raleigh," Rob said. "What else did he tell you?"

He watched her bank back the emotion, pull herself out of the pain and grief she must have felt in the early days after she'd learned of her father's death. She gave him a quick smile. "He doesn't care for what's considered a 'large' drink nowadays."

Rob said nothing.

By the time they reached the end of the inn's driveway, she had repeated her conversation with her father's friend, her Scarlet Pimpernel from the Dutch cathedral.

When she finished, Rob could smell mint in the heavy air. The inn was just up ahead. "That's it, huh? A printout of the Old Stone Hollow's Web site in Kopac's apartment?"

"That's it. There's no reason for him to hold back."

Unless everyone, including Wes Poe, was wrong, and it was William Raleigh who was out of control. Mentally ill after all. A drunk. Perhaps he was even their assassin.

A hawk swooped low over a small meadow of wildflowers. Maggie gave a small cry of pleasure, and Rob saw the shine of tears in her eyes and knew it was as much as he'd get. She was used to holding her emotions closely. She wouldn't tell him how much pain the talk of her father's secret life and of an assassin had caused her.

She didn't need to, Rob thought. He understood.

He slipped his hand into hers. "Let's

pretend we really are on vacation. At least for a few minutes."

She leaned into him, just enough, just for a second. "I hope the humidity finally blows out of here tonight."

"What humidity?"

She squeezed his hand and even smiled. "My mother loves south Florida. The humidity never gets to her. She and I have a different kind of relationship, but we understand each other. She paints flamingos." Her smile broadened, and she had a bounce to her step. "You'll have to see them sometime."

"Flamingos," Rob said.

"The most amazing flamingos."

"How does a flamingo-painting mother end up with a spy husband and a federal-agent daughter?"

"I think that's what she wonders, too."

But Rob supposed it was no more bizarre than Leola and Violet Poe raising a president, or his own parents raising a marshal and an archaeologist.

The light was green on the horizon.

The storms would be rough tonight.

He decided to wait to tell Maggie that he wasn't going anywhere. He had his room at the inn, and he was staying.

Sixteen

She'd seen him.

It hadn't been her imagination.

William Raleigh was in Ravenkill.

Libby pushed back a fresh wave of panic and kept herself from puking on the dining room floor. Her father had passed out in this very spot countless times, except there'd been no English antiques and cottage colors in those days — just ratty old junk that he hadn't been able to pawn off to friends for extra cash.

She'd always wanted control. Always. She'd fought and clawed for it as a child — for just a few moments when she was in control, for a small space that was hers and hers alone.

Taking up shooting had helped.

Now, years later, she had the thrill of her quiet work as a hired killer. The ultimate control. Someone else's destiny in her hands. Her own destiny, since even the smallest mistake could be costly.

Philip Spencer had been a mistake.

She'd known he and Raleigh were

friends. She should have killed them both. But she'd believed the stories about Raleigh's mental breakdown and his chronic drinking and assumed he wasn't a serious threat.

There'd been no money in Spencer's killing and would be none in Raleigh's.

Only survival, she thought. No sense of control, no thrill, no profit.

She hadn't become a killer because of her father.

He wasn't responsible for anything she'd become, good or bad. No credit, no blame. He'd squandered what should have been hers, and he'd provided her a miserable childhood. But she was free of him.

"Libby?" It was Star, coming in from the porch. "Have you seen Andrew?"

"No. I'm sorry."

She gave a little hiss of annoyance. "We're busy outside, and he takes off. Damn him!"

"I can help. What would you like me to do?"

"Keep the feds on the porch happy. God! I can't help it — they make me nervous. Why did they pick here?"

A good question. Now Ethan Brooker and William Raleigh were sneaking around. Libby tried not to look frozen and sick. "Because you and Andrew have done an incredible job and it's a beautiful place?"

Star caught herself, obviously embarrassed by her curt tone. "I didn't mean that the way it sounded."

"I understand —"

"I hate to ask you —"

"It's okay." Libby smiled. "I like the idea of 'keep the feds happy.' "

Star's relief was palpable. Libby stopped in the kitchen to wash her hands. Maggie Spencer. Rob Dunnemore. Ethan Brooker. Whether they knew it or not, they were all here because of Philip Spencer and William Raleigh.

Libby dried her hands, feeling less nauseous.

She wouldn't get a dime for killing Raleigh. He wasn't on Janssen's list — Janssen didn't even know he existed. She planned to keep it that way. If Janssen had known she had the CIA or whatever Raleigh was on her tail, he'd never have hired her.

She had to stay calm and make sure none of the loose ends in her life came back to haunt her. Otherwise, Janssen would fire her and hire someone else to do the job for him, and her name would get tacked onto his new hit list.

And she'd lose this one opportunity to gather her strength, then make her move and take over Nick Janssen's network. His months on the run had weakened him. He wasn't getting out of prison anytime soon. He'd left a void. Libby planned to fill it.

She had to seize the moment. There was no alternative. She wasn't going to spend the rest of her life living in a suite in a house that was no longer hers, collecting furniture, killing people here and there for extra cash — for the thrill of it. She wanted more.

Pasting an insipid smile on her face, Libby headed out to the porch and the two federal agents who awaited her.

If Juliet drove any faster up Central Park West, the cops were going to pull her over. Then she'd not only have to explain her speed, Ethan thought, but him.

And her truck.

"Did this thing pass inspection?" he asked.

She glanced at him. "Good. You didn't die on me. I was getting worried. I hate having to explain corpses in my truck." She tapped the sticker on her windshield. "Vermont says my truck's fine."

"You must have an in with someone."

"Are you kidding? I have five brothers. They're all cops and landscapers. I don't get cut any slack. Besides, just because you Texans trade in your trucks every two seconds doesn't mean we Vermonters have to. We're thrifty."

"You're cheap."

She braked at an empty parking space, yellow cabs whizzing past her. Ethan tried to sit up. His head ached. Even his eyeballs were pulsing with pain. "You won't fit."

"If we were parking a Humvee in the desert, I'd defer to your expertise," she said, looking over her shoulder as she backed up. "But since it's a truck I've been driving forever, and it's New York City, where I've been working for a few years now —"

"If you hit something, just don't hit it hard. I have a head injury."

She whipped the steering wheel around, maneuvering the truck into the space, which was, in fact, too small. But, undeterred, she inched backward, then forward, barely nudging the bumpers of the cars — both more expensive than her truck — in front and behind her.

"There." She turned off the ignition and pulled out her key. "Plenty of room."

Ethan grunted. "I'd let the air out of your tires if you parked that close to me."

She sighed at him. "Hell, Brooker, you look awful. Are you sure you don't want me to take you to the E.R.?"

He attempted a reassuring smile. "If I survived the ride down here, I can survive anything."

"How's your headache? Not severe, I hope?"

"It's fine."

"You don't have trouble staying awake, do you?"

"I did. I don't anymore. Juliet —"

"Double vision?"

He sighed. She was running down the list of trouble signs for head injuries. "No. No weakness in the extremities, no convulsions, no problem walking."

"We'll see about the walking part. I still think you should go to the E.R."

"Aren't you supposed to be at work?"

"Chief Rivera gave me the day off. A few days off, actually. I was supposed to go camping."

Ethan had met the chief deputy when the feds had questioned him after he took off in May and then came back. A tough guy. Loyal, but he expected loyalty in return. "You told him I showed up at your place?"

"I'm responsible for my own decisions."

"That's not what I asked."

"I told him. I didn't mention the call from your friend."

Raleigh. Ethan didn't want to think about him right now.

"You're going to talk to me, Major," Juliet said. "You're going to tell me everything."

"What if I have amnesia?"

She ignored him. "Can you carry your backpack?" But she peered at him again, then shook her head. "No, obviously you can't. Stupid question. I'll carry it. Wait, and I'll open the door for you."

She shoved her door open with her shoulder and jumped out, but Ethan didn't wait. His door was stiff and creaky, but he managed to push and kick it open, then climb out onto the sidewalk.

He reached into the jumpseat for his backpack, but the motion sent blood rushing into his head. His stomach turned over. He grabbed hold of the top of his seat and stood very still, waiting for his vision to clear and his nausea to abate.

"Don't pass out," Juliet said from behind him. "Damn. I'm taking you to the hospital —"

"No." He thought he spoke out loud but

wasn't positive. "Just leave the backpack."

"You don't want to fool around with a head injury."

"I'm not."

She reached behind him and grabbed his backpack, hoisting it over one shoulder. "I should have searched this thing when I had you in my place last night."

She was right, but Ethan didn't say anything. He pried his fingers loose and stood up straight. He didn't throw up, didn't pass out. He shut the truck door and followed Juliet up the stairs to her building.

"You can still go camping," he said.

"I'd go crazy. Rivera thinks I'm experiencing post-trauma symptoms from Janssen's goons, the cave —"

"Are you?"

"No."

"That kind of thing can grab you from behind when you least expect it."

"I got debriefed or whatever they're calling it now. I passed the fitness-for-duty test." She stopped herself, glancing back at him. "Not that I have to explain myself to you. Where's my cell phone?"

He handed it to her.

"You're lucky you didn't wreck it with your antics today."

"Looks like Rob Dunnemore called you

a few times on our way down here."

"How many?"

"I don't know. Maybe a hundred."

She checked the call history. "Six. That's like a hundred from anyone else. I'll call him when we get upstairs. You okay?"

"I'm okay."

Her doorman obviously remembered him from yesterday and gave him a dirty look, but Juliet smiled, as pretty a smile as Ethan had seen her give anyone yet. "This is Major Ethan Brooker," she said. "He's with me. He's had a bit of a mishap."

Ethan hated every second of the elevator ride up to her apartment.

She unlocked all her locks, and he fell onto the couch in front of a fish tank. He lay on his back and realized it wasn't just his head that was hurt. He'd done a job on his back, his shoulder, one hip.

"Who'd take care of the fish and the plants if you went camping?" he asked.

"Rivera said he would. Is your speech slurred?"

"I wish. It'd mean I'm drunk."

Juliet snorted. "If you were drunk, you'd be barfing as well as slurring your words."

"You're a hard woman, deputy."

"Keep talking. It's probably good for you. What can I get you? Beside whiskey.

Beside anything alcoholic. Is there anything I can do for you?"

He raised an eyebrow and tried to give her the sexiest look he good.

She didn't budge. "Don't get any ideas, Brooker. Never mind the concussion, you smell like a swamp." She put her hands on her hips and sighed at him. "You're sure you don't remember what happened to you?"

"I fell into the Ravenkill."

"You and your rivers."

"This one had rocks."

"If you were attacked —"

"I can't say that I was or I wasn't." He squeezed his eyes shut, trying to push back the pain and bring forward any new details about that morning. But there was nothing. "It hurts to think."

"Well, then." She hesitated, then sighed again. "Just rest."

"Your couch . . ." He wondered if his words *were* slurred. "I'm a mess . . ."

"It's okay, Ethan."

Her tone had softened, and he thought her voice might have cracked. But he knew he wasn't in great shape.

"I'm one of the good guys," he mumbled.

"Yeah. I know you are."

After that, he just heard the gurgle of the

fish tanks, and for the first time in days — maybe months — felt himself relax.

What Maggie knew about William Raleigh, now the marshals knew.

At least Rob did.

Sitting on the veranda over coffee and dessert, she saw a flicker of lightning somewhere across the Hudson. In a couple of seconds the thunder came, a long, low rumble. The green light, the still air and the unrelenting humidity were all signs of an impending storm.

"My sister had no intention of falling for Nate when we were shot in May. For anyone." Rob spoke quietly, aware of Maggie across the table. "She'd just finished a major project. She likes to say we Dunnemores are at our most dangerous when we're idle."

"You're not idle."

"I'm sitting here drinking cappuccino and eating plum tart —"

"That's now. A couple hours ago you were sneaking around after me. Before that, we had Ethan in the river. And before *that* —"

"I get your point. Sarah also says she and Nate fell for each other in a whoosh." Rob smiled, none of the blue in his eyes visible in the prestorm light. "A Ph.D. in archaeology, and that's her word. *Whoosh.*"

Maggie smiled, too. "I like it."

"All her fears and preconceptions about who she should end up with went out the window, right along with her common sense. My sister and a marshal."

"You're a marshal."

"I'm her brother."

"But her twin," Maggie said.

"You mean if I hadn't become a marshal, I would have become an archaeologist?"

"I don't know. Maybe. I can see you digging in ruins."

"Think more in terms of an old dump. That's where Sarah's been spending her time lately."

"Probably more productive than chasing me over hill and dale."

His gray eyes darkened, or maybe it was the light. "I don't know about that."

Maggie tried to ignore the flutter in the pit of her stomach. "You got hit hard in May, didn't you? Not just physically. Going through something like that . . . you must know in a way the rest of us don't how short life is and how much we're not in control, no matter how hard we try to be." She lifted her water glass and winced, self-conscious. "Listen to me. All philosophical. And I'm only drinking water."

"Getting dunked in a river must bring out the philosopher in you."

"I don't know what I was thinking, going up to Brooker like that —"

"You were thinking you'd help him."

"I'm glad he wasn't hurt any worse than he was. I wish we could have helped Tom —" She forced herself not to go that route and sipped some of her water, half tempted to dump it down her front. She was hot, restless, hyperaware of her surroundings. Of the man across the table from her. "It's been a weird few days. I'll say that."

Rob was spared answering when Andrew Franconia pounded up the porch steps and yanked out a chair at their table, sitting down without waiting for an invitation. "I heard on the news that some Russian with ties to Nicholas Janssen has turned up dead in London. Shot. Wasn't that guy you found in the Netherlands on Saturday shot? What the hell's going on?"

"You know as much as we do," Rob said.

"Bullshit."

Maggie set down her glass. "I know this kind of news is upsetting —"

"Don't patronize me. I don't care if you're both federal agents. I want to know what's going on."

"Fair enough." Maggie kept her voice

steady, reassuring. "The Russian's name is Vladimir Samkevich. I don't know a great deal about him. He and the man Deputy Dunnemore and I found dead were both shot in a similar fashion, but it's far too early to make any connection between the two murders."

Andrew's mouth snapped shut, and he sat back in his chair, exhaling loudly. "I don't know how you do this work. I truly don't. The worse Star and I deal with is the occasional unpaid bill."

"Thomas Kopac and Philip Spencer," Maggie said without warning. "Do you know either name?"

Franconia frowned at her. "No. Why? Who are they?"

"Tom Kopac is the man who was killed on Saturday —"

"Jesus Christ! Why would I know him? Why would you even ask —"

"Philip Spencer is also dead. He was killed eighteen months ago in Prague. He was my father."

"Is this personal?" Andrew asked tightly.

"I'm not sure I know the answer to that. I'd appreciate it if you could check your records and see if either name pops up."

His eyes were half-closed. "Do I need a lawyer?"

290

Rob was the one who answered. "It's a simple request, Mr. Franconia."

Star, who'd just walked onto the porch, rushed to the table, putting one hand on her husband's shoulder. "What's going on?"

He repeated what Maggie had said in terse, unemotional words, although there was still no color in his face. "Do you recognize the names Philip Spencer or Thomas Kopac?" he asked his wife.

"No," Star said, shaking her head. Her sundress, at least a size too big, hung loosely on her thin frame. She turned to Maggie. "No, I don't know either name. I can check our records. We have a mailing list, but we're not as computerized as we probably should be. We have some records on our antiques buyers, and more on our guests."

"How are reservations handled?" Maggie asked. "I filled out a form on your Web site."

"But it was just an e-mail," Star said. "Whoever's here takes the call or the e-mail and puts it in the book and provides a confirmation number. For instance, I received your e-mail reservation with your credit card information. I e-mailed you back with your confirmation number. It's fairly informal. We like that. It feels more personal."

"Can you check what you have on all your different customers?" Maggie asked. "People who've stayed here, people who've just eaten here, people who've just bought antiques?"

Star glanced at Rob, whom she seemed to think had some kind of veto power over Maggie, then nodded. "I'll check our records tonight and let you know what I find."

"It's very difficult on both Star and me having you here," Andrew said, looking directly at Maggie. "Frankly, I'm glad it's only for one more night."

Maggie managed a quick smile. "I don't blame you."

But he jumped up and spun on his heels, heading off the porch without a backward glance even at his wife.

Star smoothed the folds of her too-big dress and kept her eyes lowered. "I apologize. We're stretched thin with this place. Our cash flow's improving, but . . ." She gave an embarrassed smile. "The stress sometimes gets to Andrew. We have a lot at stake, and if your presence here . . . If there's trouble —"

"You don't want the inn's reputation

hurt," Maggie finished for her.

"No one needs that kind of publicity."

After Star withdrew, with less drama than her husband, Maggie abandoned the last of her coffee and plum tart and asked Rob if he'd like to join her for a walk before the storm hit.

They headed down the stone path, veering off into the sunflowers, like smiling faces in the fading daylight. Rob walked very close to her but they didn't touch. She breathed in the musty smell of the flowers and smiled. "Do you think sunflowers smell different in the evening? I think they might."

"I can't say I know what sunflowers smell like during the day."

"They're not very fragrant, are they?"

"Not very."

"You really are a dangerous man, Rob," she said quietly, surprising herself with her own words. "Other people might be fooled by the charm and the good looks and the education. I'm not." She turned to him, a giant sunflower taller than he was behind him. "Your future brother-in-law has a reputation as a hard-ass. I'll bet you're as big a hard-ass as he is."

"He's a hard-ass in a good way. His parents were killed in a mountain-climbing accident when he was seven. I think it made him less patient with BS at an earlier age than most of us."

"There's no easy age to lose a parent, but at seven? Both of them?" She shuddered. "I can't imagine."

"Maggie, your father —"

"I didn't know my father," she said. "Obviously."

"I have a feeling you're a lot like him. Not that easy to get to know. Self-contained. Dedicated to your work to a point that might shut out even the people you care about most."

"It's not an easy way to live, never mind whether or not it's fair to anyone else."

"We all have something. It's what we do with it that matters." He winked at her. "Now I'm being the philosopher."

"Rob . . ." She sighed. "Never mind."

He gave her a knowing look. "You see? Self-contained. We're attracted to each other. That's what you wanted to say, isn't it?"

"Maybe." She shot out of the sunflowers, onto the grassy lawn. "Doesn't this heat get to you?"

"Heat gets to me, but this isn't hot. Maggie —"

Thunder rumbled in the distance.

Taking it as a sign — an excuse — Maggie laughed. "There you go. All we need now is to be struck by lightning."

"We should go inside."

Lightning flickered on the green, western horizon, and a breeze stirred. "Rob, I —" She spun around at him, determined to say her piece. "I can't fall for anyone right now. I've been in The Hague for just three weeks. I can't do that to myself. To you."

"Who're you trying to convince?" He touched a curl by her ear. "Your hair seems lighter since you got here. Maybe there's something in the river water."

"You're having —" She made herself go on. "You're having an effect on me."

"An effect?" He laughed quietly, letting his fingers slide down her throat and skim her breast as he dropped his hand. "What kind of effect?"

"More than one kind, I'm afraid."

"Good?"

"Depends on your point of view."

He stood up straight, his expression suddenly unreadable. "I'm spending the night here, Maggie."

Hell.

"You're not choking?"

"It's my training," she said dryly.

"That'll teach you to sneak off to clandestine meetings with Scarlet Pimpernel types. I reserved a room while you were gone."

"Rob . . . you're not making this any easier."

"I'm not, am I? I was just wondering if it was my job to make this easier for you —"

"Your eyes are the same color as the sky right now. Did you know that?"

He sighed. "You're not going to make this easier on me, either, are you?"

"Not a chance."

He let his lips brush across her forehead. "We should get inside before the storm hits. The way things have been going, we *will* get struck by lightning out here."

"I swear we already have and it's affected our thinking."

"Not mine. I know exactly what I'm about."

He spoke with that mix of charm and confidence that had thrown her off balance from the beginning. Maggie pushed back a reaction to him that was physical, emotional and probably not at all appropriate.

"So do you," he added.

But the wind picked up, smashing the sunflowers into each other. Lightning and thunder flashed and cracked at the same time, the air darker, the light greener. Maggie could hear the rushing sounds of the approaching rain, and she and Rob ducked into the cellar.

Libby Smith was in her antiques room, pencil in mouth and pad of paper in hand. "Hey, there. Is the storm on us?"

"Almost," Maggie said.

She seemed delighted. "I love a good thunderstorm. We used to lose power all the time when I was a kid, but the Franconias put in a lightning rod. So boring." She grinned, shoving the pencil behind her ear. "I'm doing an inventory. It's so dull I could scream. Anything I can do for you?"

Maggie shook her head. "We're fine, thanks."

And when they got up to the second floor, it was no surprise to her at all that Rob ended up in her room.

He swept an arm around her waist and found her mouth with his, the wind pounding the rain against her window, as if to call attention to his urgency, make her stop pretending that it wasn't there.

She felt her breath catch. She tried to speak but gave up.

"Maggie." He placed his hands on either side of her face and held her within inches of him. "I'm not just being opportunistic. There's something about you —"

"About us. When we're together."

All her reserve and natural caution fell away. He seemed to feel it happening and kissed her again, even as he caught her up in his arms.

Before she could get her breath again, he was carrying her to her four-poster bed.

She'd never been carried to bed before.

They dispensed with guns and cuffs and holsters and clothes, coming together quietly, hungrily, as if it'd been a foregone conclusion from the moment he'd stepped off the plane in Amsterdam. His mouth found hers again and again, often before she had the presence of mind even to take a breath.

She didn't push back, didn't say no, just responded to the feel of him, the taste of him. His strength and obvious urgency took her by surprise. It was almost as if he'd been thinking about kissing her, sweeping his hands over her, since he'd first folded himself into her Mini.

It seemed like such a long time ago. Yet it'd only been days.

A whoosh . . .

His hands slid over her hips, coursed up her back, then cupped her breasts with a boldness that only fueled her own response.

"Maggie . . ." Rob smiled at her, rolling onto his back so that she was on top of him, straddling him. "Stop thinking."

"How did you know —"

"Because you think all the time."

She eased her palms up his abdomen, skimmed the scar from his bullet wound. In the dim light, she could see it. The round from Conroy Fontaine's sniper rifle had torn apart Rob's insides, cost him massive amounts of blood, his spleen, almost his life. But the scar was deceptively small, neat, no indication of the pain and suffering he'd endured. He was tanned and hard and muscular now.

He moved against her, and Maggie fell onto his chest, stifling a moan against his neck, tasting him, feeling his hands all over her, and whether it was her driving them toward the inevitable or him, she didn't know, didn't care.

The wind must have shifted, because a chilly breeze and rain blew against her overheated back, as if enticing her to respond to him. And she did, her heart racing as she reached over and placed her palm against his heart. Even as good a shape as he was in, his pulse was racing.

"I must be out of mind," she said.

But there was no more waiting, no more

pretending or denying. He eased on top of her, kissing her throat, taking a nipple into his mouth.

She moaned with a deep pleasure. "You're sure it's okay? I don't want to hurt you. . . ."

"You won't."

And he didn't wait. He thrust into her, filling her up. She cried out immediately, an aching need overwhelming her. She'd never wanted anyone as much as she did him, now.

He made love to her with total focus, as if he might not ever get another chance at it.

"Easy," Maggie breathed, feeling the weight of him on her, inside her. "If this is the first time since the shooting, I don't want you to kill yourself."

He looked down at her, his eyes shining in the near darkness. "I've almost died doing stupider things."

She urged him deeper into her, giving herself up to a release that came out of nowhere and overtook her, and he responded by pounding into her, letting her claw at his arms and forcing her orgasm to go on and on.

She was spent, couldn't move.

He gave her a little half smile. "I'm not done yet."

"Oh, God."

When he finally came, she came again,

with him, shocking herself as she felt him shudder, then collapse next to her.

They were both slick with sweat, breathing hard.

The storm was on them now.

Maggie pulled on some clothes and sat on a club chair in the window, watching the storm.

She could feel Rob watching her.

"I don't think I can make it to my room," he said.

He could. He just didn't want to. Maggie rolled off her chair and went to him, smiling as she traced the perspiration on his taut abdomen. "I guess I'm not as repressed as you thought."

"As *you* thought, you mean."

When he sat up, she was struck again by how damn good-looking he was. But he was serious now, brushing a hand over her hair. She took a breath. "I won't have any regrets in the morning." She smiled at him, making sure she didn't avert her eyes. "Ever."

He kissed her on the forehead, the nose, the mouth, lingering there. "I could fall in love with you," he whispered. "It wouldn't be hard at all."

Then he gathered up his clothes, got dressed and left her room without another word.

Seventeen

Maggie came downstairs early, wishing she'd brought some *hagelslag* with her from the Netherlands. Chocolate sprinkles on buttered bread would go down well after the night she'd had.

She pictured Tom in the Dutch bakery, making his crack about Krispy Kreme doughnuts not even a week ago. They'd just become comfortable with each other, and now he was dead. The image of his smile quickly changed to that first glimpse she'd had of his body floating in the Binnendieze.

She never wanted to get used to murder. Not ever.

But last night with Rob wasn't about Tom's death, or William Raleigh and his bizarre ways, or about her father. It was about something else, although she couldn't quite pin down what, except that she had no regrets and wasn't embarrassed. And yet she didn't expect ever to repeat such a night. She felt certain Rob didn't, either.

As she touched the latch to the porch

door, Maggie heard someone sobbing in the kitchen and backed up, peeking in the doorway.

Star stood at the sink in a baggy denim jumper with a white chef's apron tied around her waist. She was running water over a colander of blueberries, tears streaming down her face. "Oh, God," she whispered. "Oh, God."

"Mrs. Franconia?" Maggie stepped into the sun-washed room, the air crisp and clear now that last night's storm had pushed out the heat and humidity. "Star?"

She spun around, hands dripping. "Agent Spencer. I didn't realize you were awake." She reached behind her and switched off the water, then grabbed a dish towel and brushed at her tears with it. "I had a bad night. I'm sorry."

"It's okay."

"You're not here to take on my problems. You're here for a break." She spoke with bitter sarcasm and lowered her towel, scrunching it into one bony hand as she glared at Maggie. "But that's just a line you gave us, isn't it? You've lied to us from the beginning."

Maggie crossed the kitchen with its cheerful terra-cotta tile floor and blue pottery vase of sunflowers on a round oak table, a contrast to Star Franconia's troubled, sarcastic mood. "Why don't we sit down? You can tell me what's going on."

Star took in quick, shallow breaths, one after another, in danger of hyperventilating, but she stumbled to the table, in a corner of windows that overlooked more flowers. Sunlight shone on raindrops on vines and leaves. Maggie imagined going off with Rob for a long, romantic weekend in such a place, but that wasn't why she was here, nor was it why Rob was here. And Star knew it.

She had to have had her suspicions last night when Maggie had asked her to look up her father and Tom in any database the inn had. Staring out the window as if Maggie weren't there, Star got control of her breathing. But her hands shook, and she hugged herself, goose bumps on her bare arms. "I should have worn a sweater," she mumbled.

"It's a beautiful morning."

As if to corroborate Maggie's words, a cool breeze floated through the cracked window.

Star released several heavy sighs and gulps, until finally she pushed back her chair an inch or so and shot Maggie an angry, accusatory look. "You think my husband is involved with Nick Janssen, don't you?"

"Why do you say that?"

"You think he has something to do with your father's murder in Prague, with the murder of that diplomat in Holland and now this Russian in London." She shifted back to the view, the bones in her shoulders visible under her thin pink T-shirt. "That's why you're here. I know it is."

Remaining on her feet, Maggie tried not to let Star's emotions affect her. "We know Tom Kopac was killed on Saturday morning, because I was there. Where was your husband over the weekend?"

"Andrew? You mean did he have time to fly to Holland, kill your friend and fly back again?" There was a hard, sarcastic edge to her voice that Maggie understood but didn't like. "He was here. But he could have hired someone to do his dirty work for him. He could have arranged for Mr. Kopac's murder, Mr. Samkevich's murder. That's what you're thinking, isn't it?"

"You didn't answer my question."

Star flopped back in her chair, her arms still crossed over her chest. "He was here. We had a full house, remember? I told you —"

"I remember." Maggie let her tone soften. "Ever want to chuck it and sell the inn, travel, go back to the life you had before you got tied down here?"

"No. I don't." Tears, probably unwelcome, welled in her eyes, and she struggled not to cry. "Andrew, maybe. I'm more the homebody."

"Where is he now?" Maggie asked.

"I have no idea. Where's your marshal friend?"

"I haven't seen him yet this morning." Maggie pulled out a chair and sat down, focusing her attention on the woman next to her. "Mrs. Franconia, what did you find out about the names I gave you last night?"

With a small cry, Star jumped up, ripped off her apron and flung it on the floor, then ran outside onto the porch.

Maggie followed her, birds twittering in the flowers and shrubs, everything clean and fresh in the bright morning sun. Libby Smith lifted screened covers and cloths from the breakfast laid out on a wooden buffet table. Steam rose from a tower of freshly baked muffins. Apple-cinnamon, Maggie thought.

"Coffee?" Star asked her abruptly.

"What? Sure. That'd be fine."

Libby, obviously aware that Star was very upset, held up a hand. "It's okay. I'll get it." She filled a white mug from a stainless-steel coffee urn. She had on jeans and a sweatshirt with a picture of the inn silkscreened across its front, more appropriate for the cool air than Star's T-shirt and jumper. "Deputy Dunnemore's up. He took a mug of coffee off to the gardens a little while ago. Star? Can I get you anything?"

Star shook her head, gulping in a breath, and plunged down the steps onto the stone path.

"Maybe I should go with her," Libby said, handing Maggie the mug of coffee. "She looks like she's coming undone altogether. I know having you and Deputy Dunnemore here has bothered her. Fair or unfair, you guys make her nervous."

Maggie held the mug with both hands, appreciating its warmth. "I'll go talk to her."

"Um, cream and sugar?"

"This is fine, thanks."

The stones were still wet and slippery from last night's rain, the grass sparkling with dew, and Maggie fought a visceral urge to get away, leave Ravenkill, abandon her questions — her mission there — and just drive north along the Hudson River and see where she ended up.

She found Star on her hands and knees in front of the fairy statue, picking weeds from a bed of miniature dahlias and baby's breath. "The fairy's nose is chipped," she said. "Did you notice? Libby says her father whacked it with a wine bottle one night when he was drunk."

"Was she watching?"

"Oh, yes. She was ten or eleven at the time. But it's a beautiful statue, isn't it? I think the chipped nose adds character."

Maggie nodded, trying to be conversational and resist the urge to pelt Star with questions. "It seems to belong here."

"That's what I think." Star rocked back against her heels, shaking mud off her fingers, a brown worm wriggling out of the dirt she'd disturbed. "It's too wet still to get anything done out here."

"The gardens here are something. I have only one lowly orchid."

"What kind?"

"I don't remember. It's supposed to be unkillable, but I think I killed it."

"Nothing's unkillable," she said sadly, then got to her feet, the front of her jumper from the knees down soaked. "I didn't find a reservation for either your father or Mr. Kopac."

Maggie nodded. "All right."

"But I did —" Star faltered, sniffling as if she couldn't go on. "I did for the army captain who was killed in Amsterdam last year."

"Charlene Brooker?"

"I remembered her name from all the news stories in the spring. I thought . . . I don't know what I thought. I guess the Dutch connection got me."

"Captain Brooker was here? Or did she just make a reservation and —"

"She stayed for two nights around this time last summer."

A month before Nicholas Janssen had her killed. Eight months before he went after a presidential pardon and the Dunnemore family was nearly wiped out.

"Janssen," Star said, her voice half-strangled. "He ordered her murder, didn't he? That's what they say. And he was captured last week —"

Maggie could see that Star was very pale, her thin hands purple as she hugged herself. "I've learned the hard way to try to avoid speculating. It's natural, but it doesn't get us anywhere. Do you remember Captain Brooker?"

Tears leaked out of Star's eyes, and she choked back a sob. "Oh, yes. She was alone. She said she was taking a break. Like you."

"What did she do while she was here?"

"Took walks. Rested. She had most meals here at the inn. We talked about antiques." Star brushed idly at her tears, the anger and bitterness gone out of her. "I know I read about her death, but I never made the connection between the army captain killed in Amsterdam and our former guest. Andrew couldn't have, either. He'd have said something. I know he would have."

Who was she trying to convince? Maggie touched Star's thin arm. "We should go back to the house. You've got goose bumps. You do need a sweater."

But Star didn't seem to hear her. "We read the news accounts this spring when the two marshals were shot in Central Park and that whole business with President Poe and the Dunnemores came out. . . ."

"I was in Chicago then," Maggie said. "I remember."

Star gave a weak smile and walked back to the stone path, then stopped abruptly, doubling over as she started to cry.

"Mrs. Franconia," Maggie said, standing behind her, "if there's more — "

"There is." She straightened, her cheeks red and blotchy from crying; the rest of her skin was deathly pale. "I wasn't going to tell you. I was going to pretend —" But she stopped herself. "Never mind."

"Pretend what?" Maggie prodded.

"That I didn't know. That it never happened."

"Star —"

"Your father never stayed here at the inn, but he bought a piece from us. It's in our records. A crystal vase."

Maggie forced herself to stay focused on what Star Franconia had to say. "Here? He bought the vase from you here in Ravenkill?"

She shook her head. "No. In Prague."

Star's entire body was convulsed in shivering, more, Maggie suspected, from fear and a realization of the importance of what she'd discovered than from the cold. Her lips were stretched thin, a purplish blue, her veins in her hands and wrists bulging against her pale skin.

Maggie shoved her mug of coffee at her. "Take a sip. It's nice and hot."

"I want to find Andrew."

"Were you in Prague? You and your husband?"

She nodded dully.

"When?"

"Three months before he was killed. How —" She tensed her muscles visibly, as if to stop herself from shivering. "How is that possible? Then Captain Brooker was here a month before *she* was killed? And now you . . . you and Deputy Dunnemore, just days after . . . after —" She brushed at tears that had dribbled into her mouth. "There's been so much death."

"Mrs. Franconia, I want you to go inside. I'll get Rob Dunnemore, and I'll find your husband. Okay? Come on."

"Your father," Star whispered. "I didn't connect the two of you. I doubt I would have if you hadn't asked me to look up his name. The sale wasn't that big a thing. Even if I'd remembered, I never would have guessed he had a daughter who's a federal agent. He was just this nice man who was interested in an antique crystal vase. Austrian. Libby was the one who found it."

Maggie held her elbow and got her to start walking. "Libby was in Prague with you?"

"We met her there. She was on her own buying trip. It was our last big travel extravaganza before we opened this place. We opened in the winter deliberately, to get our feet under us before our first summer season." But Star looked abruptly at Maggie and gave a small gasp. "You have your father's red hair. I didn't think of that until just now."

When they reached the porch, the muffins and fruit were covered again, and Libby Smith was gone. "Are there other guests at the inn?" Maggie asked. "You said it was quiet —"

"It was just you and Deputy Dunnemore last night. I think . . . I think that's for the best, don't you?"

"Probably."

Maggie escorted her inside and found a sweater on the back of a chair in the kitchen. She carefully folded it over Star's shoulders.

Star tried to smile. "You're very kind, Agent Spencer. I know you have a job to do. Your father —" She wiped more tears with her fingertips, her sensitive skin raw from the chilly air and her crying. "I can't imagine. That must be so awful. This has something to do with your father's death, doesn't it?"

"I can't answer that right now. Do you have any idea where your husband is?"

"He's not . . . he's not a killer, Agent Spencer."

"I just want to talk to him."

Her shoulders slumped, and she sank onto a chair at the table, fingering a sunflower in the blue pottery vase. "In the shop in the barn, I would guess. He wanted to work on some projects there today."

"Can I get you some coffee or tea, anything warm to drink?" Maggie asked.

She shook her head. "I can get something if I want it. I'll be fine. Andrew and I haven't discussed what I found out — what I remember about Captain Brooker and your father." She sniffled, slightly more composed. "You'll let me know when you find him?"

"I will."

When Maggie left, Star was looking forlorn but not as dramatically upset as she picked bits of yellow blossom off a sunflower and laid them neatly in a row in front of her.

Ethan saw the news of the Russian arms dealer's murder when he woke up on Juliet's couch and flipped on the television.

Samkevich.

So somebody had taken out the bastard. *Hell.*

His bruises less painful this morning, Ethan rolled off the couch and tried to find coffee in the small New York kitchen. He checked the cupboards, the refrigerator, the freezer. No coffee. It was just another reason to clear out.

He and Raleigh had tracked Samkevich to London, hoping he'd lead them to Nick Janssen — hoping they could turn both lying, murdering sons of a bitches over to authorities.

Now old Vlad was dead, and Nick was in the pokey.

Ethan gave up on his coffee hunt and ducked into the bathroom to get washed up. The lump on the back of his head had gone down, but it was an ugly mix of purple, red and smudgy-looking black. He had scrapes and bruises here and there, and his eyes were sunken and bloodshot.

If he'd been Juliet, he'd have left him by the Ravenkill.

If he'd been Agent Spencer, he'd have left him *in* the damn river.

But he was lucky in that way. Always had been.

Not Char.

He washed his face and brushed his teeth, then returned to the outer room. He picked up his backpack and headed out. He didn't feel bad at all about cutting out on his blond marshal friend. Juliet would likely thank him when she crawled out of bed and realized he'd cleared out. Less complicated that way.

When he got to the sidewalk, he considered stealing her truck. The thought of navigating the New York City public transportation system didn't sit well with him on a good day, never mind the morning after he'd tumbled into a rock-strewn creek. But if he went back upstairs and found Juliet awake, hair tousled, ripping apart the place because he'd slipped out on her, who the hell knew what'd happen?

He had work to do. He had to find Raleigh. He had to figure out what was going on with Samkevich, Kopac, Philip Spencer, Maggie Spencer. What the connection among them was. And what, if anything, it had to do with Char.

Halfway down the block, he realized he'd forgotten his toothbrush.

He gritted his teeth. Goddamn it. He wasn't going back up there.

He heard footsteps approaching him from behind. Fast steps. New Yorker steps.

"You damn ingrate," Juliet said calmly, easing in next to him. "You could have left me a note."

She had on a red flannel shirt over a ribbed tank top and what looked like men's boxer shorts. Unlaced running shoes on her feet. Her short hair was tousled just the way he'd pictured it.

"You didn't have any coffee," he said. "That put me over the edge."

"There's coffee. There's always coffee in my place."

"Where?"

"The Vermont cracker tin in the fridge."

"Now, why didn't I think of that?"

She hunched her shoulders. "It's cooled off, hasn't it? I can smell fall in the air. You want to tell me where you're going?"

"No." He glanced at her strong legs. "You lift weights?"

"Three times a week."

"Good. You can carry me if I pass out from all this walking."

"You're Special Forces, Brooker. You can take on an army even with the shit knocked out of you."

He remembered how he'd found her in the cave in the bluff along the Cumberland River in Tennessee. Tied up, battered, worn out, keeping her eye out for snakes — and determined to help Sarah Dunnemore and Nate Winter no matter what condition she was in. Marshal Juliet. She'd tried to get his gun off him.

She sighed, as if she knew what she was about to say wasn't in her best interest. "There's a place we can stop for coffee on the way. Just give me two secs to put on some clothes."

"On the way where?"

"Ravenkill. That's where you're headed, isn't it?"

He didn't respond.

Her mouth was a straight, grim line. A

cool breeze blew the ends of her short curls in every direction. "You were in the Netherlands last week. You flew in to New York on Monday."

"You searched my backpack," Ethan said.

"See? I learn from my mistakes."

"Juliet —"

"You're a very dangerous guy who can't come to terms with your wife's violent death." She spoke quietly, sincerely. "You blame yourself. You torture yourself with guilt and regrets."

"Thank you, Dr. Longstreet."

She ignored his sarcasm. "It'll destroy you if you don't get a grip."

He stopped dead on the sidewalk. She didn't flinch. He faced her squarely. "Here's the thing. I don't care."

"That would make you even more dangerous — if it were true."

"Don't fool yourself," he said, turning around and starting back toward her apartment.

"Where are you going?"

"I'm taking you up on your offer to drive me to Ravenkill." He glanced back at her, noticing she hadn't made a move to follow him. "I hate subways."

"As I recall, you aren't much on my truck, either."

She didn't have the keys on her, and he didn't want to go back up to her apartment with her. Speaking of dangerous, he thought. He leaned against the passenger door and pushed back the thready start of a headache, shutting his eyes against the bright hit of sunlight.

He remembered the cool water running under him yesterday in Ravenkill Creek.

The sun bearing down on him.

Before that, he remembered the sensation of falling, an out-of-control sprawl down the steep riverbank.

He'd hit a rock. More than one rock. He could feel the bruises on his hip and the small of his back, sharpening his memory.

He went very still against Juliet's truck. He kept his eyes shut but could hear the swish of New York's morning rush-hour traffic.

He could hear the sound behind him again, an intake of breath, as if someone were summoning the strength to —

"To hurl a fucking rock at me."

Had he spoken out loud?

Opening his eyes, he became aware of New Yorkers hurrying past him without making eye contact, which didn't necessarily mean he'd been talking to himself.

But he had it now. He remembered at least some of what had happened yesterday.

Someone had beaned him with a goddamn rock and sent him sprawling, not giving a rat's ass whether he broke into a million pieces or landed in the river and drowned.

It wasn't kids throwing rocks in the river for fun and hitting him by mistake. An accident. A kid might run off in a panic but wouldn't have taken that measured breath. Ethan was sure he hadn't made it up. He *remembered.*

It could have been anyone. Raleigh. Maggie Spencer. Rob Dunnemore. The couple who owned the inn. Another guest.

Ethan hadn't thought of any suspects at the time. He'd gone into survival mode, doing what he could to limit damage to his head and internal organs even as he knew he was going to lose consciousness.

He stood up from Juliet's truck. Either someone had deliberately hit him, or he'd just dreamed up the whole scenario and he'd simply lost his footing.

His marshal rescuer came out of her building, dressed and armed.

He didn't know how he'd kept his hands off her.

Rescuer. Juliet wouldn't see herself that way. He'd played on her good instincts — her natural desire to trust and help a former army major who just wanted to find answers to his wife's murder.

Char. She'd want him to get on with his life.

But how the hell could he be thinking about taking Juliet Longstreet to bed when he didn't have all the answers to Char's death? When yesterday had raised fresh questions?

He shook off his guilt and misgivings and smiled at Juliet. "Ready to roll?"

"As ready as I'm going to be."

Ethan didn't ask her if she'd called her chief deputy before she'd headed back downstairs. Either way, she wouldn't want to tell him.

And somehow he knew she hadn't, and that she wouldn't want him to remind her she should have.

They got into the truck and Juliet started the engine with a rattle and roar. Ethan rolled down his window and smelled the soot and the cool late-summer air.

"You're taking a risk driving me to Ravenkill," he said.

"Hell, Brooker." She looked over at him and grinned. "I took a risk not shooting you on sight the day I met you on President Poe's front lawn."

Ethan didn't know if he'd tell her someone had tried to kill him yesterday.

But he might. They had at least an hour's drive ahead of them. There was time.

"That's all you marshals needed in May. One more body."

"Yeah," she said, screeching up the block. "It's all we need now, too. You're up to this drive?"

"Once you find me some coffee, I'll be up to anything."

She managed a smile. "That probably should worry me."

And he grinned back at her, as sexily as he could. "Probably should."

But she just made a hiss of mock disgust and reminded him she had five brothers.

Char had a younger sister who still hated him. So did her parents. None of them, Ethan thought, without reason.

Eighteen

Rob ran one finger through a thin film of dust on a rustic pine chest in the Franconias' antiques shop. They didn't rely on walk-in customers, which, he figured, was probably a good thing. There was no one to mind the store. A small sign urged shoppers to browse on their own and check at the inn if they needed help.

Trusting.

He'd knocked on the door to the Franconias' second-floor residence, but got no answer. On his way over to the barn, Star had waved to him from a tall blueberry bush. For all he knew, Andrew was off picking beans.

Maggie had to be up by now.

Rob shook off any thought of her and threaded his way through the furniture and glassware. His own place back in Brooklyn was a mix of hand-me-down furniture from friends and a few odd pieces he'd picked up out of necessity. He wasn't putting down roots in Brooklyn. Even in Night's Landing, his family had never been into antiques and fine furnishings — they bought what worked for the place, what was comfortable, what would last.

He supposed, by definition, antiques lasted.

He swore under his breath and stood on the wood ramp that led into the barn.

What the hell was he doing in Ravenkill?

The clear morning air, at least, provided a welcome contrast to the dust.

He'd gone to The Hague partly because of Nick Janssen's arrest, but it'd boiled down to reporters — to escaping the reverberations of his family's long friendship with John Wesley Poe. For the first time since the Central Park shooting, Rob was up against the full impact of his relationship with the president on his work as a marshal. They'd both treated their friendship with discretion, especially once Wes entered presidential politics.

But the anonymity they'd enjoyed was shattered now. Everyone knew he was President Poe's surrogate son. There was no changing it. It was a fact.

Nick Janssen's arrest had renewed public interest in the Poe-Janssen-Dunnemore connection. If it turned out Janssen had hired his own private assassin — someone who'd killed at least two people already —

the media would have a feeding frenzy.

Because of Rob's injuries and Sarah's near death at the hands of a madman, their mother had been spared some of the ordeal of being hounded to explain her past, her connections to both the criminal mastermind now sitting in a Dutch jail and the self-made millionaire and dedicated public servant now in the White House. Nick Janssen, Wes Poe and Betsy Dunnemore had all gone to Vanderbilt together. Thirty years later, Janssen had tried to use that connection to get himself a pardon, a wild flight of fantasy that had resulted in violence, death and his own exposure as something more than a tax evader.

In a candid press conference not long after the foiled pardon-extortion scheme, President Poe had admitted he barely remembered Janssen, who'd transferred after his freshman year because of money problems.

Rob still had a hard time fathoming that his mother and Wes had been an item in college, their brief romance long in the past. Both were happy in their subsequent marriages. Wes and his wife hadn't let the tragedy of losing four babies rip them apart. Instead, they'd become even tighter.

The events of the past were facts none of

them could escape, Rob thought.

He couldn't just turn the page on his own past and have it all be different.

As he walked back out to the stone path, Rob could see himself back in Night's Landing, sitting on the dock with Wes as they'd dangled their feet in the Cumberland and talked fishing and snakes and baseball.

Wes. Why couldn't you have stayed home and become a damn banker?

It was what the Poe sisters had wanted for the boy they'd found on their doorstep as a baby and raised. Roots, home, continuity, a simple life. Those were their values. Even Nashville was a long way from what Leola and Violet knew. They were suspicious of politicians and ambition, rigid in their belief that all the good life Wes could ever want — all the contribution he needed to make — could be realized on their quiet stretch of the Cumberland River.

Yet, they'd have applauded his inauguration as president in January. They'd have dressed up and gone to the balls and had a grand time, because they'd come to understand, finally, that Wes was doing what he was meant to do.

When he went home to recuperate in

May, Rob had paid more attention to the nuances of the relationships among his family and neighbors. For long weeks, he'd sat on the porch, taken the boat out on the river, explored the caves and sinkholes and trails of his home — and he'd tried to figure out what he'd missed by insisting that Night's Landing didn't matter to him. He'd never had the firm, clear connection to family and home that Sarah did. He didn't have her ability to whip up one of Granny Dunnemore's old casserole recipes and have it conjure up memory and meaning.

He saw Maggie coming toward him, the sunlight on her red hair, and shook off the assault of introspection.

"Damn," he muttered. "No wonder Wes worries."

He suddenly wished he could whisk Agent Spencer away from Ravenkill and her own memories, her own questions and doubts.

"Have you seen Andrew Franconia?" she asked, squinting at him, all professional this morning. Only the hint of color in her cheeks, the way she didn't quite look him in the eye, told Rob that last night just might be on her mind.

He shook his head. "Maybe he's gone

fishing. What're you up to?"

In a carefully neutral tone, she repeated her conversation with Star Franconia, describing Star's shattered state of mind, her recollections about Philip Spencer and Charlene Brooker. Rob knew Maggie had to be reeling from the information, but she kept her reactions to herself, under rigid control.

They continued on the path toward the inn. "I've never heard a hint that Char Brooker had anything to do with your father or William Raleigh, but that's not necessarily something I'd know. You? Do you think she could she have worked on your father's murder case?"

Maggie gave a tight shake of the head. "No idea."

"What about your pal Raleigh?"

"Nothing."

"From what I gather from Nate, whatever the two of them did is closely held." Rob gestured back toward the Franconias' barn shop. "Did your father have an interest in antiques?"

"Not that I knew of. An Austrian crystal vase . . ." She looked skeptical. "It wasn't in his personal effects, not that I ever saw. Libby was the one who found the vase. We could ask her if she knows anything.

Maybe he bought it as a gift — maybe it's got nothing to do with anything. He, Char Brooker and Tom Kopac could all have ended up sharing information on an antiques dealer and a beautiful Hudson River Valley inn. Then we got hold of bits and pieces and put them together all wrong."

"You believe in that kind of coincidence?"

She scowled. "It doesn't matter what I believe. My father —" But she broke off, refusing to go on. "Never mind. That doesn't matter, either."

There was the slightest edge to her voice, a hint of the anger she had to feel at having lost a father she'd never really had a chance to know. But she didn't want to face her resentment, her own guilt at missed opportunities — something Rob could understand.

He found himself accepting her natural reserve instead of trying to fix it. "Janssen thought my mother would leave my father when he got old. Then he'd be there. For all I know, it's still what he thinks. It's tough to know what goes on between two people, but I don't see my parents splitting up."

"My parents had been divorced for years when my father was killed." Maggie spoke quietly but not easily, without that urge to blurt out everything that Rob so often encountered. "But my mother still felt guilty. I think she believed his death was partly her fault."

"She's never said?"

"We don't have those kinds of talks. She didn't drive my father away. He had a bad case of wanderlust from as far back as I can remember. It wasn't a surprise to her. I guess she accepted it at first. But then, she just got sick of his long absences. I don't think she meant to."

"They say Charlene and Ethan Brooker spent less than a month together in the last two years of their marriage."

Maggie nodded. "Part of Brooker's drive to get all the answers to his wife's murder could be guilt. They drifted. He had his work, she had her work."

"She was killed and he wasn't there."

And she'd told everyone she was in Amsterdam on holiday, Rob recalled from his briefings. Alone.

"The Franconias' marriage is stressed," Maggie said. "For all we know, Char Brooker told my father they were a good source for a nice antique. Who knows? They got together, Libby Smith showed up in Prague. None of it could mean anything."

"People's relationships sometimes are complicated."

But Maggie wasn't touching that one. "Do we know where Major Brooker is?"

Rob didn't push her. "Probably still with Longstreet. The FBI is going to want to talk to these guys. Raleigh and Brooker, the Franconias and Libby Smith. You."

She nodded. "I'll fill George Bremmerton in when I get a chance. We need to find out if my father ever met Char Brooker — and Tom. My God. Tom was just a dedicated foreign service officer."

"Maggie —"

She held up a hand. "It's okay. I just have to accept this awful sense of impotence, that I could have and should have done more. What happened on Saturday —" She turned away, as if she needed to make herself look at the flowers and the morning sun instead of whatever images were flooding her mind. "I want whoever killed Tom caught. I want to make sure nobody else dies."

Rob touched her shoulder, remembered the feel of her skin under his hands last night. "I'll find Andrew. Then I'll call Chief Rivera and let him know what's going on."

"Can you reach Deputy Longstreet and have her sit on Brooker?"

Rob smiled. "I imagine she's not letting him out of her sight."

"I'll find Libby and hang on to her and Star." Maggie paused, her expression serious, the raw emotion of just a minute ago gone now. "We need to find Raleigh, too. I doubt he's told me everything."

Rob decided this wasn't the time to agree with her. They split up at the porch steps, Maggie heading back inside while he veered off to check around outside for the inn's co-owner.

A quick look into the vegetable and herb gardens turned up nothing.

Nobody at the fairy statue or in the gazebo.

But when he reached the side of the house, Rob saw that the cellar door was ajar and eased down the slope to it, the grass slippery from last night's rain. He had to put his shoulder into the effort to push the door open wider, its rusted hinges creaking from lack of use. He wasn't exactly making a stealthy entrance.

"Ms. Smith?" he called. "Mr. Franconia? Anyone down here?"

His eyes had to adjust after being out in the bright sun. The cellar was cool, dark and damp. He felt along the wall for a light switch, trying to remember what kind of light had been in the hall.

But he heard a moan and turned sharply.

In the dim light, he made out the silhouette of a man in the wine cellar, sunk against the wooden shelves and racks, the door wide open.

Rob recognized the white hair. "Raleigh — Christ." He shot into the small room and grabbed hold of the older man's shoulders, realized how brittle and nearly weightless he was as he helped lower him to the floor. "What happened? What the hell are you doing down here?"

Raleigh was trembling badly, sucking in quick breaths as if to ward off pain. "Tom was on to something." His eyes flickered with something like grim amusement. "All roads lead to Ravenkill."

"Are you drunk? Hurt?"

"Not drunk. Someone . . . I took a punch of some kind to the kidneys."

He was clearly dehydrated, possibly hypoglycemic. Rob placed the back of his hand against the old spy's forehead; he had a slight fever. "Whose side are you on, Raleigh?"

"Phil's side. Char Brooker's. I failed them both. I put them together. I should have known they'd become targets." He coughed, moaning in agony, but it just seemed to irritate him. He swore viciously, then took a second to calm himself. "I didn't pull the trigger, but I'm responsible for their deaths. I used and manipulated them. Now I'm using and manipulating Maggie. It's a never-ending cycle. She doesn't know about Char and her father."

"They were lovers?"

"No, not that. On a similar mission."

The man needed medical attention. "Hang on." Rob got one of Raleigh's arms around his neck and half dragged, half carried him out to the hall. "Let's get you to a doctor."

"Leave me," he mumbled. "Leave me to die."

"Not my style."

"Bastard. I deserve it."

"That's not my call. Have you seen Libby Smith? Is she down here?"

"Her room —" Raleigh coughed, a wet, nasty sound, but there was no sign of blood on his mouth, anywhere. With any luck, he wasn't suffering from internal bleeding. He pointed toward the wine cellar. "She has a workroom."

He couldn't go on. Drawing his weapon, Rob returned to the dank wine cellar. "Ms. Smith?"

Behind him, the door slammed shut, and

he heard the loud thunk of a lock twisting.

"Raleigh!"

But there was no answer, and Rob swore and kicked the door as hard as he could.

No luck. It didn't budge.

He was locked inside.

Swearing at himself, he swung his hands in the dark and caught the string to a lightbulb, pulling on it. A dull yellow light came on, but didn't reach the corners.

But he could see well enough to make out Andrew Franconia flopped against a small barrel on the outer wall, near a closed door to what had to be the adjoining workroom Raleigh had spoken about.

Rob approached Franconia cautiously, squatting next to him and placing two fingers on his carotid artery. A faint rhythmic beat said he was alive.

"Mr. Franconia?"

His eyes opened, barely focusing. "If you're here to kill me, get it done."

"I'm not here to kill anyone."

It was true, as far as it went.

Franconia tried to lick his lips, but he was only semiconscious and in obvious pain. Although his face was unmarred, his hands were shaking, his polo shirt soiled and askew, his pants muddied.

"Hang on," Rob said, rising. He checked

the office door. Locked. "Libby? Are you in there?"

But there was no response, and he returned to Franconia, who'd managed to sit up a bit more.

"Can you talk?" Rob asked. "Tell me what happened."

Franconia couldn't seem to concentrate. "My wife — Star —"

"Maggie Spencer's with her. Do you know how long you've been in here?"

"Minutes. I don't know. There was a man. . . ."

"White hair? Looks like an old drunk?"

His eyes flickered. "Yes."

"Did he do this to you?"

A feeble smile. "Christ, I hope not."

Rob didn't blame the guy for wanting his assailant to be tougher-looking and appreciated his humor under stress.

"I — I was hit from behind," Andrew went on. "It felt like a baseball bat."

Someone had been busy. Star? Libby? Had Raleigh pulled a fast one and faked an injury? But Rob didn't believe Raleigh had locked him in the wine cellar or taken a baseball bat to Andrew Franconia. Someone had been hiding, waiting for the right moment to pounce.

Andrew was very pale, shivering now.

Rob noticed a handful of dusty wine bottles in the racks. "I wonder if the wine in these bottles is any good."

His host coughed and moaned, tears of pain more than anguish streaming down his face.

The man needed a doctor.

"Well," Rob said, "wine or no wine, I don't intend to stay locked up for long."

When Maggie reached the kitchen, she found the colander of blueberries in the sink and a radio on, tuned to news on a public station. But there was no Star. The radio hadn't been on earlier — she must have returned to the kitchen and turned it on, perhaps to settle her nerves, beat back her worries and racing thoughts.

Where was she now?

Maggie checked Libby Smith's first-floor suite, knocking softly on the door. "Libby? It's Maggie Spencer. Are you in there?"

But there was no answer. The door was locked.

It was as if the sprawling house had suddenly spit out all its people. Star and Andrew weren't around. Libby wasn't around. There were no other guests. As she returned to the kitchen, Maggie noticed that her footsteps echoed on the wood floor, underscoring the emptiness of the place.

She decided to check the cellar, wondering if Libby was down there working on the inventory of her antiques. But the stairwell light wasn't on — not a promising sign.

As she started to shut the door, Maggie heard a sound from the cellar. Muffled, perhaps just a breeze catching a door.

Had someone left the outside cellar door open? Gone out that way?

For all she knew, the inn had ghosts.

She switched on the light — the Franconias' renovations didn't extend to high-wattage bulbs and fancy stairwell lights — and ventured down the steep, old stairs.

The air was cooler, drier, and with the dehumidifier off, the silence was almost complete.

"Star? Libby?" Maggie called. "Anyone down here? Rob?"

No response.

She'd never been one for strange sounds in dark cellars.

She paused at the bottom of the steps, listening, but there was still no repeat of whatever she'd heard — or imagined — a few minutes ago.

It was a large cellar, with old parts and new parts and too many doors and nooks for her to remember the exact route of her informal tour with Libby and Rob. Maggie had been far more interested in the history of the house, how weird it had to be — despite her cheerfulness — for Libby to be relegated to a small suite and odd jobs in her childhood home. That she was pulling together an antiques business was a rationalization. It had to sting to have lost a home that had been in her family for well over a century.

She'd been in Prague.

She'd arranged for the Franconias to sell Maggie's father a vase a few months before he was killed.

She lived at the same inn Char Brooker had visited a month before her murder — the same inn Raleigh had found information about in Tom's apartment the day before *he* was murdered.

As she turned a corner, Maggie noticed an arc of light up ahead. Daylight, she thought. Then someone *had* left the outer door open.

"Anyone down here? Hello? It's Maggie Spencer."

Again there was no answer.

She continued toward the light, recalling

that the outer door was near the old wine cellar. The door to Libby's storage room was unlocked, slightly ajar. Maggie pushed it open wider and realized a dim light was on inside. She moved past the tumble of pieces Libby had collected, then came to a long antique table neatly stacked with books, files and photo albums. An apple crate on the floor was filled with dust cloths, lemon oil, window cleaner and miscellaneous supplies.

One of the albums was opened to old black-and-white photographs, a series taken in front of the fairy fountain — before it had its nose smashed with a wine bottle. All the photos were of a handsome man who had to be Libby's grandfather. He looked rich, well dressed and content. If he could see his farm now, he'd probably be pleased it was as beautiful as it was, but shocked to find it in the hands of nonfamily members who'd saved it from certain destruction after his son's years of neglect.

Next to the album was a little stack of pieces of a color photograph that someone had taken scissors to and hacked into five irregular chunks. Maggie put the pieces together, like a puzzle.

The photo was of Libby Smith and a

glassy-eyed wreck of a man, red-faced and clearly drunk — obviously her father. She couldn't have been more than seventeen, smiling, her arm around his waist, probably holding him up for their picture.

They stood in front of the fairy statue, as if to emphasize that the son wasn't at all like the father.

Drawing her weapon, Maggie wove through the precariously stacked antiques to a half-open door in the corner of the small, windowless room.

"Maggie . . ."

William Raleigh crawled on his hands and knees out from the cover of ladder-back chairs stacked on top of a low wooden filing cabinet, all of them encrusted with dust and shrouded with cobwebs.

Maggie dropped down and put her arm around his thin waist. "Raleigh? What the hell is going on? Here, let me help you. Are you hurt?"

Blood dribbled out of the corners of his mouth.

Jesus.

"Libby," Maggie said. "Where is she?"

"I don't know. She's —"

He slumped, semiconscious.

"Damn, Raleigh. Don't die on me. I'll get you to a doctor."

341

"Her room . . . It's all there. . . ."

As if he were summoning his last shreds of strength, he lifted a hand and pointed to the doorway behind him.

Was Libby in there?

"Hang on, okay?" Maggie said. "I'll be right back."

Gun in hand, she ducked through the open door into a suffocatingly tiny room, windowless, a naked bulb providing scant light.

Libby Smith — or someone — was using this closetlike room as some kind of workspace. There was a second door on the opposite wall — locked. Remembering her tour, Maggie realized it must lead to the adjoining wine cellar.

A laptop was open, powered up on a worktable. A small desk lamp shone brightly on manila file folders neatly laid in a row. Pictures were tacked to corkboard on the wall above the table. Maggie scanned them quickly, her grip tightening on her Glock.

One was of Charlene Brooker, serious, confident, in her army captain's uniform. A Polaroid shot, taken here in Ravenkill.

There was Raleigh, smoking a cigarette on a European street.

Vladimir Samkevich in London.

And her father, smiling, his eyes crinkling in that familiar way. It was winter wherever he was. He wore a parka, was hatless and gloveless, but Maggie didn't delude herself into thinking he'd been missing her mother in Boca.

Had there been something between him and Libby Smith?

Before Libby killed him, Maggie thought, knowing she was right — she had Raleigh's assassin.

She quashed any emotional reaction and hit the space bar on the laptop.

On the screen was a picture of Rob with President John Wesley Poe on the Dunnemores' dock on the Cumberland River in Night's Landing, Tennessee. They were holding fishing poles and grinning at the camera, belying any pretense that they weren't that close. The picture had run in most of the world's newspapers in the spring.

Maggie quickly scanned the rest of the claustrophobic room.

Boxes of ammunition.

Pistols.

And bomb-building supplies. Wires, timers, cords, plaster.

Gunpowder. Lighter fluid. Paint thinner.

Did Libby Smith plan to kill Rob?

The president of the United States?

Below their picture were three more pictures.

Rob's parents, Betsy and Stuart Dunnemore. Sarah Dunnemore. Nate Winter.

Does she plan to kill them all?

Maggie left everything where it was and returned to the storage room, kneeling next to Raleigh, who was still. "How long have you known Libby's your assassin?" she asked him.

He was a little more lucid, but still in obvious pain.

"An hour, maybe. Less. I'm sorry. I've been so stupid."

"An antiques dealer who travels the world. Attractive, educated." Maggie's voice was tight, controlled. "What a cover."

Raleigh tried to pull himself up, but gave up, wincing as he wiped his bloody mouth with the back of his hand. "Janssen hired her to eliminate anyone who could take over his network or who might cut a deal with prosecutors in exchange for information." He spoke haltingly, but his words were clear. "It's all in that horror of a room. You have to find her, Maggie. You have to stop her before she kills anyone else."

Maggie nodded and helped him into a

344

sitting position. He had no strength left, his arms flopping aimlessly.

"Did Libby do this to you?"

"I don't know why she didn't —" He swallowed painfully. "Like Tom."

Maggie understood what he was trying to say. He didn't know why Libby hadn't put a bullet in the back of his head.

"She must not want you dead from a bullet wound. Where is she now? Do you have any idea?"

He shook his head.

Maggie put her arm around his waist and flopped his arm over her shoulder, getting to her feet with him. "She's operating from her own agenda."

"She wants to take over Janssen's network."

"Not satisfied being his paid killer, is she?"

His eyes closed, his skin grayish now as he sank against her. "Leave me, Magster. I'll slow you down."

"I'm not leaving you."

"She'll kill Brooker. Dunnemore." His voice was weak, and although he was coherent, he sounded as if he was babbling. "They're next. Rob's parents. His sister."

"I know. Come on. Let's just keep moving."

Raleigh clutched her sleeve as if he'd suddenly remembered something. "Rob is down here. Libby — I don't know what she did with him —"

Hell. "I'll take care of it."

He rallied enough to move with her at a half run; she didn't have to drag or carry him. When they reached the yard, he collapsed onto the grassy slope down to the cellar door.

"Go," he said. "Find her. . . ."

Maggie nodded and ran back inside, drawing her gun.

Just past Libby's storage room, a cracking sound — a hiss — stopped her. *What the hell?*

Libby. Her bomb-making ingredients.

Maggie dived for the floor even as the blast from the homemade bomb sent her sprawling.

As she hit the concrete floor, she smelled smoke and chemicals. She heard the distinctive sound of a fire spreading.

"Rob!" she called, scrambling to her feet. "Where are you?"

Smoke oozed out of the storage room. She couldn't risk going back the way she'd come.

She had only one choice. To go up and get out that way.

Covering her mouth with her shirt, she stayed low, under the smoke, and hoped she remembered the route back to the stairs.

Nineteen

Jarred by the explosion, Rob smelled smoke and grabbed Franconia, dragging him to the hall door. "We're crisps if we don't get out of here. Don't move, okay? I'm going to shoot the lock and get us out of here."

"My wife —"

"We'll find her."

Standing to one side of the door, Rob fired twice across his chest, shattering the lock, splintering the wood around it. He helped Franconia to his feet.

Andrew's eyes rolled back in his head. "Star thinks I love my work more than her —"

"Nah. She knows better."

He moaned in agony when Rob pulled him into the hall, but at least it shut him up. The cellar was filling up with smoke. He could hear the crackle of flames, lightbulbs breaking with the heat. Staying low, he hoisted Franconia over his shoulder and ran toward the outer door. When they reached fresh air, Rob kept moving, looking for a tree, a bench, a statue — cover was a necessity when a killer was blowing up things and beating the hell out of people.

Where was Raleigh?

Maggie?

Rob dumped Franconia onto the grass in the shade of a red maple.

It was a damn fine day. A beautiful spot.

Smoke was pouring out the cellar door.

Andrew, coughing and spitting, rolling in the grass in agony, finally noticed, finally let it sink in that his place was on fire. "Christ," he said. "Oh, Christ. Goddamnit. What —" But he coughed again, sobbing in pain.

Rob knew he had to think. "If Raleigh didn't lock us in the wine cellar, who the hell did? If he's a good guy and you're a good guy and Star's a good guy and Maggie's a good guy —" He stared down at Franconia. "I think your pal Libby wants us dead."

"I'm dying."

"You're not dying. You just feel like you're dying."

Rob scanned the immediate area and spotted Raleigh prone on the slope about five yards away, and ran to him. "Maggie," Rob said. "Where is she?"

But Raleigh couldn't answer, could barely move, and Rob swore. Libby Smith had already beaten the hell out of two men. If she found them, she'd have two hostages.

Rob couldn't leave Raleigh and Franconia for her.

Maggie was on her own.

Quashing any panic — any sense of exhilaration — Libby focused on the task at hand.

She had to get out of the house before she ended up dead herself.

She was almost there, almost to the porch door.

Her first-floor suite was on fire. She'd set a second explosive device there. The cellar had to be fully engaged now. Investigators would figure out it was arson — she didn't have the time, or even the skills, to make the fire look like an accident.

But she hadn't used bullets or poison to kill Dunnemore and Raleigh or Andrew if he ended up dead, too. He and Star were stretched thin financially and emotionally — investigators would suspect them first. By the time the authorities got around to her, Libby thought, she'd be gone, working her way down Nick Janssen's target list, solidifying her own position.

She had a contingency plan of her own. A new identity — a new life — waiting for her.

All she had to do was get out of the god-damn house before she collapsed of smoke inhalation.

Star seemed to materialize in front of her. *What?*

Her arms were flapping at her sides, and she was screaming incoherently. Libby managed to make out "my house" and "Andrew."

Libby shoved her back out onto the porch. "Go," she said. "Get to the barn. Call 911. *Hurry.* I'll find Andrew."

With any luck, he was dead in the wine cellar with Rob Dunnemore.

"I can't —"

But Libby kept moving forward, all but pushing Star, in a panic, sputtering, down the porch steps to the stone path, repeating her instructions. *Barn. 911. Barn. 911.* She'd be out of the way. She wouldn't suspect Libby of any involvement in the fire — which would further delay the police from looking in her direction.

When they reached the barn, Libby promised again to find Andrew. Star nodded, white-faced, in shock.

Libby left her.

And she ran, heading for Ravenkill Creek and freedom.

Ethan charged up a narrow path toward

350

the apple orchard and the Old Stone Hollow Inn, Deputy Longstreet a step behind him with her Glock in hand. Not for the first time in the past twenty-four hours, he wished he hadn't been so scrupulous about getting her into trouble and had scored a couple of guns for himself.

They'd been on their way down to Ravenkill Creek when they'd heard something in the distance — a crack, a rumble. Whatever it was, it wasn't normal.

Then they'd seen the black smoke rising above the trees.

"Christ," Juliet had breathed next to him. "What the hell's going on?"

Now they were on their way to find out.

Ethan wasn't accustomed to sneaking around places that were as posh as Ravenkill. His old haunts at West Point were just across the Hudson, but he hadn't been back there in years.

He wasn't law enforcement. He was military.

Or he had been. He didn't know what the hell he was now. Wanted by the marshals, probably. Juliet had made calls on the way up to Ravenkill, explaining what she was up to.

A cloud of mosquitoes followed them into the orchard. Juliet didn't seem to notice. She went at a loping run, finally over-taking him. Ethan's head was pounding. Given his injuries, he supposed he might not be moving as fast as he thought he was.

He could smell the smoke now. The ground was soft, the grass wet against his lower legs. Up ahead, the Old Stone Hollow Inn was on fire.

With her free hand Juliet pulled out her cell phone and, as she and Ethan ran toward the burning house, called for reinforcement.

Star ran around in circles in front of the barn like a two-year-old having a tantrum, her arms flapping at her sides as she screamed. She had her portable phone clutched in one hand. Maggie caught the frightened woman by both arms and held them still. "Star. Get hold of yourself and listen to me."

"Andrew —"

"He's safe. He's with Rob. I just saw them." And Raleigh, half-dead, she thought; she'd waved to Rob that she was okay and had gone to grab Star, in hys-terics by the barn. "Did you call 911?"

"No. I can't. My phone —" She squeezed her eyes shut, then flung the phone to the ground. "It's *dead*."

If he could get through, Rob would have called for help by now, but Maggie wasn't sure how much he knew — if he'd figured out for himself or if Raleigh had managed to tell him that Libby was their killer. She squeezed gently on Star's arms. "Listen to me, Star. Libby —"

"She's gone." Crying, Star withdrew one hand from Maggie's grasp and waved toward the cornfield and the apple orchard. "Running — she's scared — "

No, Maggie thought. *She's getting away.*

"I need to go after her," Maggie said, dropping Star's other hand, trying to penetrate the woman's fear and panic. "I want you to go stay with Rob. He's getting your husband and another man away from the fire. He'll see you coming — you'll be fine. You can help him."

The frenetic pacing and flapping stopped, and Star stared at Maggie, expressionless. "The marshal?" She seemed to struggle to stay focused on what she was saying. "He has Andrew?"

"Yes." Maggie touched Star gently on the shoulder. "Tell Rob I've gone after Libby Smith. Tell him she's our assassin."

"What?"

But Maggie knew Star had understood her. "Can you do that for me?"

She nodded.

"Libby's going to try to kill more people. She has a long list. Tell Rob he needs to get his family into protective custody." Maggie paused a moment, but Star didn't switch back into panic mode. "I've got to go before Libby gets too far ahead of me."

"I can do this," she said.

Maggie tried to smile. "I know you can."

She waited as long as she could to make sure Star was okay as she staggered down the stone path toward her burning inn. Then, staying within the cover of the trees as best she could, Maggie went after Libby Smith.

Nate was at home preparing for a noon meeting when Mike Rivera called with the news from Ravenkill, giving it in an efficient staccato that nonetheless relayed his urgency in no uncertain terms.

"Libby Smith hasn't had time to get to New York, never mind D.C.," Rivera said. "We'll catch her. But I thought you'd want to know."

That he and his future wife and her family were targets of a hired killer? Yeah. He wanted to know. "Rob?"

"Alive, last we heard."

After Rivera hung up, Nate walked across the lawn in the hot sunshine to the small dump that Sarah had carefully marked off for her archaeological dig. Some days she worked with college and high school students, showing them how it was done, teaching them about the history found in mundane objects — but, thankfully, not today.

When she looked up at him from her pile of dirt, her face transformed from eager welcome to concern and dread. "Where's Rob?"

In hell, Nate thought.

But it wasn't what he told Rob's twin sister. "He's fine right now, but you need to come inside."

"I've got work —"

"It can wait."

She remained calm, brushing off her overalls as she stood up, but Nate knew the realization that her brother was in danger — that she, potentially, was in danger — had hit her.

"My parents?" she asked.

"Mike Rivera just told me that two deputies from the Nashville office are on the way to Night's Landing."

"Nick Janssen? He wants us all dead?"

Nate nodded, and she took his hand and walked back across the lawn with him.

Rob grabbed Star before she collapsed

and got her to the shade of a huge maple, where he'd managed to drag both injured men, well clear of the burning house. The roof was engulfed now. It would be a total loss.

Star was shaking badly, her skin cold to the touch, but she clawed at Rob. "My husband —"

"He's hurt, but I think he'll be all right. Ambulance is on the way."

Rob released her, and she sank beside Andrew, lowering her head to his chest and sobbing. He tried to stroke her hair, but he didn't have the energy, his arm falling to his side.

Star looked up at Rob, her eyes wide and sunken with shock and fear. "Agent Spencer's gone after Libby. Toward Ravenkill Creek."

Rob acknowledged Star's words with a nod.

"You're not going after her?"

"I can't leave you all here alone."

Raleigh stirred. "Give me a goddamn gun," he mumbled. "Or a kitchen knife. I can do a lot of damage with a kitchen knife."

Rob had to give the old guy credit. "Maggie can handle herself."

"I should have known it was Libby. Crazy bitch." He moaned softly, his color better than it was. "In my younger days —"

"You managed to keep her from beating Andrew to death with her baseball bat."

"Then she turned her damn bat on me," Raleigh said with a bit more energy. "Beat the living daylights out of me."

From what Rob had pieced together from the mutterings of the two semiconscious men, Andrew had realized Libby hadn't been around over the weekend and had checked the cellar, where she spent a lot of time, discovering a treasure trove of incriminating evidence. He and Star had prided themselves on respecting Libby's privacy and the fact that the inn had been in her family for so long.

Rob heard the blare of sirens. Star jumped, startled, shaking hard.

Raleigh sat up, blood on the side of his mouth from a cut lip, not, Rob thought, internal injuries. "Go after Maggie," he told Rob. "Don't leave her to that woman. Libby would kill Maggie the same way she'd kill a cockroach. Without hesitation, without remorse. You know she would. It's how she killed Tom Kopac."

Rob was tempted, but he knew he wasn't leaving Raleigh and the Franconias until help got there. Then he spotted Juliet and Brooker on the stone path and signaled to them. They waved, picking up their pace as they pounded through a flower bed and ducked under a low-hanging branch, then joined him in the shade.

Rob quickly filled them in.

"It's your call, Dunnemore," Juliet said. "Do you want to go after your DS agent and assassin or shall I?"

"I'll go."

She managed a wink. "Thought so."

But first he turned to Brooker. "Talk to Raleigh. Your wife stayed here a month before she was killed."

Brooker had no visible reaction. "I'm going with you."

"Uh-uh," Juliet said. "You've got a concussion, Brooker, and Dunnemore here's a triathlete. You'll just slow him down."

But Rob was already on his way.

Maggie ran through tall ferns and brush in the woods below the orchard and cornfield. There was no path. She could hear the creek just below her, tumbling over rocks, almost drowning out the sounds of the sirens of the onslaught of fire trucks, ambulances and police cars.

The riverbank was steep, covered in slippery pine mulch and exposed tree roots, but she made sure she didn't trip. She couldn't risk giving Libby any advantage.

When she reached the river, Maggie stayed within the cover of a white pine as she scanned the banks.

The water, deeper here, was high from last night's rain, crashing over a mix of rounded and jagged gray boulders, forming a stretch of whitewater rapids.

Libby stood on a rock, maybe a yard into the river.

"Drop your weapon," Maggie called from behind her tree, her Glock trained on the assassin. Tom's killer. Her father's killer. "Do it now."

Without a word, Libby released her Beretta and let it fall into the water.

What the hell was she up to? Maggie stayed where she was. "Keep your hands up where I can see them."

Libby smiled in her direction. "You won't kill me. You want your answers."

And she stepped off her rock into the river, as if she were walking over a threshold. When she hit the water feetfirst, she went under, her arms flailing, but the current was too strong and dragged her downstream, smashing her against a boulder.

Maggie ran down to the water's edge, Libby a couple of yards into the river. Blood flowed down the right side of her face. She tried to hold on to the rock, but lost her grip and fell back into the water, going under again. She managed to lurch up and wrap both arms around another rock, only her head above the rapids.

"Hang on," Maggie called to her. "You'll drown if you try anything else."

She heard a thrashing sound behind her. Rob identified himself as he emerged from the woods and joined her on the riverbank, nodding toward the struggling killer. "She was trying to get to the other side of the river?"

"Apparently. She hit her head on a rock. I don't know how long she can hold on —"

"I'll get her."

Maggie shook her head. "She gets money for killing you. She doesn't get a dime for me. Motivation."

"Shoot her if she tries anything." Rob jumped onto a boulder that jutted above water a yard into the creek. "That'll take care of her motivation."

"I don't know if she has another weapon on her —"

"Well, if she lets go of her rock to get it, she'll drown. Then we won't have to worry about her trying to shoot me."

And Maggie would use deadly force if it was called for.

But when he got to Libby, she tried to scoot away from him. Rob gave her a chop to the carotid artery with the side of his hand, a move that would render her unconscious for five or ten seconds — enough time for him to pull her out of the water and toss her over his shoulder.

By the time he made his way back to the riverbank with her, she was conscious. He dumped her onto the ground just in time for her to vomit into a bed of brown pine needles.

She looked so small and helpless, Maggie thought. Yet Libby Smith was a woman who killed people for money.

Rob got Libby's arms behind her back, cuffed her and checked her for any other weapons, but there were none. She sat up, blood pouring from the gash on her right temple.

Maggie still hadn't lowered her own weapon.

Rob eyed her. "It's okay, Maggie. We're good."

But she stared at the woman who'd killed her father and couldn't make herself move. "Did my father know what you were before you shot him?"

"Yes," Libby said calmly. "I was in the nick of time. He'd have told Raleigh.

He'd have betrayed me."

"Maggie," Rob said.

She ignored him. "You weren't lovers."

Libby smiled, blood from her head wound seeping into her mouth, between her teeth. "Almost."

"And Tom —"

"I saw him before the Dutch police arrested Janssen and recognized him the next day when he showed up in Den Bosch."

"You were in Den Bosch to get your list of victims from Janssen?"

"Not victims," she said. "Targets."

Rob took a step toward Maggie, his clothes soaked with river water, stained with Libby Smith's blood, perhaps William Raleigh's blood. "Maggie, she wants you to kill her. She knows the party's over. Maggie —"

She lowered her Glock. "I'm okay. I'm not like her. I don't kill for pleasure."

Libby glared at her. "Neither do I. I kill for money."

"You didn't get paid for my father. Or for Tom."

"That was self-defense."

In a few minutes the police descended. Rob, relaxing now, gave a mock shiver. "The water's a hell of a lot colder up here than it is down home," he said, laying on his Southern accent.

Maggie stared at Libby as the local cops took her away. "She didn't get to kill you. We stopped her. Finally."

"Yeah. We stopped her." When Maggie made a move to start back up the river-bank, Rob touched her cheek. "I didn't like it when I thought you were dead."

She tried to smile. "I didn't like it when I thought I was dead, either."

Chief Deputy Mike Rivera arrived at the Old Stone Hollow Inn not long after the ambulances had left. The local police had cordoned off the entire property as a crime scene — including the car, complete with a ticket to Washington, D.C., and a New York license in a new name, that Libby had stashed on the other side of Ravenkill Creek. She'd lived in Ravenkill all her life — she knew all the places to hide things.

"Smith wouldn't have succeeded in killing your sister," Rivera said, plopping down next to Rob on a bench in front of the blunt-nosed fairy statue. "Nate would have stopped her."

"Nate was on Libby's target list, too."

"Then Sarah would have stopped her. You Dunnemores are a resourceful lot."

"Vengeance. That's the only reason Nick Janssen put our names on his damn list."

"He's not one to let bygones be bygones," Rivera acknowledged. "But we've got him now. He'll stand trial for murder."

The acrid smell of the burned house hung in the summer air. Incongruously, Rob's gaze landed on a sunflower, untouched by the violence that had gone on around it that morning.

Firefighters were still inside, making sure they'd gotten out the last of the flames.

"House is a goner," Rivera said.

"Libby wanted it that way, more than she even realized. It was still burning when the paramedics loaded her into the ambulance. She started laughing."

"Creepy." Rivera feigned a shudder, as if he hadn't heard it all before — the excuses, the reasons, for killing and maiming and setting houses on fire. "The Franconias can rebuild. They're a mess, those two. Clinging to each other, sobbing like a couple of teenagers about how much they love each other. I guess they got their priorities screwed up for a while." Rivera shrugged. "Happens."

"Where's Maggie?" Rob asked.

Rivera let the barest smile escape. "Bitching out Brooker for letting Raleigh sneak out of here."

"Longstreet was the one with the gun."

"She says he got away when Andrew Franconia started coughing up blood and she went to help him."

It was bullshit, and both men knew it. If Juliet Longstreet hadn't decided to let William Raleigh go, he'd still be there.

"She's a pain in the ass lately," Rivera said. "PTSD. But you're all right? You look cold to me."

"I had a change of clothes. It's gone up in flames."

Rivera grunted. "Whose room? Yours or the DS agent's?"

For the first time in hours, Rob let himself laugh. But he didn't answer Rivera's question, just walked with the chief deputy out past the sunflowers and the herbs, to where Maggie Spencer was standing with the sun on her hair. She was all alone, which wasn't, Rob decided, really the way she liked it. But it was what she was used to.

He'd have to convince her there was another way.

Twenty

Maggie arrived back in the Netherlands on Friday morning. George Bremmerton met her at Schiphol himself.

He eyed her as she dragged her suitcase behind her. "You don't look so good, Spencer. Any other luggage?"

She shook her head. She'd bought a few things to replace what she'd lost in the fire. Sarah Dunnemore, as beautiful as her twin brother was handsome, had flown to New York to check on her marshal brother and insisted on taking Maggie shopping in New York, somehow talking her into buying fuschia shoes and a ridiculously expensive nightgown.

"Anything happen while I was in the air?" she asked, trying to stop thinking about the Dunnemores — but she'd been trying for hours.

"No." Bremmerton gave her a grudging smile. "Somehow we all managed with you out of commission for seven hours."

Her laugh sounded tired even to her.

"You got back here alive," her boss said.

"That's what counts."

"I appreciate the thought, but Libby Smith kept meticulous records that all went up in smoke. I should have grabbed her laptop, at least."

"You did fine." He paused as they walked out to his car. "I'm just not sure I like having you come to William Raleigh's attention."

Maggie stopped. "Then you do know him."

He shrugged. "I know everyone."

As they continued to his car and she dumped her suitcase in his trunk, Maggie felt the same kind of uneasiness she'd felt the entire flight across the Atlantic — as if the other shoe was about to drop. As if Ravenkill was the beginning, not the end of what had been set into motion with the Janssen tip a week ago.

On their way to The Hague in the crush of Friday-morning traffic, Maggie sipped the last of the bottled water she'd had on the plane.

Finally she sank her head back against her seat and shut her eyes. "Raleigh told me he had contacts in Prague who notified him that Tom was asking questions about my father's death."

"Did he?"

She opened one eye and observed Bremmerton. "I don't think that's the whole story."

"Probably not."

"Goddamn it. There were no contacts in Prague who tipped him off." She had both eyes closed again but wasn't even close to relaxed. "It was you. You got in touch with him and told him to find out what Tom was up to."

But Bremmerton wasn't going any further. "You've had a hell of a week. You must be exhausted. Get some rest."

After he dropped her off at her apartment, Maggie unzipped her suitcase and dumped it out on her bed, wondering what had possessed her to buy pink shoes. Sarah Dunnemore's influence. She was so damn pretty, Maggie had felt compelled to go a little feminine.

But where the hell was she going to wear fuchsia sandals?

Her mind racing, Maggie checked her one orchid and was surprised to find it had revived in her absence. It was still alive after all.

She went down to the bakery and bought herself two soft white rolls and took them back up to her apartment. She had butter and *hagelslag*. She applied both liberally to one roll and sat in her tiny living room, thinking of Tom and Krispy Kreme doughnuts and how and why he'd done what he'd done.

Ah, Tom.

He'd been to Den Bosch *before* Janssen's arrest. Libby had said she'd seen him there.

Had Tom e-mailed Maggie the tip about Janssen?

But why her? He knew everyone at the embassy — why not alert Bremmerton?

And why was Tom in Den Bosch in the first place?

Why had he chosen it for his Saturday meeting with Raleigh? Why go to the Binnendieze when they were meeting at the cathedral?

Maggie finished her bread and chocolate sprinkles and warned herself not to do serious thinking while she was jet-lagged and dehydrated from the long flight.

So she thought of Rob and his apartment in Brooklyn and how she'd stayed with him, and they'd made love. She wondered if he'd been thinking what she had — that it'd been a great fling, a temporary thing, of the moment . . . something they'd both needed and wanted and would look back on without regret.

But it wasn't what she *really* felt. It was what she told herself. She wanted to convince herself that she didn't care about Rob as much as she did.

After her lunch and shopping extravaganza with his twin sister, he took her to Central Park and showed her where he and Nate Winter had been shot four months ago.

Damn.

Adjusting to being back in The Hague, on her own, wasn't going to be that easy, Maggie thought, tearing open a dresser drawer. She pulled out fresh work clothes and peeled off her travel clothes, changed, then headed off into The Hague's picturesque streets.

How could anything be so right and so wrong at the same time as she and Rob were?

More serious thinking.

It wasn't to be done.

She remembered the excitement and energy she'd had in her first days in the Netherlands. Meeting legendary George Bremmerton. Tom.

Her serious mood wasn't going to abate and being at the embassy didn't help. After a couple of hours, George Bremmerton caught her and kicked her out.

She needed rest.

Time to calm her mind.

But even in the morning, after a solid night's sleep, two cups of coffee and more *hagelslag,* she couldn't push back the questions and the overwhelming sense that her life was at a crossroads.

She ducked into her Mini and drove out to Den Bosch on a Saturday morning as glorious as the one Tom Kopac had died on.

She parked in the shade and walked to the Binnendieze, stopping at the open fence and staring down at the shallow, ancient waterway. Tourists eagerly climbed onto the flat-bottomed boats, carrying on as usual, no matter that a coldly calculated murder had taken place here a week ago. But the killer had been caught. That, at least, had to provide them some reassurance — if even they were aware of the murdered diplomat, the solitary assassin.

"I bought us two tickets."

Maggie recognized the Southern accent, the mix of humor and charm in the male voice. She looked behind her, and for a moment thought the events of the past week — the emotions, the jet lag, the physical demands — had affected her mind.

Rob stood next to her along the fence. "You DS agents do tend to forget what we marshals are good at."

"Tracking fugitives. I'm not a fugitive. I'm —" She broke off and frowned at him. "How?"

"It wasn't easy. Yours isn't the only red Mini in this country. I almost had my cabdriver follow an old woman and her dog."

She smiled. "You did not."

"Don't try to tell me you knew all along I was tailing you."

"I wouldn't want to bruise your marshal ego."

"You didn't know," he said. "Your mind's on figuring out what Tom Kopac was up to last Saturday."

She glanced at the river again and tried not to see Tom's body floating toward the dock, to hear the people screaming. "When did you get in?"

"This morning."

"So you haven't slept —"

Something sparked in his eyes. "I figure there's time for that. You want to see what we can do without alerting the Den Bosch police and getting them all pissed off?" He seemed relaxed, but Maggie knew he wasn't. He had the same questions she did. "Then we can do the boat tour."

She looked back down at the still water,

longing, suddenly, for nothing more than normalcy in her life. But she'd rejected normalcy at every turn. And what was it, anyway? Her father had tried to discourage her from a foreign service career not, she realized, because of the dedication and sacrifices and many rewards it offered her, but because of the choices *he'd* made. He'd let his work take over his life. He'd lost his family because of it.

Tom had never had a family.

But it didn't have to be that way. No one was more dedicated to his work than George Bremmerton, and he had a full, rewarding family life.

Maggie winced at herself. How had her mind gone off in *that* direction?

Because of Rob, she thought.

She shook off her rambling thoughts. "I don't know if I can do the tour."

"I can always give the tickets away."

He needed a shave, but that only made him sexier. And he wasn't armed — that had to feel strange when he was standing yards from a murder scene. Maggie moved away from the fence. "I never saw Libby. I've replayed every moment of last Saturday a hundred times. She must have acted fast for us — for someone — not to have seen her."

"She was brazen, that's for damn sure."

"But I can't see how she actually believed she'd take over Janssen's network." Maggie sighed, listening to the tour boat on the river below them, the guide explaining, in Dutch, what they were seeing. "Presumably Libby was in Den Bosch to get her target list from Janssen, but when did she get here? And Tom — why was *he* here last Thursday?"

"Your father was on to Libby months ago. Maybe Kopac was on to her, too."

Maggie pointed down the street toward the café where she'd spotted Tom last week. "I wonder if that's where Tom was when Libby saw him before Janssen was arrested. It's not far from where the police picked him up. He could have been drinking coffee, spying on him —"

"You think he sent you the tip," Rob said.

"Who else?" She started walking toward the café. "I just don't understand why."

Rob fell in beside her, naturally, without any protectiveness or posturing — he had nothing to prove. "Libby must have stayed around here somewhere."

"Not with Janssen at his safe house. That would have been too provocative."

They found a small hotel around the

corner from the café. It had its own café, a scatter of tables on the sidewalk. A good-looking kid of about twenty was working both the front desk and the café. He spoke halting English, but recognized the description of Libby Smith.

"She was here last week," he said, filling two small cups with strong espresso.

"Did you see another American — a man?" Maggie asked.

"He asked for her. Mrs. Smith. Like you."

The clerk seemed not to make any connection between his American and the American who'd ended up in the Binnendieze, never mind that Tom's picture must have been flashed on Dutch television and appeared in every Dutch newspaper.

Of course, Maggie thought, he could simply have decided not to get involved in a murder investigation if he didn't have to.

But he was struggling with his English to continue what he had to say, and Rob stepped in with his seven languages. In two seconds they were speaking French. Maggie, whose French was respectable but didn't roll off her tongue the way it did theirs, followed along haltingly.

The American had left a package at the hotel Saturday morning and asked the clerk to hold on to it.

He delivered his two coffees, then came back and plucked the package from behind the counter. It was a large yellow envelope both clasped and taped shut, with no writing on the front or the back.

"I give to you?" he asked tentatively.

Maggie smiled at him and showed him her badge. "It's fine. Thank you."

He handed over the package. He didn't even seem that curious about its contents or why the American hadn't returned for it. Employing all his natural charm, Rob asked the young Dutchman if they could have coffee. He pointed them to a small outdoor table.

Maggie sat facing the sunlit street and placed the package on the table. "I don't know if I should open it."

"The desk clerk says Tom left it right after Libby came down from her room. He followed her out and never came back."

"Did she?"

"Yes, but he didn't give her the package. He was waiting for her to ask for it. Then she checked out."

"The police —"

"I asked. The kid says the police haven't talked to him."

The young clerk walked toward them with two cups and saucers.

"Did he know about Tom's murder?" Maggie asked.

"He's pretending it never occurred to him the package and the two Americans he saw here that morning had anything to do with it."

"It's understandable. I wanted to think Ravenkill had nothing to do with it. I'm sure he's nervous. Think he's calling the local police?"

Rob gave a small smile. "I would."

The clerk delivered the coffees and withdrew without a word.

Maggie tapped the package with her fingertips. "It could be argued Tom meant whatever's in here for me."

"It could be argued he meant it's evidence in a murder investigation."

"It's been sitting behind the desk here for a week. We don't even know for sure it's Tom's, never mind whether or not someone's tampered with it. What if it's tourist brochures on Den Bosch?"

"You're going to open it," Rob said.

"As our friend Raleigh says, sometimes you have to break the dishes."

"Finders keepers?"

She frowned at him. "What would you do?"

"Me? I'd have been into the thing by now."

Maggie peeled off the tape and unfastened the clasp, then carefully pulled out the contents of the envelope. There were four or five separate paper-clipped stacks of papers and photographs, she realized, all held together, in Tom's typical meticulous fashion, with a larger paper clip and a fat rubber band.

On top of the first batch was the printout of the Old Stone Hollow Inn's Web site home page. "No wonder the police didn't find it in his apartment," Maggie said, pulling off the rubber band and paper clip.

The rest of the paper-clipped stacks appeared to be in chronological order, beginning with two days after Maggie's arrival in The Hague.

It was a journal entry, handwritten on pedestrian yellow lined paper. Leave it to Tom not to trust a computer, she thought, her throat tightening, his precise, easy-to-read handwriting making her feel his presence, the loss of a good man. She scanned his words.

Maggie Spencer has no idea that her father and I were friends. We met ten years ago in South Asia and stayed in touch. As different as we were, we got along. He

stopped by The Hague on his way to
New York a few weeks before he was
killed — he was flying out of Schiphol,
said he was off to check out some antiques shop in Ravenkill, New York. I had
the feeling a woman was involved.

"Maggie?"

She looked up from the paper and realized she had tears in her eyes. "I'm okay."

"We can pack up and head to the embassy —"

She shook her head. "Another minute. I
won't read every word."

In that same matter-of-fact style, Tom
explained how surprised he was to realize
that her father's trip to the States hadn't
included a visit with his daughter — it
turned out to be their last opportunity to
see each other. Shortly after he returned to
Prague, he was killed. Tom had felt guilty
for not tearing himself away from his work
to attend his longtime friend's funeral.

He'd started asking questions. Researching
his friend's death. At first, curiosity drove
him. Then concern. Other entries detailed
how he'd checked out Ravenkill and figured
out that Philip Spencer had developed an apparent interest in antiques.

But Tom didn't believe it.

He found out about the Old Stone Hollow Inn and Libby Smith and the Franconias and put the word out to a few people he knew to alert him if their names popped up. He didn't identify his sources in his log. He indicated that he believed his friend Philip Spencer had gone to Ravenkill after Libby. Andrew and Star were in Prague — but that he'd never stayed at the inn. On Wednesday, the day before Nick Janssen's arrest, one of Tom's sources tipped him off that Libby had arrived in the Netherlands and was staying in Den Bosch.

Maggie made herself look up from her reading. Her steaming coffee was untouched at her elbow, but Rob was sipping his. "You're polite," she said. "You're not reading over my shoulder."

"Your hands are shaking."

"Just what I need then, sugar and caffeine." She tried to smile but couldn't pull it off, and he wasn't smiling, either. She pushed that first stack of papers across the table. "Here. Have at it."

But he kept his gaze on her. "Your father —"

"He had his own life. It was a good one. He made his choices."

"He didn't choose to be killed."

Maggie wasn't shocked at Rob's blunt words. They were what she needed. She picked up her coffee, took a sip and focused on the beautiful day. The cars, the bicyclists, fellow travelers stopping for coffee and a bite to eat.

"I don't think I could have done this right after his death," she said. "And Tom . . . he was killed because he and my father were friends."

"He was killed because a ruthless woman didn't want to be found out."

Rob's tone was kind without being patronizing or condescending. "He was a seasoned foreign service officer, Maggie. He knew the score."

"He came out to Den Bosch looking for an antiques dealer who might know something and found an international fugitive and a killer." She pulled off the paper clip and blank cover sheet to another stack. "Jesus."

She held up a photograph of Nick Janssen and Libby Smith together on a bench overlooking the Binnendieze.

Maggie read another of Tom's journal-type entries. Rob came around the table and stood over her reading along with her. "Tom thought Libby might be an under-cover agent," she said almost to herself.

"Someone my father worked with before his death."

"An intelligence operative posing as an antiques dealer," Rob said. "He was afraid of mucking things up."

"Poor Tom. He sent me the tip because he figured I'd handle it — I'd know if we really wanted the Dutch police to pick Janssen up, or if Libby was an undercover agent —"

"He didn't mention her in his e-mail."

"He wouldn't have risked it. He gave me the chance to ignore it if he was stepping into something — if my father had stepped into something —"

"He wasn't just covering his own butt and trying not to compromise an investigation. He was protecting you."

Maggie quickly shoved the papers and photos back into the envelope.

Rob was still beside her. "That bothers you, doesn't it? Having someone looking after you."

"It's not what I'm used to, and look what happened —"

"Kopac knew your father had been murdered. He went into this thing with his eyes wide open, Maggie," Rob said softly. "Give him credit for that."

She reclasped the envelope. Tom had

said he'd keep Janssen put for an hour — he must have planned to intercede if necessary, chat him up about the boat tour, or maybe Krispy Kremes. He'd given Maggie every opportunity to do her thing.

She'd called in George Bremmerton and set Janssen's arrest in motion.

Because of Tom, Nick Janssen and Libby Smith both were in custody.

Maggie didn't need to read the explanation of what Tom had done that Saturday. He had his package of information to give to William Raleigh, but he'd stopped at Libby's hotel just to reassure himself she wasn't an innocent caught up in events out of her control.

Maggie made herself focus on her surroundings. A young couple sat at a table in the sun, their bicycles nearby. Life in Den Bosch, back to normal. But it wasn't as if people were pretending a murder hadn't taken place there, or a notorious fugitive hadn't had a safe house on its pretty shaded streets — it wasn't callousness or denial that had the locals back on the Binnendieze.

Maybe there was just a desire to get out on a pretty summer day.

"I should have pushed for more answers months ago," she said.

Rob shook his head. "Don't do that to yourself."

His words were without bitterness, but Maggie felt their impact in her gut, knew he wasn't talking just about the past week. "You think you should have pushed harder to find out what was going on in the spring. That's what haunts you. Your mother, your sister — Janssen hates them now because he didn't get his pardon. Hell, Rob. You were almost killed yourself."

He didn't answer, and looked at him across the table, taking in the blue-flecked gray eyes, the fair hair, the good looks. They could mislead, make people think he'd never suffered, he'd never had problems and obstacles — and that he wasn't meant for the work he did.

He pushed aside his coffee. "I tell myself that all we can do is get up in the morning and do the best we can."

"Are there days you believe it?"

He smiled. "Some."

"Mistakes —" Maggie managed a quick smile. "I don't like making mistakes."

She nibbled on the cookie that came with her coffee, realizing she was neither hungry nor not hungry. Her body didn't know what time it was. And she could see her father, blue eyes crinkled as he laughed, as he promised her there'd be time — years and years — when he'd be in a rocking chair and they could spend all the time they wanted together.

"Did you really take a cab over here?" she asked Rob suddenly.

"What?"

And she had him. She knew she did. "Come on, Dunnemore. Who gave you a ride?"

He smiled mysteriously and got to his feet. "Let's go offer up a prayer."

A prayer . . .

St. John's.

William Raleigh.

They found the old spook with his arms sprawled over the back of a middle pew in the massive cathedral. He was cleaned up, dressed in neat olive-green pants and a navy polo shirt. He'd put on a pair of loafers, although Rob thought they looked tight. The man had dedicated his life to public service, secret battles, putting his own life and even the lives of the people he cared about at risk. Rob had no intention of judging him. Raleigh had endured private losses that he could share with very few people.

The death of Maggie's father was one of those losses.

She sat next to him, and Rob sat next to her. She still clutched Kopac's envelope. "You and Rob were on the same flight back to Amsterdam?"

"Coincidentally, yes."

"I doubt there's much in your life that's a coincidence."

He glanced at her, his eyes no longer as pain-racked. "Or yours."

"Shouldn't you be in a hospital?"

"Nothing's wrong with me that several thousand milligrams of ibuprofen won't cure. Libby's probably wishing now that she'd killed me when she had the chance."

"She tried. She just didn't want to use bullets."

"Apparently her father was a self-centered, incorrigible drunk. It's a terrible way to grow up. He never got a grip on his alcoholism. But it's not the reason she became a killer."

"Are rumors of your drinking problems fact or fiction?" Maggie asked without judgment.

"A fiction, at least for the most part. But I knew how to play it. My own father was an alcoholic. He died in a bar fight when I was in my early twenties. There's no question his drinking had an effect on me. I just refuse to use it as an excuse."

"Raleigh —"

He smiled sideways at her. "William. Remember, it's not Bill, Will or Willie. We were a very correct family, despite my father's alcoholism. We all knew our lines. It's strange," he went on, turning away from Maggie. "No matter their failings, we always seem to say goodbye to our fathers too soon."

"My father's death wasn't your fault. Neither were his shortcomings as a father."

"I was on to Libby. I *knew* we had a new killer at work — someone both reckless and ruthless. Phil and I had tapped into the outer fringes of the Janssen network."

"Samkevich?"

Raleigh smiled, obviously pleased. "Very good. Yes, Samkevich. He gave Libby her first jobs."

"How long had she been at work at that point?"

"Months. No more than a year. Samkevich still was testing her."

"What about Charlene Brooker?"

He looked pained. "She was interested in Samkevich herself. She took the bit in her teeth after your father was killed. She focused on Samkevich and Janssen. I focused on our emerging assassin." He paused, letting his arms drop from the back of the pew. "It was a difficult time.

We had very little to go on. In essence, we were stumbling around in the dark."

Rob remembered that Captain Brooker had told everyone she was going to Amsterdam for a vacation, not to track Nick Janssen. But he was staying out of this conversation, sensing where it might lead.

"How did Char Brooker end up in Ravenkill? Did she discover that my father had been there?"

"I'm not positive, but I don't think so. I didn't know, either. It looks as if she'd discovered a connection between Libby and Vlad Samkevich and was checking it out —"

"One doesn't expect to find a paid killer in such a beautiful spot as Ravenkill, New York," Maggie cut in. "She was there a month before she was killed. But it was Janssen who ordered her murder and hired one of his men to do the job — not Libby."

"Things must have unraveled quickly for Captain Brooker." Raleigh sighed heavily, his regret palpable. "I wish I'd had half the instincts she or your father had."

But Philip Spencer and Charlene Brooker were dead, Rob thought; William Raleigh was in a Dutch cathedral, trying to learn to live with his mistakes.

"American investigators have permission now to interview Janssen in prison," Rob said. "He's crying foul over Libby's arrest. There's no such thing as assassin-client privilege. But she's not talking."

"She might as well talk," Raleigh said. "Janssen will find a way to have her killed no matter what she does. Why not tell her story?"

"Why not tell yours?" Maggie asked him quietly.

He gave her a dry smile. "Write my memoirs in my retirement?"

She smiled in return.

"Nick Janssen wants to see where his mother was buried," Raleigh went on. "She died last winter while he was on the lam. He wants to put flowers on her grave. It's something we can use."

Rob felt his stomach twist, and Maggie arched an eyebrow at her father's friend. "We?"

Raleigh shrugged. "The collective we're-all-in-this-together we."

"Right," she said dubiously.

"You're born to do this work, Maggie." The old spook faced the front of the cathedral and didn't look at her. "Your father knew it. Your mother knows it."

"My mother . . ." But Maggie didn't go on.

"She has more courage than you know.

It takes courage to paint, to express your-self that way and put it out there for others to see and comment on. She found a way to live with who Phil was, who you are."

"She and my father were divorced."

"But he was still a part of her life."

Rob wondered if he should go for a walk, but Maggie seemed to sense his awkward-ness — in restlessness — and took his hand. "I like my work in diplomatic secu-rity," she said.

"Rob likes his work in the Marshals Ser-vice." Raleigh turned and looked across Maggie at him. "Don't you, Rob?"

"Yes."

Raleigh inhaled through his nose and rose stiffly, the lingering pain of his injuries obvious. However much he wanted to pre-tend otherwise, he had suffered at the hands of the assassin he'd chased for months. "It's quite a cathedral, isn't it? It makes me wonder what would be here today if people over the centuries hadn't stepped up and done what they could." He glanced down at Rob and Maggie. "You'll find your way out of here?"

"No problem," Rob said. "You okay? Not going to collapse on us?"

"Libby's more efficient with her Beretta than with her baseball bat, but she still managed to bruise the hell out of me." He withdrew a bottle of ibuprofen from his pants pocket and rattled it, smiling. "I'm due another dose. I'll see you two around."

Rob would bet on it.

Maggie watched Raleigh make his way out of the pew into the aisle. "He'll go on awhile longer," she said, "but it won't be forever."

"I think a part of him wanted to die the other day."

"With his boots on." But she shifted to Rob, her hand still on his. "I suppose you want a ride back to your hotel?"

Suddenly he thought of her in his bed in his apartment in Brooklyn, pictured her in the early-morning light. "I don't have a hotel."

She squeezed his hand. "Good."

A week after his escapade in Ravenkill, Ethan showed up in northern Virginia for fried apricot pies, prune cake or whatever Sarah Dunnemore might have cooked up. They'd shared a tough time in Night's Landing in the spring, and he'd cut out on her when she'd been injured. Paramedics had been on their way, but Ethan had never felt entirely right about his conduct that day.

Sarah forgave him and showed him around the historic Virginia house and her archaeological dig — which he figured out was an old dump — and served him pecan pie on her shaded porch.

But he should have remembered she was on her way to being married to a marshal and was pals with the president, because he soon found himself in the back of a black sedan with tinted windows. Nate Winter and an unsmiling woman in a dark skirt and blazer were up front.

They secretly escorted him into a windowless room in a nondescript government building somewhere in the suburbs.

Presently, John Wesley Poe joined them.

The unsmiling woman did the talking. "An American contractor has been kidnapped in Colombia by a team of Colombians and American mercenaries."

"And how is this my problem?" Ethan asked.

"You can identify the kidnapped American."

He leaned back in his chair, aware of Poe and Winter studying him, as if this was a test. "Can't you identify him?"

"Actually," the woman said, "no."

The other two registered no visible reaction to what the woman, who had yet to identify herself, had said. "What's your name?" Ethan asked her.

"I'm sorry. Mia O'Farrell. Dr. Mia O'Farrell."

She had long, straight dark hair pulled back off her face and probably wasn't more than thirty-five. "Doctor of what?"

"That's irrelevant."

"You made a point of telling me your name's *Dr.* Mia O'Farrell. I figured it was for a reason."

She kept her gaze steady on him. "No reason."

"Sure there is. You're trying to establish authority over me and get me to go fetch this American out of the clutches of who-ever's got him."

"The American is important to us for reasons of national security," she said, not withering under his scrutiny.

"His name?"

O'Farrell didn't answer right away. Winter was staring at his hands, and Ethan knew if it was the marshal's call to make, he'd give the name.

But it was Poe, finally, who spoke. "This is a voluntary mission."

Ethan knew what that meant. "So its chances of success are slim to none."

Poe stood up and came around the table,

clapping a hand on Ethan's shoulder. "It's voluntary," the president said, "but I could order you to do it. Technically, Major Brooker, I'm still your commander in chief."

Ethan scratched the side of his mouth. "Problems with my paperwork?"

"Serious problems."

"I was never good with paperwork."

Winter almost smiled. Dr. O'Farrell didn't come close.

Poe squeezed Ethan's shoulder. "I need an answer, Major."

Ethan thought of Juliet. Strange that he didn't think of Char. He'd been a guilt-ridden, grieving widower for months. But he'd done the best he could by her memory. He'd pushed and prodded and hounded, and at last he had answers. Vlad Samkevich was dead. Nick Janssen and Libby Smith were in prison. And Char had been on to all of them.

Now he had to find out who he was again.

"Yes, Mr. President, I accept the mission."

Twenty-One

Nate Winter and Sarah Dunnemore were married on a warm, overcast mid-September day in the sprawling yard of the Dunnemore family home in Night's Landing, Tennessee.

They were as beautiful and happy a couple as Maggie had ever seen, but a mosquito bit her and she thought she saw a snake.

It was her first trip back to the States since Ravenkill, which all, somehow, was becoming less a raw, open wound. Libby Smith was out of the hospital and had been denied bail as she faced prosecution. The media coverage had died down. Maggie had attended the memorial service for Tom Kopac at the embassy in The Hague, meeting friends who knew him better than she had and missed him terribly. But they'd laughed about his love of Krispy Kreme doughnuts, and they'd celebrated his life.

She walked out onto the dock that jutted out into the Cumberland River and kicked off her shoes, the fuchsia-colored ones she'd bought with Sarah in New York. The heels caught in the dock's many cracks and gaps.

She heard laughter and storytelling up toward the porch. Tents had been set up, tables spread with cobblers and fried apricot pies and casseroles and fancy hors d'oeuvres. Maggie hoped she hadn't been rude and stupid in accepting Nate and Sarah's invitation. Rob had stayed in The Hague with her for five days. They'd gone bicycle riding and sightseeing, and they'd finally done the Binnendieze boat tour — and they'd gone back to the Rijksmuseum, where Nick Janssen had approached Rob's mother back in April, trying to worm his way into her good graces.

Maggie remembered with a rush of warmth how she and Rob had made love, but it didn't change the difficult logistics of their long-distance relationship.

Rob's parents were intelligent and gracious, and Nate had whispered to Maggie his theory that Betsy and Stuart Dunnemore really were wizards, making her laugh. The Winters were there: Nate's E.R. doctor sister, Antonia; his pregnant nature photographer sister, Carine; the crusty uncle who'd raised them after their parents had died on Cold Ridge. Antonia had her senator husband and their baby with her, but Carine's husband, an air force pararescueman, couldn't be there, since he'd been deployed overseas since early summer. Taking his absence in stride, Carine had tried to get a picture of Maggie's snake.

Gus Winter, the uncle, came alone, too. There was talk that he'd been seeing an ex-hippie named Moon Solaire, but she'd moved on to northern Maine and that was pretty much over. He was in his early fifties, a Vietnam vet and a mountain climber with the same build as his marshal nephew.

Maggie knew that Rob liked the Winters and was relieved his sister had married into such a tight-knit family. But Maggie had no trouble distinguishing the Cold Ridge Winters from the Night's Landing Dunnemores.

Juliet Longstreet didn't attend the wedding but apparently had sent the newly married couple a gallon of pure Vermont maple syrup.

Ethan Brooker had given them a song he'd written during his brief stay in Night's Landing.

John Wesley Poe joined Maggie on the dock. Secret Service agents were on the river, upstream and downstream. "You should dip your feet in the water," he said. "It's still warm this time of year."

"I don't know. Snakes —"

"The snakes will leave you alone."

"I like how you don't deny they're there."

"Well, they might be," he said, laying on his middle Tennessee accent, "or they might not be. But they don't have much interest in biting your feet. Trust me."

She had no idea what to say to him, but Rob, in his black tux, walked out onto the dock with them. Poe seemed to tense up, as if he might say or do something wrong, but Rob smiled at him. "Sarah's thrilled you came. Thanks for making it happen."

"My pleasure. I know it's a fuss to have me here —"

"We wouldn't have wanted it any other way."

It seemed to be enough for Poe. He relaxed, smiling at Maggie. "I'll leave you two alone. There's just one thing." He paused, but any awkwardness was gone now. Turning to Rob, he spoke. "I'm told William Raleigh has excellent instincts."

Rob smiled, but Maggie could sense his dread about what Wes Poe was about to say. "It's hard for me not to think of him as a head case."

"He wanted people to think that. It gave him room to maneuver. Agent Spencer?"

"Please call me Maggie." She'd never talked to a president before, but found Poe easy to be around, more so than she'd expected. "My father and Mr. Raleigh were friends. That gives him an edge in my mind."

"He says your father was one of the best."

Even with her security clearances as a DS agent, the details of whatever her father had done as an intelligence operative weren't for her to know. "I'm sure my father would have said the same about Mr. Raleigh."

The corners of Poe's mouth twitched in amusement. "He'll want you to call him William."

She smiled back at the president. "Yes. He's not a Bill, Will or Willie."

"He says we need people with your talent, your courage, your ethics." Turning to Rob, Poe continued. "Maggie's *and* yours."

If Rob was taken aback, he didn't show it. He shook his head. "Everyone knows who I am."

"Because of me," Poe said. "Raleigh believes it can be an advantage. He was a bit notorious after the death of Maggie's father — there were rumors Raleigh had screwed up and dived into a bottle. He looks like a heavy drinker. He used that to his advantage and was able to sneak around after Libby Smith and hook up with Ethan Brooker without anyone realizing he was up to anything."

Feeling as if the conversation was taking a personal turn and not wanting to intrude, Maggie sat on the dock and dipped her feet in the Cumberland, snakes or no snakes. As Poe had promised, the water was warm.

"Whatever you decide," the president said, still addressing Rob, "I want you to know you have my blessing."

"Do I?"

"I've known you wouldn't stay in the Marshals Service. I think all of us have always known."

Maggie glanced at Rob, who hadn't shifted his position; he was stiff, unbending, and she realized he'd been down this road before. He'd bucked a man who had become president. But the shooting in the spring — how close Nick Janssen had come to destroying his family — had given Rob pause. He didn't want to worry them. At the same time, he was who he was —

which John Wesley Poe saw now and wanted to encourage.

"Sarah? My parents?" Rob shook his head again. "I won't have their blessing."

"You have options, Rob. Consider them all." Poe himself looked stiff now, as if he expected Rob to throw his support back in his face. "That goes for Maggie as well. Both of you."

"You're making assumptions about us —"

Poe smiled then, his eyes twinkling. "I don't know about that."

Maggie had to look away. The logistics of her relationship with Rob were difficult enough. If she chose to let Raleigh suck her into another line of work and Rob didn't want to follow her? Then what?

She kicked her feet in the slow-moving river, feeling the undercurrents of her own life tugging at her.

Rob didn't respond to Poe's comment, and the president sighed audibly. "Two years," he said. "If you and Maggie give us two years, then you can go back to doing whatever you want to do."

"What if Maggie doesn't want —"

"She does," Poe said. "Bremmerton, Raleigh — they insist she does."

She placed her hands behind her on the old dock and leaned back, looking up at the two men. "Maybe Rob and I need to talk, Mr. President."

"Of course." Poe looked at her, then at Rob. "We need you two. *I* need you."

He started off the dock, but Rob raked a hand through his hair and gave a small grunt of frustration. "Wes . . . Jesus. I didn't expect any of this. Thank you." When Poe turned back to him, Rob smiled at his old friend. "Thank you for everything."

Poe nodded without comment, and he left, Secret Service agents falling in around him.

Maggie focused on the murky water. She could hear someone singing, people laughing up on the porch. Rob sat down next to her, handsome — sexy — in his black tux. "Is the tux rented?" she asked. "Because if it is, I won't throw you in the river. Damn. Why didn't you tell me Poe was going to be here?"

He shrugged. "It was a given that he was invited."

"I'm not used to having chitchats with the president, never mind deep conversations."

But Rob, she realized, was used to staying true to himself, even in the face of great authority. He'd bucked two very different but powerful forces in his life — his

402

own father, a quiet, brilliant man, and Wes Poe, a self-made millionaire, Tennessee governor and now president, to become a marshal.

He took off his shoes and socks and rolled up his pant legs to his knees. "My mother bought me this tux for Wes's inaugural balls and parties after he was elected president. She thinks all men should own a tux."

"I ended up with fuchsia shoes because of your sister."

"You'd never know Sarah's happiest in her dump-digging clothes and my mother wears sensible shoes."

"They're both very smart," Maggie said.

"That they are." He dipped his feet into the water and ran his toes along her foot, raising warm goose bumps all over her. "They want to turn us into spooks, Maggie."

She angled him a look. "George Bremmerton warned me more or less, before I headed here."

"He knows everything and everyone, doesn't he?"

"Except Wes Poe. He says they've never met."

"Not yet, maybe. So this conversation wasn't a complete surprise for you?"

She gave him a knowing look. "It wasn't for you, either. You saw this coming."

He gazed out at the river and its limestone bluffs, the familiar scenes of his childhood. Night's Landing was home for him in a way no place ever would be for Maggie. Accepting Wes Poe's offer — his *challenge* — to serve wasn't the leap for her that it was for Rob. He patted her thigh. "Maggie, Maggie."

"I've complicated your life, haven't I? You never thought you'd get mixed up with the slightly repressed DS agent daughter of a murdered spy."

"Your mother paints flamingos. I never thought I'd fall for a woman whose mother paints flamingos."

"I gave one to Sarah and Nate for a wedding gift."

But Rob kissed her forehead and whispered, "Tell me you ever imagined yourself falling for someone who's practically family to the President of the United States."

"The Southern frat-boy stuff was weird enough for me."

He slipped his arm around her and pulled her close. "I want our children to come here and catch snakes and explore the caves, Maggie. I want them to go fishing and cook up fried pies and casseroles with Sarah and drink tea punch on the porch with my parents."

"That sounds perfect to me."

"I'm in love with you." He said it softly, so that only she could hear it. "What they're asking us to do — I'll say no if it means losing you."

"Here we are talking about kids when we haven't even . . . Rob, are you asking me to marry you?"

"I am. Two years as a couple of secret agents or whatever it is Wes, Raleigh and Bremmerton have cooked up for us. Then the rest is forever. What do you say?"

Maggie smiled. "I say yes."

About the Author

CARLA NEGGERS has been writing since she climbed a tree with pad and pencil at age eleven — now she's the bestselling author of many novels of romance and suspense. An avid hiker and kayaker, Carla lives with her family in Vermont, where she's hard at work on her next book. You can visit her at www.carlaneggers.com.